Body & Soul

Body & Soul

A GHOST AND THE GOTH NOVEL

STACEY KADE

HYPERION

NEW YORK

Copyright © 2012 by Stacey Kade

All rights reserved. Published by Hyperion, an imprint of Disney Book Group. No part of this book may be reproduced or transmitted in any form or by any means, electronic or mechanical, including photocopying, recording, or by any information storage and retrieval system, without written permission from the publisher. For information address Hyperion, 114 Fifth Avenue, New York, New York 10011-5690.

Printed in the United States of America
First Hyperion paperback edition, 2013
10 9 8 7 6 5 4 3 2 1
V475-2873-0-13015
Library of Congress Control Number for Hardcover Edition: 2011030592
ISBN 978-1-4231-3527-2
Visit www.un-requiredreading.com

SUSTAINABLE
FORESTRY
INITIATIVE
Certified Chain of Custody
Promoting Sustainable Forestry
www.sfiprogram.org
SFI-01054
The SFI label applies to the text stock

To my editor, Christian Trimmer:
Thank you for giving me the chance to tell these
stories and for helping me make them better
than I ever dreamed they could be. I am so
grateful to be one of your authors.

❧ 1 ❧

Alona Dare/ Lily Turner

Malachi the Magnificent, Consultant to the Stars, had a storefront in a dingy, rundown strip mall between a sketchy-looking Laundromat and a closed-up nail salon with a big, bright orange health department sticker plastered on its door. It couldn't have been less magnificent if he'd tried.

My heart sank. This was the guy we were going to for help on life-and-death matters?

I looked over at Will in the driver's seat. "You're kidding, right?"

"What's wrong?" he asked, making the turn into the crumbling and pothole-filled lot, which was—surprise, surprise—basically empty, even on a warm and sunny Friday afternoon.

"Look at this place! It's about six seconds from being raided by the police . . . or Health and Sanitation." I shuddered.

At least Madame Selena had had her own building . . . about sixteen inches from the edge of the highway, but still. And she had a turban. Say what you will, but it certainly added an air of mystery to her, like what, exactly, she was hiding under it.

"Appearances can be deceiving." Will looked over at me pointedly.

I shoved her . . . *my* fine brown hair away from my eyes and glared at him. "Oh, ha-ha. Very funny."

I'd been stuck inside Lily Turner's body for almost a month now. My well-intentioned attempt as a spirit to simply borrow her body for the purposes of communicating with the living had backfired in a huge way. And now I had to pretend to be Lily. Or try to, anyway.

I'm an expert at pretending. I spent a lot of years and even more effort convincing people that the perfectly put together and trouble-free Alona Dare they knew and seemingly loved was the real deal instead of a carefully crafted and maintained cover.

But being a whole other person—someone I'd never met—that was a stretch, even with my skills.

I'd read Lily's diary (revoltingly full of naive gushing about Ben Rogers—barf), reviewed the contents of her pathetic closet, and dug into the depths of her medicine cabinet (cheap makeup in the wrong color palette and one bottle of expired antibiotics—boring).

But none of that told me how to *be* her, especially around her family. And I was failing . . . miserably. I didn't know Lily's favorite color, that she was allergic to strawberries (found that one out the hard way), or that she hated that old Backstreet Boys song "Everybody," which her younger brother, Tyler, played over and over again just to bug her. I'd just tuned it out and chalked it up as another example of Tyler's bad taste, in music this time instead of fashion.

Trauma and brain injury could explain away a lot, but not enough. The Turners had given me space in the beginning to "adjust," but now, unsurprisingly, Mrs. Turner was pressing for more time, more interaction . . . just more from me. And I couldn't do it; I couldn't be their Lily even if I wanted to . . . and in a funny-odd kind of way, I really did.

I didn't blame the Turners, and I didn't want to hurt them—they'd been so patient and nice to me—but I felt like I couldn't breathe with all this pressure. Pressure not only to be Lily Turner but to be the correct Lily Turner, the one they all remembered.

And Will was no help. His experiences with Lily had been mostly at school. He didn't know much of anything about her home life, at least not in enough detail to be useful.

Their friend Joonie might have had more info, given her former crush on Lily, and she'd even called from Boston a couple of times to check on "me" after hearing "I" had woken from the coma. But I'd kept the conversations short and as generically polite as possible, feigning memory loss. She sounded like she was actually doing all right living with her sister, and the last thing I wanted was to say or do anything that might cause her to worry and come rushing back here. *Not* a good idea, for a lot of reasons.

So, in short, this being-Lily thing was a mess. One I needed out of as soon as possible, but definitely before school started back up in a couple of weeks. That was the one thing that could make this situation worse—going back to school as Lily Turner. Or as a freaking junior.

But that was easier said than done. What I'd accomplished was rare—possessing a body for any length of time was virtually unheard-of. Getting me out would be one hell of a trick. Keeping Lily alive without me would be another. Her body was now, in theory, dependent on the energy my spirit provided. So, in short, even if we could find a way to get me out, I couldn't leave unless we could find a way to save Lily, too—a way to bring her spirit back from the light or some kind of energy substitute or something.

Essentially, we were looking for a two-for-one miracle. But after only a few weeks, we'd exhausted most of our semibrilliant ideas and reached desperate-measures level. We'd take anything now, any clue to point us in the correct direction.

Hence, Malachi the allegedly Magnificent.

"What's so special about this one again?" I asked as Will pulled into a parking space. "Aside from raising our chances of catching hepatitis, I mean." I looked at the nail salon and shuddered again.

Malachi would be the third "psychic medium" (a.k.a. "big

faker") we'd seen in the last couple of weeks. And frankly, he didn't seem any more promising than the others.

"He has a star by his name . . . I think," Will said, cutting the engine.

"You *think?*" I demanded.

He shifted uneasily in his seat. "It's not exactly clear, okay? I'm pretty sure it's a star."

"So, just to clarify, we're here in janky-land because of a possible doodle?"

He looked at me, stung. "Hey, we've been over this. If you have any better ideas—"

"Just . . . let me see it again." I waved my hand impatiently at him in a "gimme" gesture.

He glared at me but twisted to the side to reach into his back pocket, and I tried hard not to notice that doing so made his shirt pull tighter against his chest and brought him so much closer to me. Like, touching close.

Heat crawled up my neck into my face, and I looked away, hoping he wouldn't notice. God. This body thing—technically, in this case, I suppose it was *his* body and my reaction to it—was killing me. Could I please be noncorporeal again? Now? I did not like this . . . flesh and blood intensity. It was all out-of-control feeling, and I did not DO out-of-control.

"Here." He bumped my arm with the back of his hand, holding out a carefully folded rectangle of yellow paper.

I snapped it from his fingers, and he sucked a breath through his teeth. "Careful!"

Will treated the page like an artifact from a previous age, and I suppose, for him, it was. After our other resources (pretty much just the Internet) had failed to produce any new information on my predicament—or really, any information at all, other than calling for a priest—Will had dug into some boxes of his dad's stuff in the basement. Most of it was random useless junk his mother couldn't bring herself to throw away—a half-finished pack of gum, old birthday cards from Will's grandma, an almost empty bottle of cologne, an old answering-machine tape, grocery lists with Will's dad's illegible scrawl.

I suspect Will had been hoping for a secret journal—something detailing his father's struggle with being a ghost-talker over the years—that his mother had somehow overlooked or written off at the time as an attempt at fiction. I know he wanted to get a better handle on who his dad was, the kind of person he'd been, since his dad had lied to him for most of his life. But there was nothing like that in the boxes. And for the record, my hopes had been dashed as well, since he didn't conveniently find a vial of mysterious liquid labeled EMERGENCY ONLY: FOR WHEN YOUR SPIRIT GUIDE BECOMES TRAPPED IN A BODY.

So . . . no diary of confessions, no bottle of secret formula, but tucked into a city map of Decatur was this folded-up page torn from the *P* section in the yellow pages. The Psychic section, specifically. But what Will was interested in was the strange marks and undecipherable notes in his dad's handwriting near several of the names/ads, even though we had no idea what any of the nonsensical scrawls meant.

Will's dad was a bit of a mystery to him, so no matter how cryptic the messages on the page, it was more than Will had had before. From what Will had told me, his dad was never particularly chatty about the gift they both shared. Daniel Killian preferred to pretend that everything was normal, no matter what kind of toll that took on him and his son. I personally thought that was kind of crappy of him, especially given that he then bailed on Will and Will's mom by offing himself a few years ago.

But whatever. I guess maybe I wasn't the best judge of parental behavior at times, either.

I let out a breath and made a deliberate effort to unfold the page more carefully, and Will relaxed a little. He did have a point—the lines where it had been folded were already softening from the wear and tear we'd given it in the last few weeks. If it had been an actual historical document, it might have been faring better—parchment or whatever they used to write on back in the old days might have actually held up better than this cheap-ass paper.

The psychics shared a page with listings for property managers and prosthetic-device manufacturers. Malachi the Magnificent's ad (God, could he sound any more like a little kid's party magician?) was circled several times, hard enough to dent the page, and had what might have been a star by it.

Or an ink blot.

I sighed. Will's theory was that his dad must have been checking into these people for a reason, maybe as part of his work for the Order. The publishing date, printed in tiny letters at the bottom, indicated the page was from five years ago, right about the time Will's dad had finally quit working for them. The Order of the Guardians was essentially a group of ghost-talkers who'd taken it upon themselves to save living humankind from all of us big bad spirits. Never mind that ghosts were once living people, too. Lily and I had both almost succumbed to their relentless "protective" services. Will and I weren't exactly their biggest fans these days, and that feeling was probably pretty mutual. Will had heard from them only once after everything that happened. As far as I knew, most of the leaders thought Lily had recovered on her own, and Will was simply no longer interested in joining their organization, much to their disappointment. The one who knew better, who had witnessed what went down in the janitorial closet at the hospital—my guess was, he was staying quiet to avoid losing control over his division. He'd been abusing his authority . . . and his daughter.

Still, the Order had some serious power players, and if they'd been interested in these "psychics," maybe one of them might actually be valuable in some way. Maybe someone knew stuff we didn't. Wouldn't be hard; most days it felt like we knew nothing.

Folding up the page to hand it back to Will, though, I noticed something I'd missed before. "The other side of this is—"

He focused his attention on the steering wheel, running his thumb over a cut in the plastic. "I know."

The section right before Psychics? Psychiatrists. His father hadn't been crazy, as Will's mom and others had probably suspected at the time, but depressed? Uh, yeah. People don't generally take their lives via train because they're feeling hunky-dory.

"Are you sure he saved this because of the psychics or . . ."

He just looked at me.

Yikes. "Okay, then. Never mind." Will had few sore spots. This was one of them.

I finished folding the page and held it out to him.

He took it and put it back in his pocket. "He didn't make any marks on the psychiatrist page. Not that one or the one still in the phone book. I checked."

"I wasn't implying that he—"

"Let's just go, okay?" He opened the car door and got out without waiting for an answer.

Hey, look at that. I could upset people even when I was trying to be *nice.* Too bad I hadn't realized this talent sooner. I could have saved myself the effort of coming up with all those perfectly pointed insults.

I followed him, climbing out of the car with way more effort than should have been necessary. My left leg was stiff from sitting for just the twenty minutes or so it had taken us to get here.

I gritted my teeth, forcing myself to stand up on it anyway. I *hated* this. So broken and clumsy and . . . not me.

I'd spent years training, working out, and not eating to get *my* body, the one I'd had before. I was varsity cheerleader captain, people; that's more than good genetics. It's work.

But Lily . . . she was shorter, softer, curvier. Not fat, exactly, but not the athlete I'd been, either. Not even close. And don't even get me started on the clumsiness. If there was something to trip over in a ten-foot radius, she found it . . . the hard way. Some of that was because this body had been in a coma for the better part of a year, and some because of the accident that had put her there. I had weekly physical therapy appointments to address those issues and hopefully get this body back to the point where I could exercise on my own. But a good portion of it would never be "fixed." It was just her. And now, me.

I stepped back, shoved the door shut . . . and slipped on the loose gravel on the asphalt. I clawed for the door handle to catch myself, but it was too far away. I braced myself for the bone-crunching impact with the ground, but hands caught at me at the last second, pulling me up and against a solid, warm body.

"Are you okay?" Will's voice in my ear sounded shocked. "I was coming around to help you."

His arms were wrapped around me underneath Lily's . . . *my* sizable chest—another big change, frankly—and I could feel his heartbeat thudding way too hard against my back. I'd scared him. Me, too.

"Fine. Just . . . I'm fine. Let go already." But he didn't, probably because that would have involved dropping me. My face burned, as I imagined what I must have looked like, flailing and falling like a total klutz.

Once I got my feet back under me properly, he let go. I straightened my shirt—a hideous yellow baby-doll number—and raked a hand through Lily's blah-brown hair before turning to face him. "Thanks," I said grudgingly.

"Welcome." He towered over me now. His skin was still far too pale, and he still dressed like the angel of death in a black T-shirt and dark jeans. Three small silver hoops in his left ear caught the light and glittered beneath his black hair, adding to his whole nothing-but-trouble image. But his eyes, an icy blue I'd once thought creepy and cold, now did funny things to my insides when he looked at me intensely like this, his brow furrowed.

It made me want to tackle him, and not in the football way. Well, I mean, I guess the method was the same, but not the purpose.

A smile flickered at the corners of his mouth. "You're staring," he said.

Damn it. My face went hot again, and I turned away to limp toward Malachi's storefront. The blushing was another side effect of this stupid body. When I'd been a spirit, I'd still felt things, of course, but it was weaker, mere shades of this intensity.

"So, what's the plan?" I asked over my shoulder, doing my best to pretend the last three minutes hadn't happened. "Same as last time?"

With the other faux ghost-talkers, Will had gone in asking to communicate with his recently deceased cousin, Maria . . . who, of course, didn't actually exist and never had.

Yet they'd never failed to come up with detailed descriptions of her, obviously based on Will's appearance, and always told him how happy she was now. Not a single one of them had ever bothered to explain that some spirits—most, actually—are unreachable. Only the ones who have unresolved issues and tend to stick around after death—in Middleground, as Will called it—could communicate.

And the money they charged for all this nonsense? Ridiculous. We'd already spent almost everything Will had earned in his brief career as a busboy. There were serious dollars to be made in this area, especially as the real deal. Not that Will would ever even consider that.

Will easily caught up to me on the sidewalk leading to Malachi's storefront, and stepped ahead to grab the door. "Yeah, I think the Maria story works—"

He stopped suddenly enough that I smacked into his back, my nose colliding sharply with his shoulder blade. Short! I was short now, damn it!

Eyes watering, I stumbled back. "Walk much?" I demanded, rubbing my stinging nose.

He didn't respond, just stood there, head cocked to one side, staring into Malachi the Magnificent's windows.

A chill skittered over my skin. "What is it? What's wrong?"

"There are ghosts here," he said quietly over his shoulder. "More than usual."

Ghosts are everywhere, as I'd learned after my own death and return as a spirit. Even at the other fake ghost-talkers' locations, there'd sometimes been a few tagging along after the other clients, people they were attached to, or one or two who'd read the "psychic" sign out front and hoped it was for real.

"Really?" Holding on to Will's arm for balance, I leaned around him for a look. Not that I'd be able to *see* anything. Even though I could apparently hear spirits—a side effect of being a spirit stuffed back into a body, or maybe because I'd been trapped in Lily's body during a near-death experience, we weren't sure—seeing them was not my forte.

I squinted and all I saw were a few blurry, smudgy spots that had no discernible source. My ghost vision coming in? Or poor window cleaning on Malachi's part?

"Are you sure?" I asked Will.

"A guy in a Lincoln-type top hat is talking to a woman in a nightgown and . . ." He leaned closer to get a better look in the window. "There's some girl dressed for spring break at the beach, and a dude in the far corner is holding what appears to be a severed arm. His own."

I jerked back. "Ew. So Malachi is actually legit?" You'd think he'd have moved on up to the less skanky side of town, if so.

"Unless this is a costume party gone horribly wrong . . . maybe." Will turned to face me, tension now visibly thrumming through him. "Subtle has to be the key word here. We can't go in there and let on that we can see them."

I shrugged. No problem for me.

"Or hear them," he added.

I made an exasperated noise. "Fine, okay, whatever."

"Hey, I'm serious." He reached down and tipped my chin up with his fingertip until I was forced to meet his gaze. "You aren't my spirit guide anymore. We have no protection, no way to make them back off."

Ah, yes, another lovely side effect of this in-body disaster. Whatever bond we'd shared as spirit guide and ghosttalker was now gone. Or, at least, the most obvious sign of it. I didn't show up daily wherever he was at 7:03 a.m., the time of my death. Good thing, because that might have been kind of tough to explain to the Turners.

At one time, I'd also been able to freeze pushy ghosts in place by simply restating my claim on Will. These days, not so much. Actually, for all we knew, it might still work. But it seemed unlikely, given everything else, and it was too dangerous to try. It would mean revealing who I was inside this body and that I could hear the spirits. Then Will wouldn't be the only one being overwhelmed by last requests.

"I don't want you to get hurt," he added, his gaze softening as he took in the scar on my face . . . Lily's face.

Lily. I jerked away from him. Will wasn't immune to the effects of this bizarre situation, either. Even though he knew better, sometimes he looked at me and saw her. I know he did. And he'd never been as concerned about my welfare until it became tied to hers, it seemed.

It wasn't fair.

"*I* will be fine," I said curtly, doing my best to squelch the wounded feeling rising up in me. "Can we just do this already?"

He opened his mouth as if to say something, then closed it, clearly thinking better of whatever it was. Smart. "Yeah. Okay," he said. "I'll go first. Stay right behind me."

I nodded, not about to argue that part of it. Among the other things we'd never tested was whether I'd bump into ghosts, as Will did, or pass through them, as other non-ghost-talkers would. I hadn't found myself colliding with invisible people yet, but that was no sure indicator, as I knew from experience that ghosts avoided walking through the living whenever possible.

He turned and opened the door, and I stayed on the heels of his worn Chucks as he walked in.

Malachi the Magnificent's waiting room looked surprisingly similar to that of a doctor's or dentist's, only darker, dustier, and reeking of way more incense. There were a bunch of chairs lining the outer edges of the room and in rows toward the middle. A door in the far wall led, presumably, to the back rooms, where the "magic" would happen.

A book lay open on a desk next to that door, with a photocopied sign asking us to SIGN IN, PLEASE! ☺ Blah.

Will wrote fake names—Milli Martin and Steve Vanilli—in the book without batting an eye. (Yeah, he thinks he's funny.)

But then he turned to face the waiting room again and hesitated. I followed his gaze, and for once, I understood. The blurry spots I'd seen before were not smudges on the glass. They were in here and moving. At least four of them, maybe more. The trick was how to avoid them without *looking* like we were avoiding them.

I stood on my tiptoes, putting most of my weight on my good leg. "The chairs in the back left corner, maybe?" I whispered to Will. There weren't as many blurry spots in that direction, though we'd have to pass several to get there. The noise seemed fainter in that direction, too. I couldn't hear anything specific, just a low murmur of voices, but too many for the half dozen or so living people there, most of whom were sitting silently anyway.

Will looked sharply over his shoulder at me. "You can see—"

I shook my head. "Kinda, sorta. It's . . . I'll explain later."

He nodded and started toward the chairs I'd indicated, and I was right behind him . . . until someone caught my eye. A *living* someone.

I stopped dead, certain that I could not be seeing who I thought, especially not here.

Her normally glossy black hair was a dull and staticky mess gathered in a frizzy ponytail, and she was wearing a tank top and sweats—not the cute kind, either, but the baggy ones you only wear when you're home with the flu. Still, it was definitely her. Huddled in a chair across from the receptionist's desk and dabbing her eyes with a soggy tissue that looked about two tears away from disintegrating entirely, was my former best friend.

A rush of homesickness for my old life swept over me. "Misty?" Her name slipped out before I could stop it. "What are you doing here?" It felt like the world had tipped a bit, sliding people into places they shouldn't be. I hadn't seen her in months, not since graduation. Not mine, obviously. But hers and Will's and everybody else's that I knew.

She looked up, her eyes red and puffy from crying. Her gaze skated over my face, and she recoiled slightly, probably at the sight of the jagged scar on the left side, from my temple down. "Do I know you?"

Oh, right. I tipped my head forward, letting my hair slide to hide the damage, and buying some time before I had to answer. I didn't know what to say. She wouldn't recognize Lily, probably, but . . . "I—"

"What are you doing?" Will whispered to me, alarm in his voice. "Sorry, our mistake," he said to Misty, and then started to pull me away.

But it was too late.

"Hey, wait," Misty called after us. "I *do* know you."

In spite of everything—that she'd stolen my boyfriend and thought I was dead and gone—my heart jumped with the ridiculous hope that my oldest friend had somehow recognized me. I turned back to face her, but she was looking at Will.

I fought against the unreasonable disappointment. It only made sense, I guess, that she'd recognize him. At least he was still in the same body as the one she knew him in from before.

"You went to Groundsboro," she said, pointing at him. "You're, like, that freaky goth guy, right?"

Uh-oh. I grimaced, and Will stopped, his shoulders stiff. "Yeah, that's me," he said with a tight smile. "Let's go," he said to me.

"So . . ." She got up and edged toward us. "This guy is legit?" She waved her Kleenex-filled hand around at Malachi's office.

Now Will turned to face her with a wary look, and I could see his curiosity warring with the need to be cautious. We were starting to attract some attention. The noise level had dropped considerably, and if I wasn't mistaken, a few of the blurry spots were drifting closer to us. "Why do you ask that?" he asked finally.

To my complete shock, her face crumpled and she collapsed into her chair. "Because I need help," she said in a squeaky, high-pitched voice between sobs. "And I thought you might know if this is actually going to work."

"This" presumably referring to her consultation with Malachi.

"You're, like, an expert on all this goth/undead stuff, right?" she asked, sniffling. "And you're here, so he must be good. . . ."

Will looked at me, a little panicked. I tugged away from him and went to sit next to her, ignoring his glare of warning. No, Misty hadn't always made the greatest choices—like stealing my boyfriend even *before* I was dead—but I'd forgiven her for that . . . mostly. She was the only one—before Will—who'd known the truth about my mom's drinking problems, and she'd never told anyone or used it against me. I honestly couldn't be sure if I would have done the same with access to that kind of ammunition.

"What's wrong?" I asked, patting her shoulder gingerly.

She looked sort of . . . unshowered. Clearly, something was going on.

She took a deep hiccupping breath. "You guys remember my best friend, Alona Dare? She died?" Her voice broke on the last word, and she covered her face with her hands.

I have to admit, it warmed my heart that Misty was clearly still upset about my death, even though it had been months ago. Now, this was the kind of mourning I'd deserved from the beginning.

Will sighed heavily. "Yeah, I remember her." To the trained ear, though, he sounded far more exasperated than sorry. I scowled at him.

"So, you're here because of her?" I asked, trying to sound sympathetic while mentally sticking my tongue out at Will. See? *Somebody* missed me . . . even after stealing my boyfriend. Well, let's just not focus on that part.

Misty nodded, her head still bowed.

Oh, how sweet. She wants to stay in touch with me. I gave Will a triumphant look, and he rolled his eyes.

"I'm sure that wherever Alona is—" I began.

"She won't leave me alone," Misty said, her voice muffled by her hands.

"What?" I leaned closer, certain I must have misheard.

"I said . . ." Misty lifted her head up and met my gaze, righteous anger burning through the last of her tears. "That bitch is haunting me, and I can't get rid of her."

❧ 2 ❧

Will Killian

I've seen Alona in a lot of situations. A lot of messed-up situations, actually. Confronting angry ghosts who wanted to tear through her to get to me, discovering that her "friends" were mostly worthless jerks, and most recently, inhabiting the body of a girl she didn't know.

This, however, was the first time I'd ever seen her struck completely and utterly speechless. Her mouth worked, opening and closing several times, without a single word escaping.

Misty looked slightly disconcerted by Alona's fish-out-of-water routine. She shifted away from Alona in the chair, like she half expected an explosion of some kind. Frankly, I wasn't sure *what* to expect.

"Excuse us," I said to Misty, hastily reaching down to grab Alona's hand.

I pulled her to the far corner, near the door to the outside, and fortunately, no one followed, though the ghost in the Abe Lincoln hat (thankfully, not the real deal, just someone who apparently favored the long-dead president's taste in fashion) was staring at us now. Great.

"So much for subtle," I hissed at Alona.

"She thinks I'm haunting her." She sounded stunned.

I raked my hand through my hair. "Yeah, I kinda got that."

"I'm not, though." She shook her head as though clearing it, which made her wobble. I grabbed her elbow long enough to steady her, but she didn't even seem to notice.

"I mean, I did try it once," she continued. "Back a few months ago, right after I died."

"Yes, I remember," I said tersely. She'd almost disappeared for good then, thoroughly screwing both of our chances for survival.

"But not since then, and I can't now. I mean, look at me!" She gestured toward herself with distaste. "I'm all . . . bodified."

I gritted my teeth to keep from responding with any number of comments that would only make things worse. Yes, okay, her point was that she couldn't be haunting anyone in her current condition, but it was more than that, I knew. Alona hated being trapped in a body that wasn't her own or up to her previous standards—fine. But Lily was not exactly the Hunchback of Notre Dame, as Alona would make her out to be. Lily was cute, always had been, and yes, the scar on her face and the limp were noticeable, but they didn't make her repulsive . . . not by any stretch of the imagination.

But now was not the time for this argument.

"Look, we need to focus on the situation at hand, okay?" I glanced over my shoulder. Severed Arm Dude and Spring Break Girl had joined the faux-Lincoln ghost, and they were now talking among themselves and gesturing in our direction. Well, half gesturing, in the case of the ghost with only one arm.

Not good.

I turned back to Alona. "We need to see Malachi the Magical or whatever, and figure out what he knows, if anything, and then get out of here." Hopefully in one piece and without a trail of ghosts following both of us home.

She jerked her head up to glare at me, and the all-too-familiar fierceness in her expression made me step back. That was all Alona. I could almost see her beneath the surface of Lily. It was . . . unsettling, to say the least. "Someone is pretending to be me, the spirit of me, to scare *my best friend*." She jabbed a finger in my chest with the last three words. "How is that not a concern?"

I sighed. "Or maybe her guilty conscience is finally catching up to her, and she's seeing ghosts where there aren't any because she feels bad." It happened all the time. Sometimes picture frames just fall over. Doors slam shut, screws fall out, etc. Not all of it is the result of ghosts, but when people feel like they deserve to be haunted, that's usually the first explanation they believe. "Which do you think is more likely?"

With a sound of disgust, she shoved past me and limped back toward Misty, who honestly looked a little frightened at her approach. Faux Lincoln and Severed Arm Guy scattered to get out of her way.

I groaned silently and hurried after her. This could not possibly end well.

"I'm sorry about that," Alona said to Misty, as she reclaimed the chair next to her. "You took me by surprise is all."

Misty gave a harsh laugh. "You don't believe me."

Alona shook her head. "No, I do. Actually, *we* do," she said, giving me a "go along with this or die painfully" look.

Oh, good.

"But I'm not sure why you think it's Alona. From what I know of her, she would never—"

"Wait." Misty held up her hand with a frown. "Who are you again?"

I held my breath.

"Ally Turner. It was Lily, but I go by Ally now," Alona said. "I was . . . I am a year behind you at school." Her words sounded forced and false, but maybe only because I knew the truth.

"But," Alona continued quickly, "we have experience dealing with this kind of thing."

"We've been haunted before," I added, lying to save our asses. Was she trying to get us killed? Why not just announce to all the ghosts in the room that we could see and/or hear them?

Misty nodded slowly, as if that was not a surprise. Then she shook her head with a sad smile. "Well, whatever you know about ghosts, you did not know Alona. And trust me, it's her. She . . ." Misty hesitated. "She was my best friend. But she wasn't exactly the forgive-and-forget type, you know? Revenge. That was her thing."

Alona stiffened.

Oh, crap.

"Have you considered that maybe those people deserved what they got?" Alona demanded.

I poked her and she swiveled to face me with a frown. *Shut up*, I mouthed.

But fortunately, Misty seemed too lost in her memories to notice. "I took Chris from her. Actually, Chris and I . . . We just kind of found each other."

"Found each other, right," Alona muttered. Hmm. Maybe she hadn't yet completely forgiven Misty.

"I didn't think Alona knew before she died, but now I . . . I'm not sure. It wasn't intentional for either of us," Misty added defiantly.

"And that makes a difference how?" Alona demanded.

I cleared my throat sharply. "I think what *Ally*"— I emphasized the name, glaring at Alona, who rolled her eyes—"means is, what signs are you seeing that make you think Alona, specifically, is haunting you, not some other random ghost?"

"Oh." Misty looked startled and then confused. "Why would there be a random ghost haunting me?"

I was pretty sure there wasn't a ghost involved at all, but trying to explain to Misty that she was likely haunting herself probably wouldn't have helped. All I could do was try to show Alona that it wasn't someone impersonating her. "There probably isn't. But I'm just trying to understand why you think it's her. Other than the fact you think she'd be angry if she knew about you and Chris, *which she doesn't*," I said, aiming my last words at Alona, who slumped in her chair and folded her arms over her chest.

"Whatever," she muttered.

Misty lifted her hands in exasperation at my apparent idiocy. "Hello? Who else would it be? And why would it start right after Chris proposed?

Alona froze. "Proposed?" she whispered.

Oh, boy. With a sigh, I sat down.

Misty gave an uncomfortable shrug. "He's going away to IU and I'm staying here. He wanted us to be engaged first."

Alona sat up. "You can't do that," she said, shaking her head.

"I think what she means is you're young," I said quickly. This conversation was going to kill me. "Can we get back to the signs, please?"

Misty was looking back and forth between us like we were crazy, which wasn't far from the truth today. "Okay," she said slowly. "Picture frames knocked over, covers pulled off me in the night, footsteps in my room but no one is there, and sometimes, when I'm falling asleep, I hear someone call my name." She shuddered.

And . . . picture frames fall over, covers slip off, people often think they hear footsteps or someone calling them when they're half asleep.

"Oh, and she wrote her name in the steam on the mirror in my bathroom."

Whoa. I leaned forward in my chair. "You saw that happen?"

She shook her head. "No, it was just there one day when I got out of the shower."

Huh, well, that changed things a little. Maybe it wasn't a guilty conscience. But that didn't necessarily mean it was a ghost, either. A living person could do all of those things she mentioned, including the mirror writing. Steam up the mirror, and write the words you want. Then, when the mirror is covered in steam again, the words reappear. Maybe a living someone wasn't pleased with this new development in Misty's love life and had decided to express it as "Alona."

"I can't believe you're getting married," Alona said. "What are you going to do for a maid of honor? It better not be Leanne."

Misty gaped at her, but before she could respond, the door to the back rooms opened, catching everyone's attention.

An elderly woman in a tidy black suit and heavy black shoes shuffled out, clinging tightly to the arm of a guy who had to be Malachi the Magnificent. For one, he was wearing a cloak. In August.

The sight of that was enough to shake Alona from her sulk. "Seriously?" She snorted. "I'm beginning to think this guy doesn't understand the difference between a magician and a medium."

Probably a lot of people didn't. It was all in that mysterious realm of "might be real" to most. And if this guy was willing to play up the mystical part of it, that likely helped sell the bill of goods.

Other than his cloak, "Malachi"—no way was that his real name—didn't seem too extraordinary. He was maybe in his mid-twenties, a thin, kind of dweeby guy with curly red hair and heavy black-rimmed glasses. The effect, actually, was of someone who'd gotten lost on his way to a Harry Potter or Lord of the Rings costume party.

Great.

A few steps behind the elderly woman and the caped douche bag, a young guy in an Al Capone–era suit and hat followed, looking kind of pissed.

"You're not listening. That's not what I said at all," he shouted at Malachi.

Next to me, Alona stiffened, and I knew she'd heard the ghost, too.

But Malachi just smiled fondly at the old woman and walked her over to the main door. She squeezed his hand, leaving him with a wad of cash, which he quickly tucked inside his cloak.

I relaxed, relief warring with disappointment. Malachi was a fake. We weren't any closer to finding a solution for

Alona or figuring out what my dad had been doing checking out all these fake ghost-talkers. But at least we didn't have to claim Malachi in our ranks.

I leaned over to Alona. "When he takes the next person in, we'll get out of here."

She frowned at me. "No way. What about her?" She tipped her head toward Misty, who was staring at Malachi like he was a walking ray of hope.

I shook my head. "I don't think it's anything we can fix."

She opened her mouth to protest, but stopped as Malachi moved to stand in the center of the waiting room.

He bowed his head and placed his fingertips at his temples.

"Oh, please," Alona muttered. "Doesn't this drive you crazy?" she demanded of me.

I grimaced and looked around, but Malachi seemed to have the rest of the room captivated. "What do you want me to do?" I whispered back to her. Denouncing him as a fraud would only cause more problems for us, and we didn't need that.

Misty shushed us.

Malachi rocked back and forth on his heels. "I'm sensing several spirits here who'd like to communicate."

"Yeah, I have something to communicate," Alona muttered, maybe not quite as quietly as she should have. "Jerk."

He looked up sharply and searched the room until he identified Alona as the source, which probably wasn't too tough. She was glaring at him as if she'd have set him on fire if she could.

He gave a forced magnanimous chuckle. "I see we have a doubter in our midst."

Heads, belonging to both the living and the dead, turned toward us. *Damn it, Alona.*

Malachi approached, still smiling. "I understand your hesitation, but the ways of the dead are not—" He stopped abruptly, staring at me.

The color drained from his face, making his glasses stand out starkly. He attempted to keep his smile, but it wobbled and then fell away. "The ways of the dead are not our own," he tried again in a croaky voice, his hands at the sides of his cloak.

Then he swallowed hard, forced out a barely audible "Excuse me," and turned tail, stalking back through the door he'd just exited, his cloak flapping behind him.

I couldn't have been more surprised if he'd dropped to the ground and started clucking like a chicken.

Alona stared after him. "What the hell?" She looked to me, and I had no answer.

Except . . . he'd looked right at me and freaked. That had to mean *something*, didn't it? It was almost like he'd recognized me, but I'd never seen him before. Did he know that I was the real thing, the ghost-talker he was pretending to be? Or . . . could he possibly have known my dad?

The thought took my breath away.

My dad and I had looked enough alike; it wasn't impossible that Malachi would come to the conclusion that we were related.

I scrambled to my feet and hurried after Malachi. At least, that was the plan—catch up to him, pin him down, and make him talk. But apparently the ghost of the girl dressed for spring break had the same idea. And we collided . . . hard.

We went sprawling in different directions.

I'm not sure whose gasps of surprise were louder—those of the living people, including Misty, who saw me bounce off seemingly nothing and hit the floor, or those of the dead, who saw exactly what happened and knew what it meant.

"Will!" Alona lurched to her feet.

Misty looked astonished.

"Will?" the ghost in the Abe Lincoln hat repeated, moving closer to stare down at me.

Crap, crap, crap. Still half dazed, I rolled to my side and pushed myself to stand, ignoring the sharp pain in my elbow. Malachi's carpet had, unsurprisingly, the cushion factor of cheap toilet paper.

Spring Break Girl flipped her long auburn hair out of her face and got to her feet. "You're Will Killian? The one everyone's been talking about?" she asked, reaching through the neck of her Señor Frog's T-shirt to tug her bright pink bikini top back into place. She managed to sound surprised and disgusted at the same time.

"Another ghost-talker?" Severed Arm Dude asked, pointing the stump end of his arm at me.

The woman in the long white nightgown danced closer. She seemed, possibly, a little crazy.

I took a step back, unable to stop myself. Severed Arm

Dude, Faux Lincoln, Spring Break Girl, and Nightgown Lady . . . four, no, five—I'd forgotten about the Al Capone-type who'd been disappointed by Malachi's interpretation of his message—against just me.

If I tried to run, they'd stop me without breaking a sweat . . . Well, you know what I mean. If it came down to a physical confrontation, each of them vying for attention, they'd probably tear me apart. Attacking me might drain them of some of their energy—being violent as a spirit takes away from the resources required to remain on this plane of existence—but how much and whether that would be enough . . . there was no way to know. Not until it was too late.

I swallowed hard, my heartbeat shaking my whole body.

Alona moved toward me, faster than I'd seen her move before, at least in this body. She stepped between the ghosts and then turned to block me from them, her bad leg dragging a little behind.

"If you know Will," she said calmly, "then you know his spirit guide." The ghosts stared at her, as if uncertain what to make of her. I wondered, for the first time, what she looked like to other spirits. Could they see she wasn't like the rest of us?

"What are you doing?" I whispered, alarmed. They hadn't even known there was anything different about her. She was putting herself at risk unnecessarily.

Alona ignored me and turned to face Severed Arm Dude. She lifted her chin, daring him to come closer. "You don't want to get on her bad side, do you?"

I prayed I was the only one who could tell she was a little off, her gaze on his neck instead of his face. Several of the breathers who'd been waiting for Malachi bolted for the door. I didn't blame them. I could only imagine what it must look like to them. Misty was still in her chair, staring at us.

"The one who they say disappeared weeks ago?" Severed Arm Dude scoffed. "No one has seen her."

Spring Break Girl rolled her eyes as if the entire conversation were ridiculous.

I couldn't see much of Alona's expression at this angle, but from the sudden tension in her shoulders, I guessed she hadn't considered what the ghosts might be saying about her absence.

"Really?" Alona flipped her hair back, a classic attitude-filled move for her, and seemed startled when it didn't stay behind her shoulders. Lily's hair was shorter. But she recovered quickly enough. "I've seen her, and trust me, she is not happy."

Spring Break Girl tilted her head to one side, giving Alona a shrewd look. "Who are you?"

"No one *you* need to know," Alona said in a snotty tone that was a bit jarring to hear in Lily's voice. She reached back toward me with her left hand, flapping it until I realized she wanted me to take it. I stepped up and slipped my hand into hers. Her fingers closed over mine and squeezed almost to the point of pain, and as I drew even with her, she leaned into me the slightest bit, and I could hear her uneven breathing. She needed the help, I realized belatedly. That quick moving she'd done had come at a cost.

"We'll be going now," Alona said. "Give our regards to Malachi."

She started forward, and to my surprise, Severed Arm Dude and Spring Break Girl moved out of her way, though the latter watched us with more suspicion than was probably healthy.

I adjusted my stride to match Alona's shorter one so she could lean on me without it being as noticeable. But the slow walk across the room to the door felt interminable with the ghosts staring holes through us.

I held my breath, waiting for their rallying cry and the inevitable rush to block the door. . . .

But they let us walk out without another word.

So, maybe there was something to be said for being a bitch . . . or at least, knowing one. We'd coasted out of there on nothing but attitude and Alona's spirit-guide reputation. Problem was, that was not going to last forever.

❦ 3 ❦

Alona

"That was fun," I said through gritted teeth, collapsing into the passenger seat of Will's battered Dodge. My heart was pounding way too hard from the adrenaline rush, and pain shot up my leg in uneven bolts of agony.

"Hands in," Will warned before slamming my door shut and scrambling around the car and into the driver's seat. Once he was inside, he cranked the engine and peeled out of the parking space in reverse. "Are they coming?" His gaze was fixed behind us as he backed out.

"How should I know? Unless they're talking about following us, they could be in the freaking car for all I know." Which wasn't quite true, but I was feeling a tad irritable because once more I didn't have answers, and did have—hello?—intense pain. God, I'd forgotten how much it could hurt to be alive. And to be scared. Really and truly scared.

I squeezed my hands together to stop them from shaking. There'd been a moment when I wasn't sure, when I thought the spirits might try to stop us, and we would have been screwed. Will's abilities gave spirits physicality around him. They were as real and as capable of violence against him as any living person. I'd seen it happen before. Crowds of the dead pushing and shoving at him to get his attention. It wouldn't take much to turn it into a tug-of-war with Will as the rope.

And me, too, most likely. I shuddered at the idea. We hadn't tested whether ghosts could touch me and vice versa. I'd taken a leave of absence, sort of, from my spirit-guide duties. Since my "transformation," I'd been doing my best to stay away from disembodied voices, including those belonging to the spirits waiting for Will's help. If it turned out they could touch me—and there was a decent chance that would be the case—I would be utterly defenseless against them, just as Will was. His theory was that it was better to risk only one of us until we figured all of this out. So he was doing his best to manage them without me, relatively unsuccessfully, from what I'd heard.

"You were seeing something, though, I could tell." He spared me a glance as he shifted into drive, and I crossed my arms over my chest, hiding my hands so he couldn't see the trembling.

"Distortions, like shimmery spots in the air." I shook my

head, and he accelerated toward the exit, the tires spewing gravel behind us. "I don't know. It's—"

The car hit a pothole, jarring my leg, and I sucked a breath in through my teeth.

He slowed down and looked over at me. "Are you okay?"

I shifted in the seat, putting more weight on my right hip, trying to alleviate the pressure on my left leg, which, at the moment, felt like it was going to explode into a thousand pieces. "I'll be fine," I said, trying to sound like I meant it. "Just go, get us out of here."

He complied, but I couldn't help but notice that he also took care to avoid the worst of the holes until we reached the smoother pavement of the street. "What you did back there . . ." He hesitated.

No, no, not getting into this. "I was saving my ass as much as yours," I pointed out quickly, trying to stop this topic in its tracks.

He shook his head. "No, you weren't." He sounded almost stunned, which, frankly, stung a bit. "Until you said something, they didn't know you were different, that you were anything other than a regular living person."

Which meant I'd been dumb, dumb, dumb to stick my neck out. But I couldn't leave him like that, defenseless and trapped, even if it meant risking myself. And that was so unlike what I would have done a few months ago, it unnerved me. I definitely did not want to talk about it.

I forced a shrug. "If they'd started tossing you around or

something, somebody would have probably called the cops, and then we'd have to go through that whole is-he-crazy-or-not conversation, not to mention a hospital trip to get you fixed up." I sighed. "And I don't have the time or patience for that today."

He made a face. "Can you just let me say thank you?"

"There's nothing to thank me for," I snapped, growing more and more uncomfortable with the conversation. I . . . I cared too much about him, and this should not have been happening. It was way too big of a risk for me, leaving myself open to that kind of vulnerability. "You could have done it yourself. *Should* have done it yourself."

And short of that, what he probably should have done was find himself a new and fully functioning spirit guide to keep his ass out of a sling.

That was the real trouble. Before, at least, I'd been useful. He'd needed me, maybe even more than I'd needed him. And that was the way I liked it. If somebody needs you more than you need them, you're the one with the power, the control. But now . . . now he didn't need me at all. If anything, I was a burden, a problem to be solved. I was worse than useless, and that *sucked*. If I had truly been the person he thought I was, the one he was trying to thank, I'd have told him to dump me and find someone who could really help him, keep him safe. That's what I would have done in his position.

But I couldn't make the words come out. Because that would mean I'd be alone. No, not just alone . . . I'd be without Will. And somehow that was even worse. I'd gotten used to him being here with me, and it was getting harder and harder to imagine my life—in any form—without him. Which was terrifying in an entirely different way. Just thinking about it made me flinch.

Will noticed, of course. "Do you need to go to the hospital?" he asked quietly.

"No." I stared out the windshield, willing my eyes to stop burning with unshed tears.

He slid his hand across the seat, offering it to me. I looked at him, and he took his gaze off the road for a second to meet mine. My heart thumped triple-time in that moment, at the warmth in his eyes, the question that I wasn't ready to answer.

Hating myself for the weakness—because I knew, on some level, even this was for Lily, the person I looked like instead of the person I was—I took his hand, locking my palm tightly inside his. Holding his hand made me feel more securely tethered to the world, as if I wasn't going to float away and disappear like one of the balloons we used to release on the first day of Sunday school.

"So, why did he run?" I asked, shifting my attention to the side window and changing the topic, trying to pretend that this was not somehow more intimate than the kissing we'd done, that we weren't connected in this simple and yet powerful way that I felt in every cell of my borrowed body. "Malachi, I mean."

"I don't know." Was it me, or did Will sound a little unsorted himself?

"Better question: why did you chase him?" This time, I did look over at him.

He hesitated. "I think he recognized me."

"Really? How?" I was pretty sure Will would have remembered and mentioned meeting Malachi before; dude cut a fairly distinct figure in that stupid cloak of his.

"I think maybe he put it together, connected me with my dad."

Will did look a lot like his father in the pictures I'd seen, but . . .

I frowned. "We're talking years ago, though. *If* they even met. And he'd have to have left a hell of an impression for Malachi to recognize you from your dad and then also to run." I shook my head. "Which doesn't make sense. The guy's a fake. What would be the point of your dad talking to him at all?"

Will shrugged. "Maybe my dad was hunting down con artists for the Order or something."

"None of the other fakes were scared of you," I pointed out. In fact, based on the sheer amount of false-eyelash-batting that had gone on, I was pretty sure Madame Selena might have tried to keep him as her houseboy/love slave if I'd been paying less attention.

"That's exactly why we need to talk to him again."

"Again?" I turned carefully in my seat to stare at him. "Did you miss the part where the guy is a fraud? Totally of no use to us?"

"Maybe he can tell us what my dad was doing, give us

some direction on what to try next," he argued.

I snorted. "Hello, straws, we are grasping at you."

He glared at me.

"Look, I know you want to know what your dad was doing, I get it." I tried to soften my tone. "He was a man of mystery and secrets or whatever. But this, what we're doing? It's supposed to be fixing this, fixing me." I gestured down at myself, trying not to notice again how much smaller this hand was; though, actually, it was far worse when I caught myself *not* noticing anymore. Getting used to this was not an option. I grimaced. "And Malachi can't have anything to do with that."

Will's mouth tightened, and he gave me a look like he wanted to say something, but he just shook his head instead.

"What?" I demanded.

"Nothing." But then he kept going. "It's just, you act like Lily is some kind of horrible punishment for you."

I gaped at him and then yanked my hand free of his. "You don't want me in here, either!"

"I don't," he said immediately. "But do you know how many people would kill to be alive again, eating doughnuts, smelling flowers, talking to people—other living people— and all you care about is what you look like in her body, which, to be honest, has always been more than fine to me." The words poured out of him like he'd been holding them back for a while.

I sat back, stunned. Will had had a thing for Lily. I'd known that. It was a crush, over as soon as it started and nothing serious, but hearing him talk about it . . . that was different. "I'm not her," I said, feeling slapped.

"I know that," he said in an even tone. "I never said you were."

And yet, he still somehow managed to imply that whoever or whatever I was—not Lily!—was somehow worse. "Well, which is it, then?" I asked. "Are you offended that I'm sullying your precious Lily with my horrible personality, or that I'm just not grateful enough for the opportunity to do so?"

"Forget it." He grimaced. "I didn't mean—"

"Oh, no, let's talk about it," I snapped. "Let's talk about how great it is pretending to be someone I've never met so her family doesn't get upset, let's talk about not recognizing yourself in the mirror, let's talk about not being sure who you are anymore because everyone who looks at you sees someone else." I blinked back tears, refusing to let them fall.

He opened his mouth to speak, but I charged on. "And hey, before you bring it up, you're right. I did do this to myself. It was an accident, but it's all my fault. I love how I'm villainized for messing up, but Lily, who dumped you as a friend, fooled around with Ben Rogers, and wrapped her car around a tree, well, she's a freaking saint."

His jaw tightened. "I never said she was—"

"Please, you've done everything but turn in the paperwork. Meanwhile, nothing I do is ever good enough. Have you thought about what those other people—those spirits who would be so grateful for this chance—what they might be doing with this body? What kind of postlife adventures they might be taking with your sweet, perfect, never-made-a-mistake Lily?"

He didn't say anything, didn't even try, but I could see, by the color rising in his pale face, I'd scored a direct hit.

"I am doing the best that I can. For you, for me, even for Lily." I gestured down at myself. "And have you ever even considered what it's like for me on a personal level?" I asked, weary of fighting with him about the late (sort of), great Lily suddenly. "I live with a family that's not mine, watching them care about me and knowing it's not really for me at all. I can't even talk to *my* family about anything—other than magazine subscriptions or candy fund-raisers or whatever excuse I can come up with to be at their doors as a stranger—without freaking them out. And then there's you . . ." I shook my head bitterly. "Most girls have to hear about a guy's former crushes. I have to wear yours."

That shut up him up but, oddly, did little to make me feel better. We spent the last ten minutes of the twenty-minute drive in stony silence, which was fun.

This situation was, quite simply, a nightmare. I wanted to go home, my home, the one that didn't exist anymore. My mom had put our house on the market and moved into a condo a couple of weeks ago, according to the neighbors I'd talked to when no one had answered at home. At my dad's house, I'd turned a polite request to use the bathroom into a chance to look around and found that my old room had been turned into a nursery for my step-Mothra's new spawn, which was a girl, no less. Not that it mattered. It wasn't like I could show up at either place with a claim to belong there, especially looking like this.

More than any of that, though, I wanted my old life back. Even my afterlife had been better than this. At least I'd been me, and the people who could see me knew I was me. Now, at best, I might one day be free, back to spirit form and hoping for the light, but it couldn't go back to the way it was with Will. Not with knowing his true feelings about Lily. Like maybe he'd have rather had her back from the light than me.

Fantastic.

Will passed the Turners' street and pulled around the corner into Sacred Heart, as was our practice. The Turner house backed to an empty lot, and Sacred Heart, a huge cemetery, was across the street from that lot. It was my cemetery, in fact. Living as Lily Turner, I was now closer to my original body than I'd been since I was in it. Irony, right?

In any case, the cemetery groundskeeper's shed was on the outer edge of the property and the perfect place to hide the Dodge from view while Will dropped me off or picked me up. This additional subterfuge was, unfortunately, necessary. Will was still persona non grata around the Turner household—Mrs. Turner still blamed him for what had happened at the hospital. And my first attempt at sneaking out through the front door a few weeks ago had ended in the neighbor tattling on me, and my being forced to come up with a story that involved taking a long walk as part of my physical therapy (lie), and how if there had been a car in the driveway it must have been after I left (BIG lie).

I pulled at the handle and shoved the door open, ready to jump—well, stumble—out as soon as possible.

"Wait," Will said. "I . . . I'm sorry, Alona."

But it was one of those apologies that didn't sound all that apologetic. It was the "I'm sorry if you're upset" bullshit Chris and a couple of other ex-boyfriends had tried at various times on me. Uh-huh. There was a reason why they were exes. Well, reasons beyond my dying and, in Chris's case, his cheating. Though those were good reasons, too.

Will tapped an uneven rhythm on the steering wheel, watching his hands instead of me. "I think we should just agree that we're doing our best to find a solution to this . . . situation, and we should try not to take the stress of it out on each other."

"Fine," I said tonelessly. He could say whatever he wanted. It didn't change the fact that I still was—and always would be—the bad guy. For not being Lily, for not being grateful for the chance to be Lily. Whatever.

He sighed. "I'm going to try to see Malachi again tomorrow. It's safer if you stay here—"

"That's fine. I'm going to see Misty tomorrow." The words were out of my mouth before I even realized I'd made the decision. But I guess some part of me had been mulling it over since seeing her in Malachi's waiting room. I *knew* Misty, probably better than anyone. She was not prone to scaring easily or imagining things that weren't there. Heck, when I'd *tried* to haunt her, she hadn't even noticed. If she thought "Alona" was haunting her, she probably had good reason to, and I wanted to find out what was going on, even if Will didn't. Someone out there was taking advantage of my absence and pretending to be me, and doing it so well that even Misty, the person who'd known me best in my old life, believed it. That was *so* not going to stand. I wanted to know who was behind it so I could kick ass accordingly.

He looked at me. "I don't think that's a good idea."

I gave him a tight smile and felt the still-tender skin of my scar stretch painfully with the movement. "Then I guess we're even."

"How are you going to get there?"

Oh. That would be a small problem. Misty lived on the other side of town, closer to where I used to live. Car privileges weren't exactly up for the asking these days in the Turner household—near-fatal car accidents tend to have that effect—and walking with a bad leg was pretty much out of the question. I shrugged, hoping it looked breezy and unconcerned. "I'll figure it out."

He sighed and shook his head. "I'll take you."

"So you can spy on me, make sure I'm taking proper care of Lily?" I demanded. "No thanks."

"I'm trying to make sure we all stay safe, okay?"

"Fine," I said immediately. "Then you'll take me to Malachi's with you, if it's about keeping *all* of us safe." He'd walked right into that one. Not that I wanted to go—can you say giant waste of time?—but, by God, I was going to hold him to those stupid standards he thought were so fair. He couldn't argue, after today, that *he* would be safer without me.

He grimaced but said nothing.

That's what I thought. "Good. Pick me up here tomorrow at noon, and we're going to Misty's first." I levered myself out of the car, using the door as support.

"What are you going to tell the Turners?" He was, unfortunately, correct to ask. Mrs. Turner was the very definition of overprotective. I'd had to wait until she took Tyler out shopping this afternoon to be able to sneak out and meet Will.

"That I've made some new friends with motorcycles and we're going to have an orgy in the park," I said. It wasn't any of his business how I managed "my" family.

He threw me a dark look.

"Don't worry about it. I'll handle it. Unlike *some* people, I actually have a spine when it comes to dealing with parents."

He glared at me, spots of red rising in his cheeks. And okay, maybe implying he was a mama's boy was a bit of a low blow, but it was true. I limped out of the way and started to shut the door.

"Hey," he called.

I leaned down to see him, expecting retaliation for my slam on how he handled—or didn't—his mom. "Yeah?" I asked warily.

"I know who you are, no matter what you look like," he said quietly, surprising me.

Maybe. I nodded at him and slammed the door before the tears filling my eyes escaped. But I was beginning to think the real problem might be that who I was was just not good enough. Apparently, it had been one thing when I was the pretty face and the good body, but now, when there was nothing left of me but me, well, that was a different story. And there was no fix—easy or seemingly impossible—for that.

4

Will

I watched to make sure Alona crossed the street safely, and then I pulled away from the cemetery and headed home, her words still rattling around in my head.

She was wrong. Yes, okay, it was a little weird to watch her as Lily. And yeah, sometimes it bothered me to see her do or say things that I knew were not like Lily.

But it wasn't because I thought Alona wasn't good enough to be Lily, temporary condition or not. It was just, for lack of a better word, jarring. Like hearing a cat bark.

I was doing the best that I could, too. The friend I thought I'd never talk to again was now inhabited by the spirit of the girl I'd never dreamed I'd ever talk to at all. It was complicated and confusing, to say the least.

And every time Alona tore Lily down, I felt it. I had an obligation to look out for Lily since she couldn't look out for herself anymore. Yeah, Lily was in the light and probably could give a rat's ass what anyone said about her. But you try remembering that when she's sitting right next to you . . . or seems to be, anyway. It felt disloyal—like dishonoring her memory—*not* to defend her.

I wasn't asking Alona to be happy about it or—God help me—to appreciate it, but just not to act like getting stuck inside Lily's body was the worst thing that had ever happened to her, up to and including getting run over by a freaking bus.

Especially because I was beginning to get a little worried. It was going to be one thing to pull Alona out of there. But add to that the necessity of pulling her out without destroying her spirit and killing Lily . . . and things weren't looking so good. Even the Order, with all their tech and research, hadn't been able to work around that. They were just willing to let Lily die in order to capture Alona.

Then, even if we managed to find a way to work around all of that, there was the question of what to do with Lily. Her parents . . . they couldn't go through losing their daughter again. Even though "Lily" had never woken from her coma, they didn't know that. To them, she was back and on her way to recovery. It would destroy them to see her land in the hospital again. Even Alona knew that.

We hadn't discussed it, but there was a distinct possibility

Alona might be stuck for a while. Possibly a lot longer than either of us had hoped or imagined. Which she would hate with the fire of the sun, and which wouldn't be so great for me, either, for a variety of reasons. My life was complicated enough as it was already.

Pulling up to my house, I saw Sam's pickup in the driveway. Right next to my mom's Corolla. My mom and her boyfriend/boss were here . . . alone. *Uh-oh.*

But they were old, and it was the middle of the afternoon. Surely they weren't . . .

I grimaced and parked behind my mom's car. I'd make a lot of noise on the approach so I wouldn't catch them by surprise. I'm not an idiot; I knew what went on, but that didn't mean I wanted to witness something that would be burned into my brain, forever flaring up at the least convenient moments.

But as soon as I reached the back door, I realized I didn't have to worry. Through the window in the door, I could see my mom at the kitchen table, alone. Thank God. Except her shoulders were slumped and she seemed smaller than ever, hunched in her chair.

I opened the back door cautiously. "Mom?"

"Hi, sweetie," she said, without turning around, but I could tell she'd been crying by the sound of her voice.

"What's wrong?" I came in and closed the door behind me. "Where's Sam?"

"Oh." She waved a hand. "He's in the basement, checking the air conditioner." She frowned at me with red-rimmed eyes as I took the seat across from her. "The hallway back by your bedroom is freezing again."

Great. Only one thing that could mean. But I couldn't deal with that yet. "What happened?"

She smiled and picked up her mug of tea. "It's nothing. I'm fine."

"Mom, you're not fine. Crying alone in the kitchen is not—"

"Shhhh." She frowned. "Not so loud."

Okaaay. So Sam didn't know she was crying, which meant . . . what? "Can you please just tell me what happened?"

She smiled again, and this time I clearly saw sadness there as well. "Sam . . ." she began slowly.

"Did he break up with you?" *Damn it, Sam.* I liked him, thought he was good for my mom, who needed someone to make her laugh. "If this is because of what happened at the diner . . ." I'd had to quit the diner a couple of weeks ago, after a ghost just would not get the message that I was off duty as a ghost-talker when I was working as a busboy. Said ghost had decided to express his displeasure by sweeping a table clear of dishes . . . while the people were still eating, unfortunately.

Sam had been pretty cool about it, and no one had blamed me. The customers had been stunned at first and then eventually blamed it on the table legs being uneven. Yes, most people will find a way to explain the inexplicable so as not to acknowledge the existence of the supernatural. But clearly I couldn't continue to work there without risking exposure . . . or someone's injury by flying dinnerware.

"Will you let me finish?" my mom asked in exasperation.

"Okay, okay." I held up my hands in surrender.

"He wants me to move in with him," she said carefully, her attention focused on the mug in her hands.

"Oh. Uh . . ." I'd not been expecting that, and, as with other moments in my life where my next words would be essential . . . my mind was blank. "Shouldn't you, uh, at least be engaged first so that he . . ."

She looked up at me, amused. "So he's not taking advantage?"

My face burned. "Well, uh . . . yeah."

She set her mug down and patted my shoulder with a laugh. "Thank you. I love you, too."

As always, my mom seemed to understand where I was coming from even when I couldn't quite get the words right. I guess that's what made her my mom.

"And if Sam had his way," she said, "that's exactly the way it would be."

I tilted my head to one side, trying to follow what she was saying. "You mean he asked you to marry him?" I demanded. If so, this was the first I'd heard of it.

"Not so loud," she reminded me with a frown. "And yes. Several times."

I sat back in my chair, my words gone again. "And you said . . ."

She took a breath and let it out slowly, studying the

mug in front of her. "It's complicated. I'm not sure I'm ready for that."

"So, he's suggesting moving in as an alternative," I said, finally getting it. "He's trying to work up to the getting-married part."

"He didn't exactly position it that way," she said wryly. "But I suspect that's his goal, yes."

It took a second to imagine Sam with a place at our table here, a chair that would be his. Unless . . . maybe it wouldn't be him at our table, but us at his.

My stomach dropped a little at the thought. Moving into Sam's place? I couldn't picture it. I'd never even been there. It was an old fix-it-up farmhouse on the edge of town; I knew that much. Old and isolated; that could either be really good . . . or really bad for me.

Then a second thought struck, just as hard as the first. Maybe they weren't planning on my tagging along.

I was starting classes at Richmond Community College in a couple of weeks. Apartments were available near campus, but living so close to that many people—and the ghosts following them around—without a spirit guide seemed like a bad idea. At least my mom knew what was going on when she saw me seemingly talking to open air. Not that I wanted to live with her for the rest of my life, but it was going to take a little more time to figure out a workable solution, now that Alona was . . . unavailable.

I glanced involuntarily toward my bedroom. The temperature drop my mom had referenced likely meant a spectral visitor, or ten. I could hear vague whispers coming from the hall as they talked among themselves. At least they knew enough to know I wouldn't like finding them here and were trying to be discreet. Without a spirit guide to keep them in line, they'd been breaking all kinds of rules lately, like coming to my house and waiting for me in my freaking bedroom.

But I'd find a way to deal with it, if I had to. I wasn't going to hold my mom prisoner with my problems. She'd already been through that enough.

I cleared my throat. "So, uh, whose house?" I asked. "I mean, are you going there, or is he coming here? And when is—"

She shook her head. "I'm going to tell him no."

"Because you're not ready or . . ."

She avoided my gaze.

I sighed. "Because of me."

"You're my son," she said fiercely, looking up at me. "And we take care of each other."

I nodded, recognizing the words as similar to those she'd said in the hours following my father's funeral. It had been only the two of us for years now.

She straightened up. "Besides, you need me right now with Alona off flitting around somewhere, paying no attention to her duties." Her mouth tightened in disapproval.

I grimaced at the lie I'd given her to explain Alona's absence and the increase in ghost activity around me. I couldn't tell her that Alona was directly responsible for Lily's amazing "recovery." My mom had handled the ghost-talker thing fairly well, but Alona's spirit in Lily's body? That was beyond even her most liberal thinking. And she'd never particularly liked Alona to begin with, so I didn't want to make things worse.

"Mom, as much as I appreciate that, there's nothing you can do," I pointed out, trying to be as careful as I could not to hurt her feelings. "This is something I have to work out on my own."

"I know that," she said, with exaggerated patience. "I'm certainly not capable of helping you resolve any of your"—she eyed the basement door, which was open a crack, checking to see that Sam hadn't returned—"issues." She reached out and took my hand, squeezing it. "But I can at least make sure you have a safe place to be yourself until you figure it out."

I shook my head, feeling the sting of tears in my eyes and nose. "You shouldn't have to give up your life, not any more than you already have."

She waved my words away. "Who says I'm giving up anything?" She stood and took her mug to the sink. "That farmhouse of his is a wreck still, especially the kitchen. And in six months or a year"—she shrugged—"his renovations will be done and maybe you'll be ready to be on your own. It's not the end of the world."

But I could hear the forced note of cheeriness in her voice. Sam had already proposed multiple times, and moving in together was less than what he wanted. How long would he be willing to wait for that? Especially without knowing the truth about what was going on with me.

My mom had decided that she didn't want Sam to feel forced into believing something that most people found pretty far out there. Okay, fine, but without that context, he might think she'd never come around. That we were like those permanently messed-up, codependent mothers and sons. Norman Bates and his mom, or whatever.

"Do me a favor," I said.

She turned away from the sink and raised an eyebrow at me, her hands already covered in bubbles from scrubbing the tea mug. She always cleans when she's upset, especially when she's not admitting that she's upset. "What's that?" she asked, obviously suspicious that I was going to try to talk her into something.

"Just . . . don't say no yet."

She opened her mouth, but I kept going before she could speak. "Give me a couple more weeks. Tell him you need time to think about it, if you have to, but don't tell him no. Please."

"Nothing is going to change that quickly." She looked tired suddenly. "I don't want to give him false hope."

"I'm working on something, okay? I just need a little more time." If I couldn't at least find a lead by then, it probably wasn't going to happen any time soon. In which case, contingency plans would need to be made. And living at home forever was not one of them.

My mom narrowed her eyes at me. "William, if you're putting yourself in danger—"

"Totally safe, promise." Which was true . . . to an extent. Leaving things as they were would be far more dangerous—that much was certain.

She nodded slowly, not quite sure whether to believe me. "All right."

"Thanks." I stood, shoved my chair in, and, before leaving the kitchen, took the extra couple of steps to kiss her cheek, startling her. "I got this. Don't worry," I said, wishing I felt as certain as I sounded.

But first things first. Before I could continue working on a way to get Alona back in spirit form—and consequently, giving my mom her life back—I had to address a more immediate problem. I left my mom at the sink, with the sound of Sam's footsteps coming up the basement stairs, to head back to my bedroom.

Once upon a time, my house had been a ghost-free zone. I had done my best to hide my identity as a ghost-talker, and the few ghosts who'd figured it out had never managed to follow me home.

Ghosts are not omniscient. They don't know anything more than they did when they were alive, other than what they learn by watching, listening, and, well, walking through walls. So my exact address had remained a mystery to them, thankfully.

The trouble was, as soon as my reputation started to spread—thanks in part to Alona's initial desire to make sure everyone knew she was *my* guide and therefore better/more important than the rest of them—more spirits started recognizing me on sight. And constantly staying on guard and making sure I wasn't followed became more difficult. When Alona had been my guide, she'd kept everyone in line, literally. But now? Not so much.

Unfortunately, the dead look pretty much like the living, unless their clothes are obviously outdated or you catch them passing through a solid object, which they can't do when they're around me anyway. So, checking to make sure the strange guy behind you on the sidewalk is, in fact, breathing and not a ghost trying to stalk you is a little tricky.

As it turns out, ghosts don't usually mind being asked about their status in the living world—it's attention, and for most of them, they've been running short of that for years— but the living tend to kind of . . . freak out.

I'd done the best I could to be careful when coming to and going from my house, but it only took one or two of them to track me down and then spread the word. Consequently, my bedroom at times now had more ghosts in it than a hospital, cemetery, and funeral home combined. Fun.

As soon as I hit the hallway, someone noticed me, and the whispers that I'd been able to ignore in the kitchen started to rise in volume until they hit what could only be described as a clamor. Five or so ghosts were crowded into the hall in a half-assed kind of line that started at my bedroom doorway and crossed in front of the bathroom.

Doing my best to project a calm that was in complete contrast to the sweaty nervousness I was feeling, I ignored the voices and the hands reaching out to grasp me.

"Will, please—"

"I need you to tell them—"

"—you help us?"

"—stop him from selling the house?"

No one tried to pin me down—that was good—and I managed to slip through into my bedroom. I shut the door, catching someone's fingers between it and the frame. An indignant and surprised yelp followed.

Yeah, some of them were still trying to adjust to the idea of having physicality around me. That was actually a good thing. It meant they weren't as likely to try physical coercion or violence to get what they wanted . . . yet.

In my room, the ghost situation was worse—probably ten of them—but at least I recognized most of them as people from the list Alona had begun assembling for me a few months ago. They knew I'd been working on helping them. They'd seen Grandpa B., one of their former fellow haunters, go into the light, and I'd told them about how Liesel and Eric had finally found their peace last month. So they wouldn't get too pushy . . . most likely.

"Any luck?" a ghost in a poodle skirt asked hopefully, her ponytail swinging as she got off the foot of the bed to greet me. A bunch of faces turned toward me expectantly, including that of a vaguely familiar-looking woman wearing a tight blue business suit, her dark red hair in a fancy twist. She actually pushed her way forward from the back to hear my response.

They all thought I was looking for Alona. It was, again,

a story I'd been forced to come up with on the fly to explain her absence and my diminished ability to help them. There were too many of them, and without Alona, I couldn't get as much done. Not to mention the time suck that researching anything and everything to try to separate Alona from Lily had turned out to be.

Leaning back against the door, I shook my head. An audible groan went up from them at once, as if they'd rehearsed it. And I suppose, in a way, they had. They were showing up here two or three times a week now, with the same question, and I was always forced to give the same answer.

Telling them the truth would have been a mess. If other ghosts knew what Alona had been able to do—taking on a body, possessing it, for lack of a better term—there might be a run of them trying to do the same on anyone they found who seemed to be in an unconscious or comatose state. And that was the last thing we needed. Most of them probably wouldn't succeed . . . or not for very long, at least. It took a great deal of power, apparently, to do what Alona was doing. A red-level spirit or above, according to the classification system the Order used. Still, we weren't entirely sure of the effects these attempts might have on the living, nor did we want a rash of five-minute-long possessions, which would, frankly, be creepy as hell.

So as far as anyone in the spirit world was concerned, Alona had taken off for locations unknown after we'd had a fight. That last part, at least, didn't require much of an imagination stretch.

The poodle-skirt girl shook her head, ponytail bobbing with the movement. "You should have apologized right away," she said disapprovingly.

"How do you know I was the one in the wrong?" I asked, offended in spite of the fact that we were talking about an argument that had never happened.

"Please." She rolled her eyes and flounced over to perch at the foot of my bed again.

"I keep telling you, she's gone." Evan, the creepy janitor dude from my former high school, spoke up, smashing his mop down impatiently into the bucket/wringer that was always with him. "Disappeared, poof, vamoosed. She doesn't respond when you summon her. She's not here at her time of death." He shook his head. "The bond is broken. She ain't coming back."

Which was all true, but not the direction I wanted this conversation to go. I held my hands up and tried soothing. "We don't know what—"

"No, I think we do." He jabbed a finger in my direction. "And you need to start focusing on what's important, not chasing after your piece of ghosty tail." He smirked.

A barely muffled round of snickering emerged from the crowd, and I felt my face get hot. Evidently, Alona and I had not been as discreet as I'd thought. Technically, there wasn't anything wrong with our relationship. Except, I suppose, the part where I was alive and she was . . . not. Still, it wasn't like *that*. We'd known each other when she was alive, and we were the same age . . . Oh, forget it.

I tried to rally and regain control over the room, despite all the smirking faces. "And I take it you want me to start by helping you?" I asked Evan.

"I've been waiting." He leaned his mop against the wall and stepped forward, hands out in an "I'm here" gesture and a grin stretching across his acne-scarred face.

Except he'd been sent to the back of the line by Alona, I knew, which meant that most, if not all, of these people should have been ahead of him. To my surprise, though, none of them protested his advancement, which could only mean they'd given up on the order Alona had established and were desperate enough to see someone, anyone, helped to give them hope that they would one day be in his position.

Not good.

It was also a problem because it was Evan.

"Well, come on, then." He stepped around several of the others and patted my desk chair eagerly. "Turn on your machine and let's get cracking." He looked from my computer to me expectantly, and the ghosts shuffled and shifted around in my room, moving closer like they wanted to be sure not to miss any of the show.

I sighed. "Evan, you killed people."

"It was an accident!" he protested.

"I know," I said wearily. Sort of. To hear Evan's side of it, he'd only intended to scare the kids he'd caught tagging and egging the school in the middle of the night. Actually, he hadn't even caught them. He'd heard gossip about the intended midnight prank during the day and planned to stake out the school until they showed. It had, apparently, become a point of pride for the Groundsboro students in the early nineties to torture him by making messes they knew he'd have to clean up. And he'd become equally determined to catch them in the act and turn them over to the cops. Unfortunately—or not, as it turned out—they'd moved up their plans, and by the time he arrived, they were already done and trying to make a not-so-clean getaway. Per Evan's description, it looked like a chicken factory and a paint factory had exploded simultaneously—minus the feathers . . . and the fact that there is no such thing as a chicken factory. But whatever. This was Evan's story.

The perpetrators scrambled to get back into their pickup, even as they taunted Evan on his late arrival. Infuriated and humiliated, he'd accelerated at them in his van, intending to brake and swerve at the last second. Except he didn't.

He said his brakes had failed, but the police hadn't been able to find evidence of that. Two kids had ended up dead, and a third one was badly injured. It didn't help that one of the kids who'd died was the son of a prominent lawyer. Evan had been convicted, given the death penalty, and executed by lethal injection in 2002, right before they put a moratorium on the death penalty in Illinois, which still rankled him to this day.

"You've already tried apologizing," I pointed out. He'd attempted to make amends to the affected families before his death, but it hadn't helped. He was still stuck here, in between. "What else do you want to do?"

"I don't know!" He folded his arms over his jumpsuited chest. "That's your job to figure out."

Like I didn't have enough to do? Like my own problems weren't already trying to hold my head under the water until I quit breathing? At least I was *trying* to solve them instead of dumping them in someone else's lap. So, blame it on frustration, momentary insanity, or just forgetting for a second that the guy was a killer—no matter what he said—but suddenly I couldn't keep my mouth shut any longer. "How about telling the truth, for a change? You didn't swerve because you didn't want to, and that's what's keeping you here."

Dumb, Will, definitely dumb.

He lunged at me, and the room exploded in noise.

The woman in the suit, the one who I'd noticed earlier, appeared in front of me suddenly, blocking Evan's path. "Back off." She shoved at him, and he stumbled, looking stunned. "And the rest of you, shut it already," she said to the others. She glanced at me, as if expecting my gratitude and/or approval.

But I was too distracted. I recognized her now. It was Spring Break Girl from Malachi's place . . . except she was dressed differently. She'd ditched her bikini top and shorts for a suit that clung to her curves and a fancy, twisty hairstyle, both of which made her look older than the nineteen or twenty she'd probably been. How was that even possible? Ghosts couldn't change their appearances, not like that.

"Do you really think this is going to get you anywhere?" she demanded of the other spirits, hands on her hips. With her attention on them again, I got a better glimpse of the back of her head, which appeared slightly, uh, dented.

I grimaced.

"Who are you?" Evan asked her, sulking. Defeated by a girl—one more float for his pity parade.

She turned and beamed at me with determination and maybe the faintest hint of crazy. "I'm the help he's been looking for."

Oh. Crap.

❧ 5 ❧

Alona

I waited until Will's car pulled away before I crossed back over to Sacred Heart. I wasn't ready to be Lily Turner, even for pretend, at this exact moment. Fury and hurt burned in my gut in a potent mix.

I didn't object to Will caring so much about her; my problem was more that he didn't seem to care nearly as much about me. I was the spirit here, the soul. Lily, the real Lily, not this body, was probably up on a cloud laughing her ass off at all of this. Or . . . since this wasn't a cartoon, in the light, completely at peace, unaware and unconcerned about the corporeal struggles of the rest of us. That was more likely.

Bitch.

I'd been there once. In the light. I don't remember any

of it, other than fleeting memories of this sensation of overwhelming peace and acceptance. Then I'd found myself back here on this ball of dirt, stuck between the living and the dead once more, no explanation, no "thanks for playing," nothing.

I'd told Will what I'd had to, what made the most sense—that I'd been sent back to learn more and to help him. It was easier than explaining that I'd been rejected—me!—and I didn't even know why.

Actually, if I were being honest, it was even worse than that. Getting rejected without knowing why was one thing. But I'd been in the light for nearly a month before they'd decided to boot me. Like there was some flaw with my character that was visible only upon closer inspection. Or someone had decided I needed a further taste of karma, and offered acceptance only to yank it away, just as Misty and I had done on occasion to those petitioning for first-tier status. At the time it had seemed almost a kindness to at least let them believe they had a chance when most of them didn't. But now . . . now I saw things a little differently.

I didn't think the light was vindictive like that—it kind of went against the whole principle of what the light was supposed to be—but who knew for sure?

Everything since my return had been one big guess, including saving Lily last month when she was dying in that broom closet and I was disappearing.

And what did that get me? Nothing but more trouble.

Whatever.

It took me a while to find my grave again. I hadn't spent a lot of time here since my funeral. To be honest, graveyards are kind of, well, dead. The only people who come here are the living, and they are always respectful and fairly boring when here. The dead who are stuck in between have only each other and watching the living as their entertainment, so they aren't sticking around places like this. Cemeteries are, in that respect, a good place to go for some alone time, for those on both sides of the great divide.

The other problem, I eventually realized, was that I was looking for the temporary placard they'd put up immediately after the funeral to mark my grave. But when I found the right spot, it was only because I recognized the headstone my father had special-ordered. It had finally come in.

Made of Italian rose marble with weeping angels on top, the stone was big and beautiful and a little obnoxious, standing about six inches taller than the stones on either side. But that was my dad for you. He'd given me the headstone he thought his princess deserved. Which was pretty much the last thing he'd done for me, by the looks of it.

The marble was dirty with clean splotches from the last rain, and the built-in vase was empty, without so much as a dried leaf hanging around. The grass had finally grown in over the bare dirt, but it was a tough old summer green rather than the baby stuff of spring, and it was starting to rise above the base of the stone.

Had my dad even been here since they'd put up the stone? It didn't appear so. He'd been busy with Gigi, my step-Mothra, and the new baby on the way. His replacement daughter.

Tired suddenly and my leg aching, I knelt awkwardly at the edge of the new grass, careful to avoid sitting above any portion of my former body. That would be just too weird.

Neglect I would understand—had understood for years—from my mother. She was not capable of focusing on anyone other than herself, even now that she was trying to get better. Maybe even especially now that she was trying to change. She needed every bit of willpower she had to keep herself on track, and I'd seen all too well what happened when she went off the rails.

But my dad? I was special, his favorite. The one good thing that had come out of his marriage to my mother, or so he used to say. He spoiled me, and I would have done anything for him. And I had done plenty—corralling my mom into resembling a reasonable human being when he needed her for legal meetings or whatever, not complaining when he'd left me to manage our bills and the money we received from his monthly check, keeping my mom from pestering him every thirty seconds, taking the calls from the neighbors when my mom was parked halfway on the front lawn again so my dad wouldn't have to interrupt his staycation with Gigi, etc.

He was always grateful, quick to tell me he knew he could count on me. That I was a "team player."

Except I wasn't. Not really. Because no matter how grateful my dad claimed to be, no matter what he bought me to say thank you . . . he never did anything differently. To be a team player, there had to be an actual team, people working toward a common goal. And all I'd had was one parent making a mess of everything while the other avoided acknowledging said mess, leaving all the responsibility to fall on me.

I cleaned up after him.

I froze, the realization ringing through my head loud and clear. Yes, my mother had needed me to take care of her alcohol-induced messes . . . but my father had needed me to take care of her so he'd have the luxury of avoiding it. He'd used me, every bit as much as my mom had.

I felt sucker punched. He'd dumped his responsibilities on me and then forgotten all about me as soon as I was gone. Buying one pretty headstone was all it took for his guilt to be assuaged, apparently.

My mother had long accused him of always chasing after the newest, shiniest object in the vicinity without feeling or regret, be it the latest car, gadget, or wife. I'd thought being "special" had exempted me from that. Guess not.

With effort, I leaned over and yanked some of the too-tall grass away from the base of my ridiculous headstone, my eyes stinging suddenly.

This is why people shouldn't stick around after they die. It's lonely and miserable, and it makes you think too much. Or, if you have to stick around because of unresolved issues, then you sure as hell shouldn't be sent back after you've addressed them. I mean, what is that about?

I tossed the loose blades of grass away, but the breeze

caught them and sent them fluttering across my grave, just as it would the leaves in a few months and then the snow after that.

I pictured my former self snug in the white casket in the ground below, immune to all the drama and chaos going on up here. And for a second, I wished I was with her. Just gone.

"Why am I here? Why did you send me back?" I asked for probably the millionth time in the last two months, this time aloud instead of in my head.

But the answer was the same. Silence.

Of course. Because that was *so* helpful these days.

I spent longer at the cemetery than I meant to and had to hurry to get back home before Mrs. Turner and Tyler returned. Still, hurrying or not, I should have known something was wrong the second I reached my bedroom window. If I'd stopped and thought about it, I would have remembered that I'd left the window open, and it was now closed. I might have checked things out before barging in.

But my brain was on a constant loop of unhappy thoughts, and I was in a rush. So, it was only after I'd pried the window up from the sill—it's much harder to do that from the outside than you'd think—and stuck my head into the room that I realized two very important things.

First, unless I wanted to end up on my face, it would have been better to start with my feet.

Second, Tyler Turner, Lily's younger brother, was

standing in the middle of the room and glaring at me, his arms folded over his skinny chest.

Busted. "I went for a walk," I said weakly.

Tyler was the second hardest thing about this gig, coming in just behind Mrs. Turner. It wasn't his fault, exactly. I had no idea how to be an older sister, any more than I knew how to be *his* older sister, specifically. He was three years younger than Lily (four years younger than me) and a complete and utter mystery to me.

Sometimes he seemed to hate all the attention his parents, particularly his mother, put into me. He constantly pointed it out when I answered their questions incorrectly ("No, purple is your favorite color") or I didn't "remember" something I should have ("But you hate mustard!").

Other times, like when I had a headache (or found it convenient to say I did), it seemed to send him into a panic. He would sneak around to check on me every fifteen minutes, while pretending not to, or bring me a glass of water and Tylenol with an anxious frown.

I couldn't figure him out.

But Tyler was the one who'd first noticed that something was different about Lily, the day that I'd first taken over, even before I'd grabbed his wrist. He saw it somehow. He knew his sister well.

And sometimes I wondered if he knew I wasn't her. That would be trouble. Big trouble.

Tyler shook his head at me. "You went out for a walk through the *window*?" he scoffed. "Right. Better not try that one on Mom."

This is what I'd been missing by not having siblings? No thanks. My only experience with younger brothers came from being around Misty and her family. But her half brothers were still in diapers, and the worst they ever did was steal a lipstick to use as a crayon.

I sighed and backed out of the window, preparing to climb in properly. If he was going to sound the alarm, I wanted to be inside, at least.

In an awkward motion, I swung my bad leg and then my good one over the sill. I grimaced, bending my head to fit beneath the frame, and let myself down in a barely controlled fall to the floor. The impact sent a jolt of pain through my injured leg, and I stumbled forward a step, bumping into the desk. The desk lamp and a bunch of books and magazines crashed to the ground.

"Shhh!" With a quick glance at my bedroom door, which was half open, Tyler edged closer to me. "Do you know how close it was?" he demanded in an undertone. "Mom sent me down here to tell you we were back early. What if she'd come down here herself instead?"

I stared at him as if he were speaking a foreign language. So he wasn't going to tell on me? "She would have been pissed?" I felt that was a fairly safe—and true—answer.

Now it was his turn to stare at me. "What is wrong with you? Of course she would have been—" Tyler shook his head impatiently. "Never mind. You didn't even tell me you were going this time."

He sounded almost . . . hurt. I shifted, uncomfortable. I really wanted to sit down, take the weight off my leg, but obviously he wasn't going anywhere anytime soon without some kind of conversation. Great.

"Okay," I said slowly, trying to piece all of this together and come up with some kind of Lilyesque response. Clearly, because Tyler and I had never had a discussion about my sneaking out before, he and Pre-Coma Lily must have. So, wait, Pre-Coma Lily had been sneaking out? Where? Why? I knew she wasn't perfect, but this went even beyond what I'd suspected. Then again . . . Lily had "dated" Ben Rogers for a while, and he wasn't exactly the show-up-at-the-front-door-and-meet-and-greet-with-the-'rents type. Kind of interfered with his whole pillage-and-plunder-the-naive-but-willing plan.

But she hadn't mentioned sneaking out to meet him in her diary. Then again, maybe Lily was brighter than I'd given her credit for. It was one thing to describe a date you probably weren't supposed to be on; another to spell out in big bold letters the specific crimes for which you could be punished if a parent went snooping. Besides, everything she wrote about back then was Ben-related. The getting-out-of-the-house part probably hadn't been all that important to her.

I realized Tyler was still waiting for a response. "Uh, sorry?" I offered.

"Forget it," he muttered. He plopped himself down on the edge of my bed.

Fabulous. Was there a polite way to say "Get out"? How would Lily have said it? She probably wouldn't have. For all

I knew, she and Tyler had been best buds, blah, blah, blah. You know, it would have been so helpful if Lily had written about this kind of stuff in her freaking diary instead of pages full of her name intertwined with Ben's in every conceivable fashion.

"So, were you with Ben and those guys?" Tyler asked.

Aha, I *knew* it!

"Not this time," I said carefully. "Just visiting some other friends."

He nodded. "Don't forget, though, Ben said that one time he'd let me try driving his car."

Um, okay. I didn't know what to say to that.

Tyler looked so hopeful . . . and relentlessly dorky with the cowlick at the back of his head and his oversized polo shirt (orange, this time) and khakis. I had no idea why Mrs. Turner kept dressing him like a middle-aged golfer, or why he let her.

Huh. By comparison, Lily was the cool one in this family.

I straightened up a little as the realization dawned. Wow. That kind of explained a lot. Tyler was a geek and two weeks shy of starting high school. Hanging out with Ben, then, last year, even with his older sister along for the ride, must have seemed like the epitome of awesomeness.

Except . . . what kind of sister introduces her younger brother to an ass like Ben? And why would Tyler still want to hang out with him after what Ben had put Lily through?

Ben had been part of my crowd at school, but we certainly weren't friends. He thought way too much of himself, nice body or not. He was slick and incredibly skilled at putting on the charm until he got what he wanted. Which, to my mind, wasn't fair. Why give people—specifically girls with ridiculously low self-esteem—such hope? It was no challenge. Ben won every time . . . including with Lily.

From what I could tell in her diary, Lily had still been hoping for some kind of long-term thing with Ben all the way up to the end. Her final entry was about getting ready for that last party, the one where he'd publicly and brutally humiliated her and she'd driven off in tears . . . and crashed her car.

I bit my lip. Was it possible Tyler didn't know the full story about what happened with Ben or at the party? I wasn't even sure if her parents did. So, in Tyler's mind, maybe Ben was still the good guy Lily had bu   him up to be. Ugh.

"Maybe next time," I said to   r finally. That was the easiest answer. Telling him that Be   nd Lily had broken up would only bring on a barrage of qu stions that I didn't have the energy or information to answer in a Lilylike fashion. And since there was no way I was going near Ben Rogers in this body, and even less of a chance of my bringing Tyler . . . problem solved.

Tyler looked at me strangely. Probably because it was taking me about two minutes too long to respond to everything he said, but, hello! I had no idea what he was talking about most of the time. He should have been taking it easier on his potentially brain-damaged sister.

"You still owe me twenty bucks," he said after a long

moment, his head cocked to the side in evaluation.

"Yeah, right. Twenty bucks for what?" Feeling my patience evaporating along with my strength—God, who knew siblings were so much work?—I limped my way over to the desk chair, turned it around, and lowered myself into it with a sigh. It was wooden, old, and hideously uncomfortable, but still better than standing.

"For playing lookout? For keeping Mom away?" He threw his hands up in exasperation. "I had to tell her you were in the bathroom."

I rolled my eyes. "That's a terrible idea. What if I hadn't shown up when I did? You were going to tell her I was in the bathroom for hours?"

He popped up from the bed, face all red with fury. "Well, if you'd told me you were going to be gone, like you're supposed to, then it wouldn't have happened that way, would it?"

Oh, so there we go. The final piece clicked into place. Lily used him as her cover when she sneaked out, and she paid him. Got it.

"Twenty bucks to cover for me when I'm gone, and all I have to do is tell you I'm leaving. That seems fair," I said cautiously. I could really use a setup like that when I went to Misty's. And yet, looking at Tyler's wary expression, I couldn't shake the feeling that I was doing something—everything—wrong. You'd think I'd have been used to that sensation by now, but I wasn't. "I don't have any money right now, though. Can I owe you or—"

He made a frustrated sound and looked away, seemingly close to tears.

"What's wrong?" I asked, alarmed. Somewhere along the way I'd stepped in it again, apparently.

"What's wrong with you?" he demanded, his voice breaking and his fists clenched at his side. "Who are you?"

I froze. "I don't understand."

"It's like you don't remember *anything*. You're not even the same person—"

I gritted my teeth, feeling my grip on my temper start to slide. "Look, I said I would give you the money, but—"

"When have you ever given me money?" he shouted, flinging his skinny arms out wide. "You always tell me no! Just like you always tell me that Ben was only being nice and didn't mean it about driving."

I gaped at him. "Were you testing me?" The little creep!

"No!" He swiped the back of his hand against his face. "I was just—"

"Then why were you asking when you know I always say no?" I asked, starting to get angry. This was hard enough without someone deliberately setting me up.

"Because that's what the two of you do," Mrs. Turner said from the doorway.

Tyler and I jumped in surprise, and it took everything I had not to look back at the window, which was still open, and the desk in the wrong place. It all screamed "unauthorized exit." And how much of our conversation had she heard?

"You argue back and forth over silly things. That's what you've always done," she said to me. Then she turned her attention to Tyler. "Ty, baby, remember we talked about this?" She stepped into the room and pulled him to her in a sideways hug. "Personality changes, memory loss, it can all be part of your sister's condition. We need to accept the differences until she finds her way back."

But looking at me over the top of his head, she frowned, seemingly less than convinced suddenly.

Great. I felt a swell of frustration. This was all I needed: one more person watching my every move, holding it up to the Lily standard, a level of imitation I would never be able to attain.

Tyler pushed away from her, sniffling loudly, and fled the room. Mrs. Turner watched him go, with a sigh. After a second his feet thudded up the steps, and the door to the upstairs creaked open and then banged shut.

Mrs. Turner turned back to me, looking weary. "I know things are difficult for you," she said. "But we're trying, Lily . . . Ally. It would be nice if you could, too."

I jerked back as if she'd slapped me. "I am trying," I said through gritted teeth. In fact, all I ever did was try.

She shook her head. "You don't want to talk to us."

Because I kept saying the wrong things, which only upset everyone even more.

"You don't want to look at the photo albums or home videos to help you remember," she continued.

Hello, photos and videos without context don't *mean*

anything. And if I tried to ask questions to get that context, it would only highlight exactly how much I didn't remember, i.e., EVERYTHING. I was trapped.

"I offer to take you shopping, like today, or out to dinner, or whatever you want, but you always say no. You spend most of your time down here alone, like you're hiding from us." She lifted her hands in exasperation.

I fought the urge to shout at her, Duh! Sometimes I retreated to my room because I was avoiding the ghost of Granny Simmy, who haunted the armchair upstairs and spent a lot of time yelling at her living relatives. But yeah, most of the time I was dodging the fam. Who wouldn't? Nearly every word out of my mouth was the wrong one and resulted in people crying or staring at me like I'd grown another head. It was a little stressful being constantly on edge about what I said and did and how I said and did it. Even worse in a one-on-one situation like a mother-daughter outing. And shopping? God. I couldn't even act like Lily; how was I supposed to shop like her? Based solely on the contents of her closet, I'd have to assume that she was *trying* to look bad. She'd had no sense of her own body shape or the correct color palette for her skin tone.

"So . . ." Mrs. Turner said, leaning back against the door frame, as though she needed the support. "I'm beginning to think maybe Tyler isn't the only one. Maybe I don't know who you are, either. My daughter isn't a quitter." The look she gave me was full of hurt and more than a touch of resentment.

Like this was all my fault? I dug my fingernails into my palms, struggling against the urge to scream.

Yes, technically, it was my fault I was stuck here, but I wasn't failing intentionally. I don't fail. I NEVER fail. But this . . . this was an impossible task. Maybe if I'd known Lily better, or if we'd been more similar to begin with . . . but that was not the case. Instead, I had to keep banging my head against a wall that was never going to fall, tiptoeing across a minefield without so much as a map. And no matter what I did, no matter how hard I tried, I was never quite good enough. And nobody even appreciated the effort; that was the worst part. The Turners, of course, had no way to know, but Will did, and he was right up there on the bitching bandwagon.

Something inside me snapped. Screw it. All of it. Will could have his perfect Lily, Tyler his confusing and contradictory sister, and the Turners their innocent and naive little flower of a daughter. I was done. If I was going to be stuck in here for God only knew how long, then I was going to be stuck *my way*.

I stood up, ignoring the jolt of pain in my leg. "I am not her. I am not the Lily you knew." My words were cold and precise. If Will were here, he'd have been freaking out. Too bad.

Mrs. Turner flinched, but I kept going. If there was even a hope of me sticking it out with the Turners, things had to change. Right now.

"I am sorry, more than you know, but I can't do this. I

can't be her," I said simply. "And every time you compare me to her, it makes things worse."

"You make it sound like you're a totally different person," she said with a weak laugh, dabbing at her eyes, which were overflowing.

"Are you the same person you were five years ago? Ten?" I demanded.

She looked surprised at the question. "I don't—"

"It may not be time that's the issue here, but I'm not who I was before the accident." That was as close as I dared come to the truth. "I don't remember what you want me to remember. I don't know the things you want me to know."

I heard the desperation in my voice and hated it. I raked my hands through my hair, too fine and flat to my fingers. I was wearing it that way because that's how Lily had. God, everything was about Lily, how she would act, what she would say . . . I couldn't stand it anymore. "I can't even say I want mustard without everyone acting like I'm speaking Russian or something. It's just a freaking condiment!" I swiped at the dampness on my face, cursing Lily's overactive tear ducts.

"Honey, it's okay . . ." Mrs. Turner began, starting to cross the room toward me, her hand extended.

I shook my head. "No, it's not."

She stopped and lowered her hand to her side.

"I wish I could be her for you. I wish this was easier. But I can't, and it's not." For that matter, I wished I was a better actress and Lily had left behind transcripts of her life for me to read. But that wasn't to be. I was doing the best that I could, and please, God, I needed that to be enough for *someone*.

"What do you want us to do?" Mrs. Turner asked, almost warily, as if she feared I'd suggest leaving me alone forever or tell her that I was moving out.

I took a deep breath, trying to get the tears under control. "We start over. New memories. No comparing me to who I was before, no forced attempts to get me to remember things. I try to be someone you're not ashamed to call your daughter, and you try to accept me for who I am now." For as long as it lasted, anyway. Lily wasn't here anymore, but for the moment, I was. I had to be.

Mrs. Turner paled. "I was never ashamed," she said. "I know this isn't easy for you, either, but we're only trying to help."

"A fresh start," I persisted. "Can we do that?" Because even though I understood her pain, if I had to hear one more time about how "I" never did, said, or thought something before, I was going to lose it. Run away screaming, which was not only impractical, it would also probably result in my being locked up somewhere for my own good. I knew she had brochures for a rehab center that specialized in brain injuries and mental trauma—I'd seen them on the kitchen counter.

"We can try," Mrs. Turner said slowly.

Yes. I let out a small breath of relief. She wasn't completely convinced, but that was okay. I hadn't expected her to be. Any amount of wiggle room, any chance to not feel like a complete screwup would be worth it.

"Is that shopping trip you offered still on the table?" I asked, suddenly filled with a fierce determination and a captivating idea.

Mrs. Turner looked startled, but nodded. "Sure."

Good. If I was failing at pretending to be the old, badly dressed, poorly accessorized, and seemingly color-blind Lily, well, then, what did I have to lose by ditching her? Being a new Lily—one whose changed interior was reflected by an external shift as well—might make everyone, if not happier, then at least slightly less miserable and confused. Except Will. He'd hate it. But he'd get over it when he saw it was for the best, right?

I held my hands out at my sides. "I'm ready when you are."

It was *so* time to ring in the new.

✤ 6 ✤

Will

It didn't take the ghost from Malachi's very long to hustle everyone out of my room and the hall, even Evan, who was still sputtering at me in incoherent fury. She just . . . shooed them like they were nothing more than vaguely annoying pigeons, telling them to come back tomorrow between two and four (even though I had no idea if I would actually *be* here tomorrow between two and four and felt pretty sure she had no way of knowing that either). Her tone brooked no argument, and her confidence left little room for doubt.

It was almost Alona-esque, actually, and kind of impressive.

Except . . . it might have been more impressive if I'd done it for myself. Once again, I'd needed someone else to step up and defend me, I realized with a grimace. That idea bothered me more now than it had before, especially with relying on someone other than Alona. It felt like the beginning of a pattern, and I didn't like that.

"So, I heard you're in need of a new spirit guide," the ghost from Malachi's said, turning her attention back to me, when the last ghost passed through the outside wall. She folded her arms beneath her chest, further amplifying the cleavage peeking out of the unbuttoned top of her white button-down, and gave me a too-bright smile.

"Maybe," I said cautiously. Getting a new spirit guide would solve several of my problems, but also create a huge new one: Alona would kill me. Though we'd never discussed it, I was fairly certain she would see a new guide as both a replacement and a sign that I was giving up on getting her back in spirit form. Neither one of those things would be good.

"Great," she said, her Miss America–pageant expression still firmly in place. "My name is Erin, and I'd like to volunteer."

I fought not to show my surprise. She *wanted* to be a spirit guide? No one ever wanted to be a spirit guide. It meant giving up a certain amount of freedom and tying yourself to a ghost-talker who might or might not even be able to help you. Alona had done it only under duress. There was definitely something . . . odd about this girl. Aside from the whole hanging out at Malachi's and the ability to change her appearance so drastically, which was strange enough. If

I had to guess, I would have said she was probably rocking some serious power to be able to do that.

Keeping an eye on her, I moved warily away from the door. Standing against it would only allow her to pin me there, blocking my exit, if she so chose. "Why would you want to—"

"I've been dead for five years, and I'm aware of that fact." She ticked facts off her fingers. "I'm familiar with how this in-between place works, people trust me, I'm very friendly, I, like, love to help people and whatever . . ."

Jesus, she was rattling this stuff off like it was a job interview.

"How did you change your appearance?" I asked, interrupting her while she went on about being dedicated.

"Oh, that?" Erin shrugged. "It's not hard. Just have to concentrate." She closed her eyes and the outline of her spring-break look shimmered into view over her current appearance for a brief moment before disappearing. "See?"

It was . . . impressive. Even Alona couldn't do that. Or, if she could, she was unaware of it. Because there was no way that she would have stayed in her gym clothes for all those weeks if she'd had another option. "But what's the point?"

"Looking professional makes the other ghosts take me more seriously," she said, sounding as though the answer should have been obvious.

I frowned. That made no sense. "Why do you care if—"

She made an impatient noise. "I've got to get the

information somehow, don't I? It's not like *Malachi* can get it for himself." Her smirk and the odd emphasis she placed on his name confirmed my suspicion that it was a fake.

"Wait, wait." Confused, I held up my hand as though that would slow her words down long enough for me to process the meaning behind them. "You work for Malachi? He's legit?" If so, he could have fooled me. In fact, he did fool Alona and me, both.

Her expression cooled. "I don't work for anyone. He owes me, and we've worked out a mutually beneficial relationship. Until now."

So Malachi was for real? My brain was spinning trying to keep up. Why would he pretend otherwise? To keep the ghosts at bay, maybe. But then why go into business as a freaking medium? Sensing that my hundred-and-one questions about Malachi would only piss Erin off, I forced myself to stay on topic. "What happened?" I asked.

She stared at me mutely.

Apparently, asking about Malachi's fakery was not the only way to piss her off. I sighed. "All right. Fine." No questions related to Malachi at all, apparently. But what kind of job interview was it when I couldn't ask about her previous employer . . . or whatever? Not that I had any intention of "hiring" her, so to speak. Also, Alona would kill me twice if she ever heard me implying that a ghost-talker was a spirit guide's boss.

Erin rolled her eyes and sat on the bed, giving an extra bounce on the mattress, seemingly just to hear the springs creak under her weight. Alona had done stuff like that, too, when she'd first realized my presence would give her physicality. "Look, he's small-time. Lacks vision. He always has."

I had absolutely no idea what that meant. Either he was a ghost-talker or he wasn't. Except there were varying levels of ability—maybe that was what she meant. Might also explain why he needed her to get information and relay it to him, as she'd implied.

"Whenever I want to make things better for us, he's always dragging his feet. I have to do everything. It's pathetic." She heaved an exasperated sigh. "But you?" She grinned up at me, again with a little bit of crazy greed in her eyes. "You're different. I thought you were the stuff of rumor and suburban legend, the powerful ghost-talker who came out of nowhere."

Huh. I wondered where she was getting her information. The undead rumor mill moved with frightening speed and terrifying inaccuracy. I was a little scared to think about what she'd heard.

"Imagine what we could accomplish together. All those people we could help, the good that would be done." She shivered as if in anticipation. "It would be amazing."

"Uh-huh." I edged back from her. I had, believe it or not, learned my lesson about mysterious girls—both living and dead—who showed up with offers that sounded too good to be true. It hadn't worked out very well with Mina Blackwell when she'd tried to recruit me into the Order, and

I doubted this would be any different. "I need to think about it." Which was a lie. She'd freaked me out plenty in less than ten minutes. She was way too eager and interested in something most other ghosts saw as a form of punishment. Something was not right. Any kind of a more permanent arrangement was definitely off the table.

Erin pouted, cocking her head to one side. "What is there to think about? Are you still hung up on your old spirit guide, the one who left you high and dry?" She eased up from the bed, swaying into my personal space. "She's gone for good, I promise you that." She tapped a finger against my chest, seeming all too pleased with herself. "And I can be very comforting."

Holy crap. "Uh . . ." I scooted away from her, my brain still processing her words. "What do you mean, she's gone for good? How do you know?" I knew the others thought that, but Erin spoke with such confidence it sent alarm bells ringing in my head.

She backed off a step, looking cagey. "Let's just say I have my ways."

"Like?" I persisted.

She drew back, her mouth pinched in anger. "You know, if you can't appreciate what I'm offering, I'll just talk to the other one, then." She spun on her heel and started walking away.

"The other one what?" I asked warily.

"The girl you were with this morning, the one who was talking to the crying chick," she said over her shoulder with some exasperation, as if I should have known. "She's a ghost-talker, too, isn't she?"

"Leave her out of this," I said immediately, before I had time to realize exactly how panicky and paranoid that sounded. *Smooth*, I heard Alona say in my head.

Erin turned to face me, eager interest written all over her face. "Something's different about her, isn't it? I could see it." She raised an eyebrow. "Maybe *she* would be open to some help."

"No, you offered it to me first. And I said I'd think about it, okay?" I didn't want her anywhere near Alona. Whoever (or whatever) Erin was, she was powerful and up to something, and Alona was too vulnerable in her current state.

"You know," she said with a tight smile, "I don't actually need your permission."

Uh-oh. I'd been kind of hoping she wasn't aware of that fact. "Wait, let's just—"

She shut her eyes and said in a loud dramatic voice, "I claim you as my ghost-talker."

Panic lit up my insides. "Stop!" I started toward her, not sure what I could do short of tackling her.

"I am yours and you are mine." She finished in a hurry before I could reach her.

I winced, waiting for a cold blast of air and the supernatural-feeling shift in the atmosphere, the sense of two pieces fitting together. That's what had happened when Alona had claimed me.

But . . . there was nothing.

Huh.

She cracked one eye open to look at me. "I am yours and you are mine," she repeated slowly.

Still nothing. I started to smile.

She opened both eyes and made a frustrated noise. "What the hell?"

"Maybe it knows that tying yourself to someone who doesn't want you around and can summon you up on a whim is a bad idea," I said, giddy with relief. I had no idea what "it" was, other than some kind of otherworldly force that seemed to control these things, and I certainly had no way of knowing if it had any kind of opinion on the matches it made. But something had kept the connection from going through. . . .

Erin folded her arms across her chest. "Are you threatening me?"

Yes. "No. Just making sure we understand each other," I said.

She narrowed her eyes. "It's not like it worked, so you don't have anything to worry about from me." She turned away and stalked toward the opposite wall to leave.

I resisted the urge to call after her and ask if she was going to try to track down Alona/Lily, but I'd already done enough damage in that area. Asking now would only make her more likely to do so. Plus, what were the odds that she'd be able to track Alona down?

"You know, you seem to be in a big hurry to help people 'and whatever,'" I said instead. Not that I was complaining; just really, really suspicious.

She paused halfway through the wall and gave me an over-the-top phony smile. "What can I say? I'm a people person." Then she vanished.

A people person? Yeah, right.

I spent the rest of the afternoon and evening trying to find anything on Malachi or an Erin who'd died five years ago. She was a loose cannon that I'd rather not have rolling up behind me, catching me unawares.

But I didn't have any last names, and at least one of the names was fake (Malachi), which didn't really help in the information-gathering process.

I found Malachi's Web site again, but it held no new information. The only thing strange I noticed this time around was in the testimonial section. First, that he even had a testimonial section implied that he'd been able to help people, all evidence to the contrary today. Erin certainly seemed to believe he was for real, though, and while she might have been slightly off her rocker, she wasn't completely crazy. But beyond that, four out of the ten blurbs mentioned receiving a letter from Malachi and a coupon for the initial consultation right when they needed it most. The recipients seemed to take this as a "sign" they should contact him for help with their otherworldly problems.

More like a sign that Malachi had somehow gotten his hands on a mailing list targeted to the vulnerable, like from a cemetery or funeral home, or that he spent his free time scouring obituaries. People who'd recently experienced the death of someone close to them were probably far more likely to buy into what Malachi was selling. What a user.

After a few more fruitless "Malachi" searches—nothing but Bible mentions—I resorted to searching Facebook, thinking I might be able to pick Erin out of the crowd of Erins in Decatur, Illinois, with a photo. But either she hadn't been on there when she was alive, or her page had been memorialized, which apparently would block it from outside searches.

Great.

Before I could log out, the chat box in the corner popped up with the sound of a suction cup being removed. It flummoxed me for a second. I wasn't on here all that often, and most of my friends weren't the chatting type. Then I saw the name and it made sense . . . sort of.

Lily Turner: Oh, good, you're here. I can't figure out her freaking e-mail password.

Oh, Lord.

Will Killian: What are you doing?
Lily Turner: What? No cell, no privacy on house phone, and I don't have your e-mail. How else was I supposed to reach you? Smoke signals?

This was surreal. It was one thing to have Alona talking to me through Lily in the same room. I could hear the different cadences, see her body language and her expressions, all of which helped make it clear she was Alona, not Lily. But this . . . this was eerie.

Will Killian: How did you log in?

Lily Turner: Duh. She told her browser to remember her log-in info. Very sloppy, but useful for me.

Will Killian: I'm sure.

Lily Turner: You think I should have logged in under my own name? Like that wouldn't have caused a stir.

I imagined, for a second, the reaction of however many friends Alona had when they saw her status button go green, and I was grateful suddenly that she'd had the forethought—and wisdom—not to do that. Actually, I couldn't believe she *hadn't* done that. It must have taken everything she had to resist the temptation.

Lily Turner: Also, you have only seven friends? That's kind of pathetic.

Will Killian: I don't measure friendship in kilobytes.

Lily Turner: Yeah, you know who says that? People who have only seven friends.

She sounded alarmingly chipper. More like herself, in a way that I hadn't heard from her since before the whole Lily debacle had started.

Will Killian: Whatever. Is there a point to this?

Lily Turner: Yes, you can meet me tomorrow at Misty's house. Noon. I don't need a ride.

Will Killian: You don't? Why?

Even I heard the suspicion in those words.

Lily Turner: Don't worry about it. All part of the plan.

Will Killian: I don't think scarier words have ever been spoken.

She didn't respond right away, and I thought she might have logged off or walked away.

Lily Turner: Have you seen my page?

It took me a second to figure out what she meant, and then I still wasn't sure which "my" she meant.

Will Killian: You mean your Alona page?

Lily Turner: What else?

Of course.

Will Killian: No. Only seven friends, remember?

Will Killian: Wait. How can YOU see it w/out logging on?

Lily Turner: Apparently, Lily sent me a friend request at some point. I must have accepted it.

Probably when Lily had been dating Ben Rogers. That would have been the only time, knowing Lily, that she would have felt confident enough to approach the great and almighty Alona Dare and for her to even have a chance of Alona accepting, not that it had made much of an impression on Alona, obviously.

Will Killian: You don't even know who your friends are?
Lily Turner: That's not the point!
Will Killian: What is, then?
Lily Turner: Never mind. Forget it.
Will Killian: Alona . . .
Lily Turner: It's a ghost town, ok?
Lily Turner: There's a bunch of stuff after the funeral, people I didn't know talking about me in the 3rd person, creeeepy . . .
Lily Turner: And then a whole slew of mean stuff.

I grimaced, not surprised.

Lily Turner: And then nothing.

Well, that at least explained why she hadn't logged on as Alona Dare.

Will Killian: I'm sorry.
Lily Turner: Whatever. It's fine. Should have expected it.

I sat there for a long moment, not sure what to type in response. The Alona I'd first talked to a few months ago would have been devastated, shocked, unable to believe that others would speak poorly of her and then abandon her. This Alona, though . . . She was different.

Will Killian: Want a few of my seven?
Lily Turner: *snort* No. You need all you have.

That was more like it.

Lily Turner: But thanks.
Lily Turner: And don't forget. Don't pick me up. Meet me there. 643 Fairmont.

She logged off before I could respond, and that overwhelming sense of trouble on the horizon suddenly returned. No matter what else happened, how much she changed, Alona was a schemer. She planned and manipulated until the world fell into order, or as close as she could manage it. Why did I think tomorrow was not going to be a good day?

I was bleary-eyed, cranky, and generally not my best when I went to meet Alona at Misty's at noon.

It had taken me forever to fall asleep the night before. It might have been all the Mountain Dew I had drunk to keep me awake for a few more completely useless Internet searches, or worrying that Erin was going to suddenly show up again, or hoping my mom's life wasn't wrecked because of me. But then again, it also could have been that, right as I dozed off, two dead middle-aged brothers—Tim and Bob? Jim and Bill? It was never clear, as they were too busy shouting—strode through the wall into my room, still arguing and wanting me to take sides.

From what I'd gathered, they'd inherited a piece of land from a grandfather, and each had different ideas about what should be done with it. And they'd killed each other over it . . . about forty years ago.

That alone might not have been enough to do more than piss me off, except they both still had the shotguns they'd used against each other. You die with it, it's yours even in the afterlife. Would those work against me? No idea. Didn't particularly want to find out, especially at two in the morning. Well, really, at any time, but in the middle of the night, ghosts with guns take on a certain amount of creepy intensity. It was almost enough to tempt me into finding Erin and having her try again.

I'd tried pointing out to the brothers that they were dead, so it didn't matter anymore. However, it was the principle of the thing, apparently.

I'd only gotten rid of them—after more than an hour of trying to get them to shut up and listen—by saying that they should have split the land in half evenly. Not that they thought this was a reasonable solution. Dividing it up made it far less valuable, I guess. But my utter stupidity, proven to them by the fact that I'd bothered making this suggestion, gave them something to agree on for the first time in years. I love it when I can help families come together.

I'd finally dozed off after they left . . . and promptly overslept. So now I was running late to Misty's, on top of everything else, which didn't help my mood, either.

The neighborhood was between mine and Alona's, in location and wealth. Misty's house—which I missed the first time down the street because they had all these huge hanging flowerpots covering up the number on the porch— was a rambling multilevel house. It had a three-car garage with one of those big turnarounds for the cars. I recognized Misty's Jeep in the driveway on my second pass and pulled to the curb across the street to park.

There was no sign of Alona, of course. If she'd gone in without me, I was not going to be happy. Correction: I was already not happy. If she'd left me out here to ring the door- bell at Misty Evans's house, which was not exactly my home turf, on my own, I was going to be pissed.

Gritting my teeth, I started toward the driveway, already trying to think of what I would say when someone answered the door. Misty's house wasn't as ritzy as Alona's, but I didn't fit in here any better than I did over there. It wasn't that I particularly cared what Misty or her family thought about me, but I didn't feel like defending myself against potential stalker accusations if Alona hadn't bothered to explain that I was coming along. Plus, it was a giant waste of time. I was almost positive Misty wasn't being haunted; not in the tra- ditional sense, anyway.

About ten feet up the driveway, I caught movement from the corner of my eye. I turned, half expecting Misty's angry dad or an unwelcome ghostly tagalong. But it wasn't either of those; it was a girl, who'd obviously been waiting on the edge of the lawn, her presence hidden by the overgrown shrubs on the side of the drive (someone in the Evans family loved plants, evidently).

She smiled almost shyly, tipping her head down so her blond-streaked hair would fall forward over her face. It took me a second to put the pieces together. Not because I didn't recognize her. That would be dumb. It was more like my brain refused to make the connection between this girl and all the data and images previously stored in the "Lily" file in my brain.

"You're late," she said, edging closer, the limp on her left side pretty much the only familiar thing about her.

I couldn't think, couldn't speak. The words wouldn't come, fighting against each other and the shock. Of all the things I'd thought Alona might be planning—and trust me, I ruled out very little when it came to her ambitions—*this* hadn't even made the list.

It was Lily . . . but not. Her hair was blonder and shorter, barely reaching the base of her neck, and it was ragged on the ends but in that way you could tell it was supposed to be. She was wearing makeup—sparkly stuff on her eyes and something that made her scar much less noticeable—and clothes I'd never seen before. Tight dark jeans that stopped at her ankles, and a loose-fitting shirt in a shade between pink and red that brought color into her face. It also had a V in front that dipped low enough to reveal something white and lacey underneath, which made me feel like I should look away. I felt heat rise in my face.

"You like?" she asked, as though asking my opinion on an ice-cream flavor. "It was harder than I thought." She looked down at herself with a frown, toying with the long, beaded necklace that hung down almost to her waist. "My old look doesn't work for her. She's more funky-free, you know? And then there was working with that stupid budget." She rolled her eyes.

Slowly but surely, the surprise was wearing off, and I could feel my words returning to me. None of them were good. My God, who did she think she was? She hadn't just crossed the line; she had completely obliterated it. Blood was roaring in my ears.

"We still need to do something about some more color," Alona continued, seemingly unconcerned with my silence. "I used a little self-tanner. Not the craptastic turn-you-orange stuff, of course. But that's not enough. It's still August, so maybe—"

"What the hell is wrong with you?" The words burst out of me. So, yeah. Not exactly my best opening argument, but you've got to go with what you've got.

She stopped, her mouth partially open, but Alona being Alona, she rallied quickly. "Excuse me?" she demanded, narrowing her eyes at me. She managed, somehow, to jam more indignation into those two words than other people would have with a whole speech. It should have been a warning to me, but I was already too far gone.

I grabbed her elbow and tugged her down the driveway, where we would be less noticeable from the house. I couldn't help noticing she smelled good, like oranges and flowers, and her skin was smooth and soft beneath my hand. These changes in her . . . No, I did not like this. "Lily is not some doll you can play dress up with when you're bored," I hissed. "She's a real person—"

She threw her head back with a harsh laugh. "Believe me, I'm all too aware of what you think of Lily." She turned on me and jabbed a finger in my chest. "What you're forgetting is that, for all intents and purposes, I am Lily right now. If I want to cut *my* hair or buy more flattering clothes for *my* body, then *I* can do that."

I gaped at her.

She smirked. "Remember yesterday? 'Be grateful for this chance, take advantage of life, Lily's body is just fine with me'?" She smoothed her hands down her sides, a deliberately seductive motion, and I had to look away. "I decided you were right." The challenge in her tone was unmistakable.

I felt punched. "So this is some kind of revenge or something?" I asked numbly. "Because I wanted you to treat her with respect?"

Hurt flickered across her face for the first time. "Not everything is about you," she said, but her words lacked the force of a few moments before.

"She doesn't even look like Lily anymore," I said, the break in my voice taking me by surprise. Was it really a bad thing if she didn't look like Lily anymore? She *wasn't* Lily.

But what Alona had done wasn't right, either.

I turned away from her, focusing my attention on a point across the yard until I could get myself under control. My emotions were ricocheting all over the place. I couldn't land on any one of them for more than a second.

"No, she doesn't," Alona said. "She looks better. *I* look better."

I glared at her over my shoulder.

"No." She shook her head fiercely. "You don't get to argue with me about this. You know damned well that if she was here and I was alive, this makeover would have made her day, probably even her year."

I rubbed my forehead and felt the start of a new headache. "You are impossibly full of yourself."

She threw her hands up. "What do you want from me? No matter what happens, no matter what we do, the girl you knew, she is gone, okay? Even if we could figure out a way to drag her out of the light—"

I winced.

"Which, trust me, would be about as much fun as it sounds—she wouldn't be the same person you knew." She shook her head, her new haircut framing her face until she tucked the strands back behind her ear. "You can't preserve her as some kind of walking, talking museum exhibit. It's not fair. To any of us."

"So *this* is your solution?" I said, gesturing at her new appearance. Even I could hear that the disgust in my voice was too much, too over the top, but I couldn't stop.

Alona flinched but then looked up, a defensive cant to her chin. "Yeah, it is. And you know why that matters? Because for whatever reason and for however long, I am still here." She stepped closer, staring me down, her dark eyes filled with fury and hurt. "Whether you like it or not, the light sent *me* back, not her."

Her words struck like a slap, and I stepped back involuntarily.

"Is everything okay out here?" a female voice called from the house.

Startled, I looked up to see Misty on the front porch, wearing pajama bottoms and an oversized T-shirt with an image of a megaphone on it.

She frowned at us. "What are you guys doing here?"

Next to me, Alona forced a smile and waved. "We just wanted to check in with you after yesterday."

Misty nodded warily and then tipped her head back toward the door. "Come on in."

Pointedly avoiding even a glance in my direction, Alona started up the driveway.

I followed. "Just because the light sent you back doesn't mean you've got a free pass to do whatever you want," I said under my breath.

She ignored me and kept walking.

I should have just shut up. Some small part of me knew that. I was tired, overwhelmed, and more than a little freaked out. It was one thing for her to try to change Lily; I didn't have to like that. But what was really bothering me was that

I *did*. Lily had always been my friend. But *just* a friend, not anything more. And watching her walk up the drive a few steps ahead of me, I realized my problem wasn't simply that Alona had changed the way Lily looked; it was that I liked the way she looked now more. She looked like Lily's distant, more confident, more attractive cousin.

I felt like a complete shit for thinking that, disloyal to the core; and irrationally, I wanted to punish Alona for it, find some way of making her feel as bad as I did. Which was a stupid, stupid idea, but as unstoppable as a speeding car with burned-out brakes.

"You know, you can't just use Lily to walk back into your old life. Haven't you learned anything?" As soon as the words were out of my mouth, I wished I could call them back.

She stopped, her shoulders stiff. Then she turned to face me with that haughty expression I recognized all too well. But what was eerie was how well it fit on this new face. This new version who was both Alona and Lily. A true Ally.

"Bye, Will," she said with a coolness that reached into my insides. "Let me know if you buck the trend today and find out something that's actually useful."

Then she walked away.

❦ 7 ❧

Alona

Here's the thing. I knew Will would be angry when he saw me. I'm not stupid. That's the reason I had him meet me at Misty's. I'd known there was a possibility he might storm off, and I didn't want him leaving me at home . . . or across the street at the cemetery, as the case may be.

However, what I'd failed to estimate correctly was exactly *how* angry he would be. Mrs. Turner, once she'd gotten over her surprise yesterday, had been cautiously encouraging, excited to see her daughter attempting to interact again. This morning, she'd taken me to get the highlights I wanted, putting down her credit card without hesitation. Then she'd dropped me off at Misty's house, requiring only Misty's name and phone number in return. That was a big stretch in my freedom and could only mean she was pleased with my "progress."

I guess I'd thought it would be the same with Will. He'd yell and kick up a fuss about the changes I'd made but eventually realize that I'd done a good thing. Lily looked better than she ever had. There could be no doubt about that. Okay, and yeah, I benefited, I suppose, but it wasn't like it had come at her expense or anything.

And he knew that. Just as I knew he liked what I'd done but couldn't deal with it. He was, once again, punishing me by holding me accountable for a past that wasn't mine. Like it wasn't hard enough to be Lily; I had to be Lily in a specific way to meet his expectations. Whatever.

Would it have killed him to admit, even grudgingly, that I looked nice? I felt my eyes well up. Being that mean was just uncalled-for and so not like him. He'd left me no choice but to walk away before he saw my reaction. I wouldn't give him the satisfaction of seeing me cry.

"Are you okay?" Misty frowned down at me from the top of the porch stairs.

"I'm fine," I said, wiping away a tear that had escaped, careful of my mascara. Despite my new look, I didn't have any better control over the tear ducts. Lily had been and always would be faster to cry than me.

I climbed the steps, holding on to the rail, and the screech of Will's tires on the otherwise quiet Sunday morning drew our attention momentarily back to the street.

"He's kind of a jerk, huh?" Misty asked, cracking her

toes against the floorboards, a habit that used to drive me crazy but now seemed nothing but achingly familiar.

I shrugged. "Sometimes."

"Come on in," she said, pulling open the screen door and leading me into the dim front hall. "You want to use the—"

Without thinking, I'd already detoured around her to the small bathroom just inside the door to grab a tissue for my stupid teary eyes.

"Oh, good, you found it." She frowned at me.

"Sorry . . . My grandma's house is set up like this," I said. I was going to have to be more careful. I'd spent as much time at Misty's house as at my own; probably more, actually. Remembering to pretend I was a stranger to it would be tough.

She gave me a strange look but nodded.

"This way." She headed down the hall toward the kitchen.

I followed slowly, caught up in absorbing how little her house had changed from what I remembered. I couldn't begin to count how many times I'd eaten dinner over here or stayed the night, and Dr. Everly, Misty's mom, had included me with Misty and her three younger half brothers without batting an eye. Looking back on that time now, I suspect she knew things were not so great for me at home, though she probably hadn't figured out exactly how bad, or she would have been on the phone with some kind of agency to get me out. For that reason alone, I was grateful that Dr. Everly's new husband, Kevin, and the "Screaming Three," as Misty referred to the three boys her mother had produced with Kevin, kept Misty's professor mom pretty distracted.

Being here in this place from my past, one of the few left intact for me, breathing in all the same smells, a wave of longing for the familiar swept over me. Maybe it would be worth swallowing my pride, forgiving Misty, and trying to forget everything that had happened, in exchange for a small portion of the comfort and feeling of safety I'd once experienced here.

If I did that, though, I'd be doing exactly what Will accused me of—using Lily to walk back into a form of my old life. The larger question was, did I care what Will Killian thought when he so clearly did not care what I thought . . . about anything?

I might have gone on considering this question—and my various options—except that as soon we walked into the kitchen I received the clearest sign possible that the past was just that, and there was no going back.

Dr. E. and Kevin must have had the kids out somewhere, because the normally chaotic kitchen was quiet and empty except for a curly-haired girl standing in front of the open fridge in her pajamas, eating what appeared to be raw cookie dough from the tube with an oversized spoon.

Leanne leaned around the fridge door and raised an eyebrow at us, or, more specifically, me. "What's this?"

Leanne Whitaker was now Misty's go-to friend for weekend sleepovers? Seriously?

I struggled to keep the hurt and anger from showing on my face, knowing it would only make things worse.

When I'd been alive, the three of us had mostly gotten along fine, all on the varsity squad together. But Misty and I had been a pair, with Leanne a little on the outside. That's just the way it was. I'd never particularly cared for Leanne. She was always too eager to enjoy someone else's misfortune, which was, frankly, tacky. And I'd experienced that firsthand a few months ago, when I first came back as a spirit to find her talking trash about me. *Bitch.*

I knew Will would have lumped the old me in with her, but I never saw Leanne and me as being anything alike. Yes, people thought I was cruel, but I think there's a difference between giving a brutally honest assessment of a situation, which may cause pain, and causing pain so you can take some kind of delight in it. *Yuck.*

That same trait made Leanne someone you didn't want as an enemy, though, so a friend she was. But not the kind of friend you trusted. At least, I hadn't, and I couldn't believe Misty was being naive enough to do so.

Then again, Misty had never been a great judge of character. That had been my job in our friendship.

"Leanne, this is . . ." Misty looked at me. "What was your name again?"

See what I mean? She'd let a virtual stranger into her house. Not that I was complaining, in this particular instance, as it benefited me. "Ally Turner," I said.

Misty nodded, rubbing her eyes like she wasn't quite

awake yet or hadn't gotten enough sleep. "Right. Ally." The dark circles beneath her eyes looked even more pronounced than they had yesterday.

Leanne cocked her head to one side, evaluating me.

Crap. I held my breath. This would go a lot easier if I didn't have to deal with whatever impressions they might already have of Pre-Coma Lily. Misty hadn't recognized this body, of course. *I'd* barely remembered Lily's existence. There was no way Misty would have. But Leanne . . .

Her eyes narrowed, and an evil grin spread across her freckled face. "I know you." She slammed the fridge door shut with the bottom of her foot, sending the magnets holding the twins' artwork to the floor, and pointed her spoon at me. "You're that girl who lost her shit in front of everyone at one of Ben's parties last year."

Damn it.

"What?" Misty frowned at Leanne.

"Yeah, yeah," Leanne said, waving her spoon around in excitement. "Ben was being his douchey self." She rolled her eyes. "He showed up with his hands all over that freshman. Henley? Hanley?" She scrunched her forehead in concentration, trying to remember. "You know which one I mean. And this chick *freaked.*" She sounded delighted.

"Hello, standing right here?" I muttered.

Leanne ignored me. "Anyway, there was this huge scene. And then she drove off and crashed her car." She paused to give me a skeptical look. "I thought you died."

"I was in a coma," I said tightly.

Misty turned to me. "That was you?" she asked, sounding worried for the first time that maybe she'd let someone who was less than stable into her home.

Thanks a lot, Lily. I could feel my face burning even though I'd had nothing to do with any of that Ben Rogers stuff. I wished, for once, that I could remember this giant confrontation between Lily and Ben. I'd been at the party, but either I'd missed seeing it, or it hadn't registered as anything out of the ordinary. And given the way Ben was, it might very well have been the latter. Girls were always either fawning over him or yelling at him, postfawning. Still, while I was wearing Lily's face, it would be helpful to know if that scene had been as bad as Leanne was implying, or whether she was amplifying it for her own entertainment and my discomfort. I supposed I could have played the memory-loss card and had someone tell me exactly what had gone on, but finding a trustworthy eyewitness— in other words, *not* Leanne—was the trick. So I'd have to roll with it.

"That was a long time ago, and not why I'm here," I said, shooting a death glare at Leanne, who grinned in response. "I came to make sure you were okay," I said to Misty, which was kind of true. "You seemed really upset yesterday, and I wasn't sure if Malachi was able to help you. . . ." *Gag.* Like Malachi was helping anyone but himself.

"She was at the psychic's yesterday," Misty said to Leanne, wrapping the end of her ponytail around her fingers, another nervous habit. "The one who's been trying to help me?"

Leanne made a sour face that could have been in response to the fact either that I'd been somewhere with Misty or that Misty was going to a psychic. Apparently more than once, I realized, as her words clicked through.

"You've been there before?" I asked incredulously.

She shrugged. "He said it would probably take a few times before he could cleanse my aura."

Such a scammer. "Please," I said at the same time as Leanne, who gave me a disgusted look.

Whatever. She didn't *own* the word.

"But he didn't come back yesterday, like, not at all," Misty said to me. "He missed the rest of his appointments."

"Sweetie, I told you, he's only after your money," Leanne said with a condescending smile. "Someone was probably on to him, and he bailed."

Wow. So Leanne and I actually agreed on something. Though she'd obviously let Misty go to Malachi in the first place, which I would not have allowed.

"No." Misty shook her head vigorously. "I'm telling you he's for real. He knew stuff about me and about *her*." Her voice took on a hushed urgency. "Stuff he couldn't have known."

Leanne rolled her eyes and spooned another bite of cookie dough into her big fat mouth.

Misty turned to me. "You know," she said defiantly. "You saw them. The ghosts in his office. The ones he says are his guides."

Interesting that Malachi was apparently aware of his

spirit companions. Maybe he wasn't the fake he seemed to be. Or maybe he was really good at being that fake. Having spirit guides wasn't an uncommon fact about mediums/psychics. He'd probably just done his research.

"She was with that creepy dude from school, Will something. Remember him?" she asked Leanne.

I winced on Will's behalf, and Leanne gave a noncommittal grunt.

"They were both seeing something that wasn't there. It was the weirdest thing." She gave a shudder and then turned back to me. "Ghosts, right?"

I hesitated before responding. I needed Misty to believe me if I was going to figure out what was really going on here. But if I spoke up now, I'd be cementing Ally's reputation as a freak, which I might have to live with for a while.

What to do?

Finally, I nodded. Figuring out who was pretending to be me was more of a priority at the moment. Besides, I'd be out of this body before too long . . . probably.

Leanne snorted, and I hoped she'd choke on a chocolate chip. "Ghosts don't exist, Misty. I told you."

"Then why did you insist on sleeping in the guest room last night instead of my room?" Misty demanded.

Leanne focused on digging out another bite of dough. "Whatever," she muttered. "It was warmer in there."

Misty looked to me. "She's here again. Alona, I mean." She twisted her fingers together nervously. "Since last night."

My ears pricked up. "She's here now? How do you

know?" I tried for a discreet look around the room and saw nothing out of the ordinary, no blurry spots.

Misty shook her head. "I just feel it sometimes. Like there's someone watching me." She smiled sadly. "I know it sounds ridiculous, but I'm not crazy. I know it's her."

"Do you want to show me where that feeling is strongest?" I forced myself not to sound too eager. "Maybe I can take a look?"

Leanne smirked. "Miss Pathetic here suddenly has special spooky powers."

Forget choking. I hoped that cookie dough was chockfull of salmonella.

"It's called a near-death experience. You should try it sometime," I said sweetly. "Maybe without the 'near.'"

Leanne gaped at me.

I turned to Misty. "So?" I asked briskly.

She nodded, wide-eyed. "Uh, sure."

I stepped out of the way and let her lead me back into the hall and up the stairs. I couldn't help noticing the changed photos on the stairwell wall. I was no longer in any of them.

Not that that was entirely shocking. Kevin, who was about ten years younger than Misty's mom, was obsessed with documenting his new family, which had included Misty and me at one time. He had a bunch of these artsy, wrought-iron picture frames/art pieces all the way up the wall. He changed the photos out about every month, swapping in the latest family images.

This particular selection appeared to be about summer

activities. The twins, Owen and Ian, with their older brother, Colin, all in matching water wings. Colin attempting to drink from the hose but mostly spraying his face. Misty and her mom sitting together on the porch swing, talking to each other, their faces serious and their dusty toes dragging across the boards. And some kind of picnic with all of them . . . and Chris, my ex and Misty's current boyfriend.

There were a few pictures of Chris, some with him in the background, as I would have been once, and others focused on him.

In the one closest to me, he had Colin on his shoulders and a twin (don't ask me which was which, I'd never mastered that) wrapped around each ankle. He was pretending to struggle to move forward, but I could tell that beneath the faked strain on his face, he was having fun. His eyes were crinkling up at the edges like he was fighting not to laugh. And behind him, Misty was out of focus, but I could still see her grinning.

They were happy. Kevin was a good photographer, catching the truth in a moment like that.

"So you and Chris Zebrowski, huh?" I asked, and immediately wished I could pull the words back.

She glanced warily over her shoulder at me, pausing on a step.

"I don't know what you've heard, but it wasn't like that," she said.

"Yeah, that's what you said. So what was it like?"

I could see her weighing the moment, deciding whether

she should have to answer me or not. After all, who was I to her? "He sees me," she said. "And I see him."

I frowned. *Huh?* "I saw . . . I mean, I'm sure Alona saw you." I mean, I'd been a lot of things, but visually impaired was definitely not one of them.

But Misty wasn't done yet. "Alona . . . Alona was like this giant storm, you know?" Her voice was distant, like she was seeing something other than the stairway. "You got swept along with her, and after a while you weren't really sure where you were or who you were except as it related to her. I wasn't Misty. I was Alona Dare's best friend. Chris was Alona Dare's boyfriend." She shook her head. "Know what I mean?"

Not exactly.

"But Chris and me, we found each other, and it's real." Her voice rang with fierceness, and her gaze met mine without hesitation, as if she was daring me to challenge her words. "We see each other for who we are, not as accessories to somebody else."

In that second, I felt a wave of envy so strong it nearly knocked me backward down the stairs. Not because it was Chris, but to have someone know me like that . . . I wanted that with a craving I felt in my borrowed bones.

She started up the steps again.

I followed, taking each stair one at a time with my hand on the railing, and wrestled with the mix of emotions churning in me. I'd had Chris in my life, but he'd never looked one-tenth as content as he did in those photos. It hurt, seeing proof that it wasn't him but me who was flawed.

My eyes stung with tears. Every instinct told me to blame the two of them—Misty and Chris. They had been greedy, selfish, and cruel. They'd done this to me. But how can you deny something when the proof is right in front of you? The truth was, they'd done this regardless of me. I was a nonentity, which somehow hurt more than if it had been a deliberate strike against me.

She reached the top of the stairs and turned to wait for me.

"So why aren't you wearing his ring?" I asked in a voice that was probably harsher than it should have been. I wasn't sure if I wanted to know, but I couldn't stop myself from asking, either.

"I didn't say yes yet," she said, looking at her bare left hand as if making sure the ring hadn't somehow appeared there suddenly. "I'm eighteen. We're going to different schools." She gave a little shrug.

On the top step now, I waited, sensing, *hoping*, there was more.

"And how am I supposed to say yes to him when Alona is still so upset?" she asked in a small voice. "She's, like, not at rest because of us."

I let out a silent breath of relief. I hadn't lost her completely. I still mattered to her, even if it wasn't really me who was doing the haunting that had her so concerned. That somehow lifted a burden from my shoulders I hadn't even known I was carrying.

"Well." I cleared my throat against the lump of unshed tears. "Let's go see what we can do about that."

She gave me an odd look—and why not? Ally Turner had no reason to be emotional about any of this—and gestured for me to walk ahead of her. Her room was the last one at the end of the narrow hall, past the tiny guest room and the former master bedroom that her three brothers now shared. Dr. E. and Kevin had renovated the study downstairs last year, turning it into their room.

Misty's room looked much the same as when I'd been there last, a couple of months ago. Yeah, I'd visited her a few times after I'd died. Her grandmother's quilt was still on her bed, rumpled from where Misty had slept beneath it. The television on her dresser blared a rerun of *The Hills*, and all the dresser drawers hung open from the last time she'd searched them for socks or whatever. She always did that, left the drawers open, arguing that it saved time. Over the years, I'd banged my hip or knee on their sharp edges more times than I could count.

The major difference in her room appeared to be the pile of college stuff—a new comforter still in the plastic, a laundry basket stuffed full of notebooks, folders, and other school supplies, and a stack of plastic plates and utensils—in the corner.

She caught me looking at it. "Millikin in the fall." She rolled her eyes. "Free tuition because of my mom. But at least I get to live on campus."

I nodded, knowing that had been the plan for years. I'd

been considering going with her. The school had fit my dad's requirement of being close enough for me to drive home to check on my mom on a regular basis; hence, the car I was supposed to get as a graduation gift. Only, that car had been traded in for a minivan with a car seat for my new half sister, as I'd discovered last month.

I forced away thoughts of my evil stepmother—and her potentially evil spawn—to focus on the task at hand. "This is where you sense her presence most often?" I asked, trying not to squirm at the supreme cheesiness of that line.

But Misty apparently saw nothing amiss in it. She nodded, rubbing her hands over her arms as though chilled.

I didn't feel anything out of the ordinary besides amped-up air-conditioning, which I knew was Misty's standard protocol whenever her mother was out of the house. Dr. E. was very environmentally conscious and probably wouldn't have installed A/C at all if she could have handled the whining from the other members of her family.

I didn't see any obvious blurry spots, but seeing ghosts still wasn't something I was particularly skilled at. So I focused on listening instead, trying to screen out the noise of the television for the sound of whispers or movement nearby, but all that garnered me was Leanne downstairs, apparently yapping away on the phone.

"No, seriously, she just showed up here. Can you believe it?" She gave a bark of laughter. "I should invite her to Ben's party tonight. Now, that would be worth seeing, I bet. Freak-out of the Century, part two, you know?"

Wonderful. News of my arrival and recently acquired weirdo status would reach the entire graduating class before I could even leave here. Fortunately, most of them would be going to college in the next week or so, and I wouldn't have to deal with them much after that.

Though, of course, there was no way I'd be stuck in this body for that long. Right?

Riiight.

"Anything?" Misty asked anxiously, looking around the room as well.

I shook my head with a grimace. I really wanted to catch this jerk who was pretending to be me. "She was here this morning? Are you sure?"

Misty nodded rapidly, then hesitated before adding, "Well, I'm pretty sure. Nothing was knocked over or anything. It was just that feeling again." She shivered.

Great. Maybe Will had been right, and this was all in Misty's head. "Anywhere else we can check?"

She thought about it for a second and then gestured to the half-closed door to the attached bathroom. "That's where the message showed up on the mirror."

Might as well check it out while I was here. God, it was going to suck if I had to leave without anything. Will, assuming he ever spoke to me again, would never let me live it down.

I crossed the room, feeling Misty's gaze on my uneven stride, and yanked open the door, expecting nothing scarier than the heap of wet towels Misty was prone to leaving on the floor until they mildewed. Gross.

Instead, though, I almost walked face-first into a spirit, a big blurry spot leaning over the vanity, probably hard at work on another message.

An embarrassing and involuntary squeak escaped me before I could stop it, and I took a step back.

"Oh, hey." The spot shifted and swirled in front of my eyes as it turned toward me, a distinctly female voice emerging from it. "I was wondering when you were going to show up."

❧ 8 ❧

Will

I couldn't believe Alona. I pounded my fist against the steering wheel in frustration.

Though, really, shouldn't you have known she was going to pull something like this? my logical side asked, deciding to put in a belated appearance. After all, Alona was not one to heroically suffer looking anything less than the best she thought she was capable of at any given moment. In fact, it was a little surprising it had taken her a month to get to this point.

And my reaction? *You definitely could have handled that better.*

Shut up, I told that censorious voice in my head.

That icy expression she'd worn before kissing me off had given me a sick feeling. It reminded me too much of the one she'd paraded around behind at school, back in her original body. That was Alona Dare—perfect, cool, untouchable. The irony was, of course, that it proved I was right in my long-running argument with her: it was more about attitude than actual appearance. But I didn't feel I'd be helping myself by bringing that up today.

She looked good, and she knew it. For a second, I could see her stepping up and taking this life for her own, becoming the "Ally" she'd created in the space that used to be Lily's.

True, she didn't have her original body, and I was sure that that would have been her first choice if it had been remotely possible, which it wasn't. But with what she'd done today— the clothes, her hair—it was clear she was growing more comfortable with being Ally, making that persona her own.

It was conceivable that one day she'd be comfortable enough with the new and improved Ally that she might not want to leave.

And if she didn't want out anymore, she wouldn't, in theory, need me any longer. There would be nothing keeping us together. That realization struck with cold, hard force, distracting me. A car horn blared, and I looked up to find myself crossing the yellow lines. Heart pounding, I jerked the wheel to keep the car on my side of the road.

I'd always considered, in the back of my mind, the possibility of losing her. To the light, to her own stubborn refusal to keep her energy level up by being positive. But the longer we'd been together, the less I liked to think about it, shoving it further and further down in my thoughts. I couldn't imagine my life without her, in one form or another, and I didn't want to think about her being taken away. I'd never thought about the fact she might *walk* away.

I swallowed hard, fighting against the panicky feeling clawing at my chest. Yeah, in Lily's body, she could hear and sort of see ghosts, which would make her life more complicated; but it wasn't like I could help her with any of that. I'd needed *her* to help *me*.

Besides, she didn't seem to need much assistance in that area. She was handling it better than I was.

No. I shook my head. I was being ridiculous. There was no way that she'd ever voluntarily stay in Lily's body.

The only reason she'd even pulled this extreme-makeover routine was because she was unhappy with how she looked, finding Lily's appearance inferior to her original body. Hadn't we been fighting about that only yesterday?

So our problem was still the same as it had ever been: we had to find a way to get her out without hurting Lily.

I tried to feel as reassured by this line of thought as I had been over the last month, but it wasn't working this time.

And then what? that pushy voice returned to ask.

Having started down this path of thinking, the conclusion was impossible to avoid. Assuming I could get Alona back as a spirit guide, things would go back to normal. We'd be helping ghosts between make-out sessions, and all would be great with the world . . . for a while.

But I was getting older and she wasn't. I'd go to Richmond for classes and meet people who didn't know her. If I wanted to go out and grab pizza with someone, either Alona couldn't go or she'd have to tag along as a spectator and keep quiet, a state I couldn't even imagine.

One day I'd be twenty-five and then thirty-five, forty-five. . . . She'd still be eighteen. At some point, that was going to get creepy, even beyond the living/dead issue we had going already. And maybe not now, or even in ten years, but I might want the possibility of a family. I couldn't see any woman, even one cool enough to handle the fact that her husband talked to the dead on a regular basis, being okay with a spirit guide who looked like an eighteen-year-old cheerleader hanging around, especially if she knew there'd once been kissing. And, for that matter, I couldn't see Alona being happy in that situation, either. I might not have been Chris Zebrowski, but sharing attention was not something Alona did well with *anyone*.

I imagined an argument with a wife or a girlfriend on one side, Alona on the other and me in the middle. I shuddered. No way.

Suddenly I was afraid that no matter what happened, I was going to be saying good-bye to her, one way or another.

As soon as I pulled into the strip-mall parking lot, I noticed with a rush of dread that Malachi's window sign—a neon outline of a hand with an eye in the center—was dark.

Crap, crap, crap.

I parked as fast as I could and approached his storefront cautiously. I didn't particularly want another run-in with Erin. But the lights were off and the waiting room was empty, of ghosts and living alike.

I pulled on the door handle. Locked. Malachi the Magnificent was closed, despite the decal in the lower part of the window proclaiming hours that would have indicated otherwise.

I resisted a stupid urge to punch the glass. Without any other way to contact him, I was out of luck if he'd holed up somewhere. Apparently, he'd been really scared yesterday, another piece of this that made no sense.

Putting my hands up to block the light, I tried to get a better look through the window. Most of the chairs were now stacked three or four high, and the receptionist's desk had been shoved back against the wall. Either Malachi had a very dedicated cleaning team, or he was gone . . . for good.

And it keeps getting better.

But as I started to move away from the window, I caught a flicker of light. Pressing my hands tighter against the glass to block out more of the sunlight, I searched for what I'd seen.

There. Underneath the door to the private consultation area, territory Alona and I had not managed to breach yesterday, a fine line of light flashed and then dimmed. Like someone was moving around back there.

Malachi.

I considered knocking, hammering on the door in case he hadn't heard me trying to open it a minute ago, but what were the odds he'd actually open it if he saw me standing there?

At times like this I wished for Alona to be here in spirit form. She'd have slipped through a window on the far end and unlocked the door to let me in.

But maybe there was another way.

One of my responsibilities during my short stint as a busboy at Sam's Diner had been taking the garbage out to the Dumpsters in the alley. The strip mall on the block behind the diner had its back to us. If I remembered correctly, all the units had doors in the back. And on any given day, most of those doors remained unlocked or even propped open for the ease of employees' coming and going.

I jogged around to the side of the building and then to the back. As I'd suspected, several of the green doors stood open, and a couple of employees from a cell-phone store stood outside smoking. The door corresponding to Malachi's location was closed, but a battered blue van was parked in front of it, with the cargo doors open.

Score.

I approached the van cautiously, wary of Erin and afraid Malachi might bolt if he saw me.

But Erin was nowhere to be seen, and Malachi wasn't in the van, at least as far as I could tell. Hastily filled cardboard boxes dominated the cargo area in the vehicle, and the driver's seat appeared to be empty.

I stepped away and started toward the back door to Malachi's storefront. Before I could reach it, though, the door opened, and the man himself emerged, carrying another worn-looking box. Minus his cape and with his hair sticking up in several directions, he looked more like a harried delivery guy than someone with "Magnificent" in his title.

He saw me and froze, the box slipping in his hand, like he might drop it and run. Then his shoulders sagged and he just looked exhausted. "We're leaving, okay? In a matter of minutes." He brushed past me, heading toward the van.

"Wait," I said, hurrying after him. "I just want to talk to you."

He shoved the box into the van and turned to face me, raking a hand through his already rumpled hair. "Look, we got the message the first time. We shouldn't have stayed, but no one else came around." He shrugged helplessly. "We were subtle, careful not to overdo it—"

"I know," I said. "That's what I want to ask about."

He stared at me. "Who are you again?"

"Will Killian."

He nodded slowly. "I think I met your—"

"My dad?" I ventured.

He nodded. "That was a few years ago," he said, seemingly trying to piece something together. "You're not a member of the Order."

It was a statement, but I could hear the uncertainty in it, the question.

I shook my head. "No."

"Well," he said, "that's a relief." But he looked almost disappointed, which made no sense. "So, what do you want?"

"Just to talk," I said again. "There aren't many of us who can . . ." I hesitated, glancing at the cell-phone store employees, who were watching us with unabashed curiosity. "Not many who can do what we do." Assuming he was legit, which I still wasn't sure about. But if he was, he might have some major skills worth learning. Like how he'd managed to ignore the ghosts in his office so completely.

"No, no." He shook his head. "If you figured us out, someone else isn't far behind, and I can't take that chance." He slammed the van doors shut and headed for the front of the vehicle.

I followed him. "I didn't figure anything out. Your name was on this paper my dad left, that's all." I pulled the page from my pocket, unfolded it, and held it out to him.

He glanced at it, his face tightening.

"I was hoping you might have some answers," I said.

He laughed, but it sounded bitter. "Kid, the day I have anything other than questions, you'll be the first to know." He pulled open the driver's-side door and levered himself into the seat.

Kid? He wasn't even ten years older than me. I'd thought it was bad when the Order had been bent on recruiting me as some kind of prodigy. But it was infinitely worse, as it turned out, to be treated like a nonentity, someone not important enough to talk to. I'd expected that in high school, from people who didn't understand. But from this guy? No way.

"Look, I don't need the mysteries of the universe explained," I said, getting pissed. "I just want to know how you keep from being overwhelmed." I wanted to ask him about Alona's situation, too, but I wasn't stupid. He was a stranger with potentially shady business practices and an overly aggressive spirit guide. Caution seemed like the smarter route, at least until I got a better feel for his character. He might not be a member of the Order, but I couldn't be sure that he wouldn't trade information on us to save his own skin.

He shook his head at me again, like I was speaking Japanese despite having been told that he wasn't fluent. "Don't you have anyone else to ask about this? Where is your dad?" he asked.

"Dead." I folded up the page from the phone book and tucked it carefully into my pocket. "Killed himself. Almost four years ago." Those words came out more readily now, after so much time, but they were never easy to say.

Malachi sat back in his seat, startled. "I'm sorry," he said after a long pause. "I didn't know."

It wasn't something discussed openly at our house, obviously, and I doubted my mother had given much information publicly, in an obituary or anything, if at all. I didn't like bringing it up now, feeling like I was somehow using what had happened to get sympathy or manipulate him into giving me answers. But it was, in fact, the truth. I couldn't go to my father because he was dead. And he was dead because he'd wanted it that way.

So I made myself wait, squelching the intense urge to say, "Forget it," and walk away.

Malachi gave a heavy sigh. "All right. He did me a favor

once. I suppose I owe you the same."

Guilt and relief competed for priority, with relief winning out only by a slight margin. "Thanks," I said.

He stepped down from the van. "Five minutes. That's it."

The back room in Malachi's storefront was decidedly utilitarian and boring, not at all what I'd expected. Walking through the door, I saw a small kitchen/storage area to the right and a tiny bathroom to the left. The main area, where'd Malachi had obviously performed his spirit "consultations," was a wood-paneled room with cheap white shelving lining the walls and a table and chairs in the center.

There were signs, though, that the decor had once been more exotic, or at least aimed to be. Puddles of purple candle wax stained almost every square inch of the shelving. The metal curtain rod that hung behind the door to the waiting room still held a strand or two of dark beads.

"Crystal ball is already in the van," Malachi said from behind me, as if all too aware of how mundane the space appeared now.

I couldn't tell if he was kidding.

He pushed past me and dragged a chair away from the table and gestured for me to sit in it. "Ask. Let's go."

He hadn't been joking about the five-minutes thing, evidently.

"Uh, okay." I sat down, even though his nervous/twitchy energy was enough to make me want to pace instead. "When I was here the other day, you had me fooled. I would have sworn you were a fake. It was like you didn't even hear or see the ghosts in the waiting room. Where did you learn to do that? To tune them out like that?"

He gave me a tight smile. "I'm not sure that's something I can teach."

"Seriously, you're going to pull this 'it's a trade secret' bullshit on me? This is my life. I'm just trying to survive." Before he could respond, I pushed further, struck by a sudden idea. "Is it something Erin does?" She was powerful beyond anything I'd ever seen.

He paled. "Erin. You talked to her?"

Uh-oh. Maybe not the best idea to bring up disloyal spirit guides when I was trying to get the guy's help. "Yeah, she came to see me, but—"

He stalked forward until he was right in front of my chair. "What did she say? Did she claim you?" He leaned over me, suddenly much too close.

Whoa. He'd gone from zero to crazy intense in the space of a few seconds.

I shifted away from him. "Look, I didn't say yes or anything." Not that it had mattered. But whatever; Malachi didn't need to know that. "She was just—"

"You said no?" he asked in disbelief. "Did that stop her?"

My head was spinning, trying to keep up with this conversation. "Uh, no. But it didn't work. I think the bond with my spirit guide might somehow still be active, even though she's not exactly here anymore." That was the only explanation I'd come up with that made any kind of sense.

He laughed, too loud and long. "It didn't work?" He straightened up and raked his hands through his hair. "Of course not. The first one strong enough to tempt her, and it didn't work. Unbelievable." He dropped to his knees, as though his legs wouldn't support him further, and rubbed his forehead as if he were in pain.

"Are you okay?" I asked cautiously.

"I'm great. Can't you tell?" he snapped, his face still in his hands.

Okaaay, then. He wouldn't be the first ghost-talker to have lost possession of his marbles.

Fighting disappointment, I looked past him toward the door. I could make a run for it, no problem. But that would be the end of this conversation, and any future conversation with him, guaranteed. I wouldn't get this opportunity again. And the answers I wanted might be here, just buried under a few layers of whack job.

"Did you want it to? Work, I mean?" I asked carefully, digging a little to piece together what was going on without making him completely flip out. If Erin was the source of his ability to control what he heard/saw, why would he want to get rid of her? Yeah, she seemed to have that same attitude problem Alona occasionally had, but it would be worth it for the kind of peace he appeared to have.

He looked up at me, dark circles under his eyes clearly visible for the first time. "For the last five years I've been haunted every single waking minute of every day," he said, and laughed, but it sounded weak and sad. "Hell, for that matter, sometimes she wakes me up."

"I don't understand." Which was a massive under-statement.

He stood up abruptly, pulled out the chair next to mine, and sat in it, leaning toward me. "You want to know how I ignore all those other ghosts? The ones you said were in the waiting room?"

Given the strange, almost fevered expression on his face, I wasn't so sure I did want to know anymore. But I was in it too deeply already.

I nodded.

"I don't. I can't see them."

It took me a second to catch on. "You mean you can only hear them." It wouldn't be all that surprising, given what I'd learned from Mina. There were varying levels of ability among ghost-talkers. Even Mina herself had trouble track-ing ghosts when they moved.

"No," he said with exaggerated patience. "I mean, I can't see them, hear them, or even tell they're there."

I frowned. "I don't—"

"I can only see and hear one ghost." He held up a fin-ger to illustrate his point. "That is, if I'm not completely crazy, which is always a possibility." He threw his hands up. "Maybe this is all part of one giant hallucination. Maybe I'm lying somewhere in a drug-induced coma, and this is all in my mind." He sighed and then shook his head. "Wouldn't that be nice?" he asked, more to himself than me.

I gaped at him.

Malachi noticed before I could recover myself. "Happy now?" he asked. "Got all the answers you want?"

I shook my head. "That doesn't make any sense."

"If it's any consolation, that's pretty much the reaction the other guy—your dad, I guess—had, too."

"You're talking about Erin?" I asked, to be sure.

"The one and only," he said with a bitter smile.

That wasn't possible. You either had the gift or you didn't, with varying degrees in between. It wasn't localized to specific ghosts. It couldn't be. It would be like being able to smell only one scent or see one color. "Well, she's not a hallucination," I said. "I can tell you that much. I've seen her, too."

He just looked at me. "Reassurance from someone else who might be a hallucination doesn't really help."

I opened my mouth and closed it before trying again. "Maybe you should start at the beginning." I was starting to think he might not be crazy; crazy people don't usually bother to question their own sanity. "Has it always been this way? When did you start seeing her?" Maybe he'd suffered some kind of traumatic brain injury or something. That might explain why he could see only one ghost . . . or why he thought he might be hallucinating.

"What's the point?" He laughed. "You're going to help me? You came to *me* for help."

"Just . . . start talking," I persisted. If there was ever anyone who could have been helped by the Order and their tactics, it would have been this guy. But he'd clearly been afraid of them tracking him down, even running from me when he'd thought I was one of them. So my curiosity was going to get the better of me on this one. And who knew, maybe I could help him. He looked like he needed it.

He sagged back in his chair. "I don't . . . Everything was fine until Erin died."

"You knew her before, then?"

He looked as if I'd asked the stupidest question possible. "She's my sister. My twin?"

"Oh," I said. I never would have guessed that. Maybe some resemblance around the eyes. Maybe. Her hair was a darker red and not nearly as wild as his. The features that made her look pretty and petite kind of gave him a happy-gnome appearance.

"My fraternal twin, obviously," he said, sounding huffy.

"You're twins and your parents named you Malachi and Erin?" I asked in disbelief. He'd definitely gotten the short end of the stick there.

"My real name is Edmund," he said stiffly.

I grimaced. Not much better than Malachi. I thought about apologizing but figured it would only make things worse, so I stayed quiet and waited for him to continue.

"Erin had an accident at school. When we were freshmen in college." He looked down at his hands. "When they called me to the hospital after she fell, she was already . . . gone. I was standing there, staring at this empty body that used to be my sister, trying to figure out how I was going to do this. You know, life. How I was going to be alone, you know? For the first time ever." He rubbed his eyes as if the image was burned onto the back of his eyelids and he wanted to remove it.

He forced a laugh and opened his eyes. "When I was seven and joined the Cub Scouts, Erin would scream and cry until she made herself sick while I was gone at meetings. Eventually, it was easier not to go."

That sounded a little unhealthy, actually.

"In the summers, our grandparents wanted us to visit for a week separately, part of that whole giving-twins-individual-attention thing." He lifted his shoulders in a defeated manner. "She pulled the same crap, carrying on and screaming until they brought her home. After that, we always went together."

Scratch that. A lot unhealthy.

"Erin was always the one who decided everything. What clubs we should join, who we should take to the prom, where we should sit at lunch. It was just easier that way. She's three minutes older than me. She always knew what we wanted. Or," he said with heavy sigh, "what she wanted and what I'd go along with."

He looked up at me. "It was my fault, too. She was pushy and controlling, but I let her. She was the one who faced the world, and all I had to do was follow along in her wake. I didn't have to stand up for myself, didn't have to fight."

I shifted uncomfortably in my chair. That sounded a little too familiar, maybe.

"I didn't know what to do when she died," he said. "It

was like losing part of me, an arm or a leg or something." He shook his head. "I didn't know how to function without her. I needed her, so I wished for her to come back. Harder than I've ever wished for anything. I was desperate."

I leaned forward in my chair, suddenly aware of where this story was headed.

He sighed heavily. "And then she just showed up . . . and started talking. Yelling, actually," he amended. "Even after my parents got to the hospital, I was still the only one who could hear her. It freaked me out at first. I tried to ignore it—her—but she saw me, knew I was looking at her." He shrugged helplessly. "After that, she never left. The doctors said it was grief or shock or depression. Then my parents got involved and tried to have me committed."

Oh, I knew that feeling. I thought I'd had it hard, but to live an otherwise normal life for eighteen years and then to start seeing your dead sister everywhere . . . that was worse. What I could do was difficult, but at least it had the potential to be beneficial. What Malachi/Edmund had going on was torture.

Although I'd never heard of anyone developing ghost-talker abilities overnight like that. That was odd.

"Erin warned me about what my parents were planning, and we left in the middle of the night." He lifted his shoulders heavily. "Haven't been back home since."

"What does she want?" I was ashamed to realize I hadn't even bothered to ask her that myself, when she'd shown up at my house. Then again, she'd *shown up at my house.*

"What do you mean?"

"I mean, ghosts usually have unresolved issues, unfinished business keeping them from moving into the light," I said.

He stared at me blankly.

"You've never seen the light." Of course not. If he could only see one ghost, and she was still here, he'd have had no opportunity to do so. "Well, look, it's there. It works, trust me. There's a system. All you have to do is figure out what she wants, what issues are holding her here and—"

He shook his head with a harsh laugh. "You're not getting it. Her unresolved business? She wants to be alive again. Isn't that what they all want?"

I didn't know what to say. If that was the case, there wasn't much hope for Erin. She must have been holding on to her in-between state with sheer strength.

"As long as she's with me, someone can hear and see her," Edmund said wearily. "She can have indirect contact with the living world. I've tried to leave, but she always finds me."

Erin was using her brother as a lifeline. I was beginning to see why he was stuck and why my dad hadn't called the Order down on him. She was wrong to be taking advantage the way she was, but how could you ask him to turn on his sister?

"And from what your dad told me about his gift—and yours, too, I guess—with someone like you, she'd have the ability to touch stuff again, pick things up." He sighed. "That's one step closer."

"That doesn't happen with you?" I asked.

He shook his head. "Your dad didn't understand it either."

I was beginning to wonder if he was even a ghost-talker at all. The ability didn't develop overnight, at least not that I'd ever heard of. He could see and hear only one ghost, and he didn't have to deal with the added effect of giving her physicality, probably the most common (and dangerous) effect of our gift. It sounded more like he was being haunted by someone he was specially connected to. The twin thing, operating even postlife, perhaps? Like he'd pulled her spirit to him, and the bond between them allowed them to communicate still.

"Don't worry. Now that she's tried it with you once, and it didn't work, she probably won't try again," he said, trying to be reassuring. "Besides, we need to be moving on anyway. We've stayed in one place for too long as it is." He stood up and shoved his chair back in place at the table.

I shook my head. "If you stay, maybe we can find a way to—"

"Someone's going to run the numbers soon, like the Order did when they sent your dad to investigate. Too many hauntings, too close together. It raises a red flag with the statistics they track, I guess. He covered for us last time, but it'll happen again, and I'm betting we won't be as lucky with whoever they send to investigate."

Actually, given what I knew about the Order and the dwindling number of those qualified enough to be considered full members, he and Erin might be safer than they thought just from the Order's sheer lack of manpower to investigate things like wonky statistics. But that wasn't what caught my attention. "Too many hauntings? Why would you have any control over that?"

He looked uncomfortable. "I thought you understood. She's the only one I can see."

I still wasn't getting it.

"I can't go out and find business on my own," he said with exaggerated patience. "She passes messages along from those she finds, but sometimes making a connection between a ghost and someone who lives locally and is willing to come in . . . It's a bit iffy."

In other words, Erin didn't feel like doing the work, and without her eyes and ears, he couldn't do it for himself.

"So, sometimes we have to help things along," he said, studying the carpet with more intensity than it deserved.

Wait. I sat up straight in my chair. "Are you saying she haunts people to drive business?"

"Only when we need the money," he said defensively. "And it keeps her busy."

Jesus. Pieces of this began to fall into place. Misty thinking Alona was haunting her. The letter/coupon that his testimonials had mentioned. "You send Erin out to haunt someone if they know someone who died recently?"

"Depends on what the newspaper says," he mumbled.

And Misty had probably been featured prominently in the articles about Alona's tragic, untimely death, as her distraught best friend.

"What, like, if they have money?" Misty didn't have money, but it wouldn't take much research to figure out her parents were probably doing okay.

He didn't respond, just shifted his weight awkwardly.

"And then once you've scared them, you send them that stupid letter and coupon, bringing them right to your door." It was brilliant. And utterly creepy.

"Do you think this is fun for me?" he demanded. "I'd have a regular job if I could, but she won't let me! Besides, it's not your problem anymore," he said pointedly. "As soon as Erin gets back, we're leaving, remember?"

So they could inflict this scam on innocent people in some other town? No way. Not if I could stop it. "Where is Erin, anyway?" If she couldn't stand to go a minute without being heard or seen by a living person, as he claimed, then she'd been gone for a while now.

He grimaced. "I couldn't tell her we were leaving. It . . . it would upset her. She's out visiting clients."

"You mean, she's haunting people." I shook my head in disgust. "I can't believe I was feeling sorry for you, and you're—" I stopped, struck by a horrible, awful thought.

"Who is she 'visiting' today?" I asked, forcing the words out, caught in the inescapable conclusion that I could see barreling toward me.

He appeared taken aback by the intensity in my voice. "I . . . I don't know."

I stood up and shoved him against the shelving. "Think!"

"We don't have that many on the line right now," he

said, his voice shaking. "Just Mrs. Baxter, the guy who owns the dry cleaner's, and the girl."

Misty. Which was exactly where Alona happened to be at this particular moment. *Damn it.* If Erin tried to claim "Ally," that would be bad. I didn't know what would happen. It would be worse, though—much worse—if Erin figured out what made Ally so different. A powerful ghost who wanted nothing more than to be alive again in the presence of a body she knew was currently occupied by a spirit?

Not good.

I let go of Malachi/Edmund and ran for the back door. "You stay here," I called to him over my shoulder. "We're not done yet."

I just hoped the same could be said for Alona and Lily.

❧ 9 ❧

Alona

"**I** figured you wouldn't be able to stay away," the blurry spot continued.

It took a second for the full implication of her words to sink into my brain. She recognized me. She *knew*.

My breath caught in my throat.

Up until now, I'd been assuming whoever was pretending to be me to haunt Misty was someone who'd decided to take advantage of "Alona's" absence to have a little fun at "her" expense, maybe a ghost from the list who'd gotten pissed at something I had (or had not) done for them.

But this . . . this was not that. This spirit, whoever she was, obviously knew exactly who I was. She'd been waiting for me. Me, as in Alona Dare.

Crap.

"Took you long enough, though," the ghost said. "Listening to those two jabber on all night was almost enough to make me want to kill myself again."

Movement at the top of the blurry spot gave the suggestion of someone tossing her hair in disgust. In fact, if I squinted hard enough, I could almost make out a face in the haze before me. God, this would be so much easier if I could *see* her.

"Not that I killed myself in the first place," she added. "Whatever. You know what I mean." She waved dismissively. Or at least, that's what it looked like. A smaller piece of the blurry area moved in a half arc.

I shook my head, my brain whirling with possibilities. Will was the only one who knew what had happened with Lily's body. So who was *she*? Someone who'd eavesdropped on Will and me and heard too much? Her voice didn't sound at all familiar, so she couldn't be someone I'd talked to on a regular basis.

But more important, what did she want? I was afraid I didn't want to know. You don't go to this much trouble to set up a power play without a really good reason.

I swallowed hard against the rapidly developing pit of dread in my stomach.

"What is it?" Misty whispered. "You see something, don't you?"

I'd almost forgotten about her in the room behind me. "Misty, go downstairs," I said over my shoulder as calmly as I could. "I'll handle this." *How*, exactly, I wasn't quite sure, and for the first time I wished Will was here. Not that he could have done anything, but he definitely had more experience with being defenseless in the presence of ghosts and might have had some tips. But with or without Will, one thing was certain: I couldn't have Misty up here listening to me as I tried to talk to this . . . faker.

"But what if you need me?" she persisted. "What if she wants to talk to me? She was my friend."

"Oh, how sweet," the ghost purred, oozing closer.

My pulse spiked, and I backed up, giving the ghost room to exit the bathroom. I didn't know who she was or what she wanted, which was bad enough. But if it turned out that my presence gave her physicality—you know, like the ability to *hurt* me—that would be much, much worse. I didn't know for sure if I had that aspect of the ghost-talking "gift," but now didn't strike me as a particularly good time to find out.

"If I need you, I'll call you," I said to Misty. "Just go, please." I dared another glance back to make sure she was listening. Figuring out what was going on and who this was would be tough enough without worrying about blowing my cover.

With an unhappy expression, Misty started for the hall but stopped to linger in the doorway.

I gritted my teeth. "Seriously? I'm trying to do my job here." Or at least pretend to, anyway. But I was rapidly losing patience with Misty and her softheartedness. True, she had no idea what was really going on, but even so, this ghost had been haunting her, terrifying her for who knew how long, and she wanted to hang around and have a chat?

"I know," Misty said. "But I just wanted to say . . . Alona, for what it's worth, I am sorry." With pleading in her eyes, she addressed a spot high on the wall above the bathroom door. How tall, exactly, did she think my ghost would be? "I shouldn't have done that to you, no matter how Chris and I felt about each other. And I would have told you eventually. I was just afraid that you would be so angry. . . ." She trailed off and looked down at her hands, fidgeting with her thumbnail. "I didn't want to lose you as my friend. I was selfish. I wanted you both. I never wanted to hurt you, and I'm even sorrier I didn't get the chance to tell you that before. I hope you can forgive me."

I stared at her, stunned. There it was. The apology I'd been waiting months to hear but never expected to receive.

Misty took a deep breath and nodded, more to herself than to me, and walked out, her steps lighter, as if having said the words had cleansed her in some way or lifted a weight from her.

"Such devotion. It's adorable," the ghost drawled. "She's been so upset lately."

I whipped around to face her, reinvigorated suddenly. She was not Alona Dare. I was, no matter who I looked like. She shouldn't even *be* here, and that apology was not for her. "Shut up," I snarled.

"So much hostility," she said with an amused gasp. But she still moved back slightly, proving she wasn't as tough as she thought she was.

"You've gone to a lot of trouble to get my attention. What do you want?" I folded my arms, though I supposed any effort to make Lily look fierce was probably wasted. She was too cute, scar and all.

The ghost laughed. "What, Misty? That's just business."

Which meant what, exactly? "What do you want?" I repeated. The more she dragged this out, the worse it was going to be. I could feel it hanging above my head, like the proverbial piano on a fraying rope.

The blur edged closer, and I caught a glimpse of dark red hair and brown eyes before the particles reshifted into a messy, undefined swirl. Was my ghost vision finally improving? That would be nice . . . or not.

"I'm here to make you an offer that is going to rock your world," she said.

"Please." I rolled my eyes, angry at her for playing me and at myself for falling for it. I'd walked right into her trap, and now I was stuck. She knew who I was, and the only thing stopping her from blabbing it all over the undead world was her own greed. She wanted something. The only question was what.

Actually, no, that wasn't the only question. Would I be able to do what she wanted? That was a good one. I wasn't Will. I was blind in this world and limited by a far less flexible situation at my current home. I couldn't go traipsing off to strange places, alone, in the middle of the night.

And here was the big question. What was she planning to do if I couldn't give her what she wanted?

My stomach ached at the thought. If word got out about me, I'd be flooded by ghosts, not only with final requests and messages but also with questions about how I'd done what I'd done with Lily—Body Wrangling 101. Like I had any satisfactory answers on that topic other than, "It just happened."

Regardless of my knowledge—or lack thereof—the results would be the same. Eventually, I wouldn't be able to hide my "issues" from the Turners. And those rehab center brochures would lead to applications and being shipped off to Arizona or some other godforsaken place . . . if not worse. Will's mom had once come very close to having him institutionalized. In a neat little twist of fate, I could end up facing the same situation.

"Can we skip the buildup and cut to the part where you get to the point?" I snapped, fighting the urge to move farther away from her. I refused to give her the satisfaction.

"I'm going to be your spirit guide," she said in a rush. "And we are going to rule this in-between place."

I opened my mouth with an automatic "forget it" hanging on the tip of my tongue . . . and stopped. *What?* That was not the blackmail scheme I'd been expecting. It didn't sound like a blackmail scheme at all, actually. It was . . . I didn't know what it was.

I shook my head, confused. "What did you say?" I had to have heard her wrong.

"You're a ghost-talker. You need a spirit guide. I'm it," she said, her voice full of pride.

Wait . . . what? I started to speak but stopped myself

before trying again. "You think I'm a ghost-talker?" I asked in disbelief. No way. Did she actually think I was a regular—well, relatively speaking—ghost-talker?

"We're having this conversation, aren't we?" she scoffed.

I resisted the urge to laugh in giddy relief. Could I have really gotten it that wrong? She did seem to know me, though. How was that possible?

I hesitated, and then finally asked, "How do you know me?" What did I have to lose? If she knew I was Alona Dare in another body, she'd have said so, probably in a scathing tone. If she didn't, it would still be a reasonable question for me to ask as a run-of-the-mill ghost-talker.

She rolled her eyes. "Figures that you weren't paying attention yesterday."

"Yesterday?" I asked with a frown. She'd seen me yesterday? Where had I been that she would . . .

Oooh! Malachi's. It had to be. She was one of the angry ghosts in that faker's office, that was all. She'd noticed my intense interest in Misty's problems and bet on the fact that I'd follow up, giving her the chance to propose this spirit-guide idea. Smart.

Now it all made sense. It was laughable, knowing what I knew, but I could see how she'd arrived here, both physically and with her logic.

With that final piece of the puzzle in place, a huge weight of worry rolled off my chest. I let out a slow breath of relief. She honestly had no clue. I was just another ghost-talker to her, not a living dead girl, so to speak.

"Look, I appreciate your offer, but I don't think that's a good idea," I said firmly. It was, in fact, a ridiculous idea. I was a spirit trapped inside a body, the last person in the world qualified to have a spirit guide. If she attempted to claim me as her ghost-talker, I was almost positive it wouldn't work. But explaining that was kind of out of the question.

"You think I can't do it? You think I'm not worthy?" Her tone held a challenge, and I caught a glimpse of a stubbornly pointed chin in the swirling haze where her face would likely have been.

I shook my head and put my hands out, palms up in a gesture of peace. "No, that's not it at all."

"Because you don't know me, you don't know what I'm capable of. I get what I want. Always," she said in a tone that brooked no argument.

Whoa. That sounded very familiar, like something I would have said not so long ago. If she, whoever she was, had even half my stubbornness, let alone a similar temper . . .

A faint warning bell sounded in the back of my head. "I can still help you," I said quickly. Well, Will could, assuming we could get back on speaking terms. "You just need to need to stay calm and—"

"Do not tell me to stay calm," she said through clenched teeth. "This is not up to you."

Oh, not good. Spiraling out of control here. "Uh, okay, look, it's totally not a reflection on you or anything," I said in my best attempt at soothing. If she got angry enough, we might yet find out if she could shove me around or not.

The blur straightened up, almost as if she were coming to attention. The first trickle of real fear climbed up my gut, along with the urge to run. I took a slow step back.

"I claim you, ghost-talker," she declared.

I gaped at her. Seriously? Was there a spirit orientation class—Dealing with Ghost-talkers—that I'd somehow missed? How did she know what to say when I'd just sort of fallen into it? Clearly she'd done her research. This didn't bode well.

"Wait!" I said quickly. Just because I didn't *think* it would work didn't mean I was actually right. I'd been wrong more times recently than I cared to remember. "Don't—"

"You are mine and mine alone," she finished in that same overly loud and formal tone.

My eyes snapped shut out of instinct. Holding my breath, I found myself waiting with dread for the supernatural breeze that had marked my connection to Will.

But the room around us remained silent and still except for the dull roar of the central air-conditioning kicking on outside.

Huh.

I opened my eyes slowly. No supernatural breeze, and I didn't *feel* any different. Guess maybe I was right . . . this time.

I laughed, more out of relief than triumph. Okay, maybe there was a little triumph in it. It felt good to score one in my column for a change instead of everyone else's.

"What the hell?" the ghost demanded.

I grimaced. So much for relief. I might not be tied to

this ghost as a ghost-talker, but she was still here, and she'd still have to be dealt with.

I took a deep breath, steeling my patience. "Like I said, I don't think it's a good idea to—"

"Two of you? How can it not work on either one of you? That makes no sense." The ghost sounded distinctly put out.

"—try to claim me," I said, and then stopped, her words finally penetrating. "Two of us?" I asked, hearing the deadly chill in my voice. "You tried this on someone else?"

"Of course." She didn't even hesitate in answering, too preoccupied and annoyed to notice my tone. "Like you were my first choice. I'd never even heard about you before yesterday." The ghostly haze shrugged. "Other than rumors that the ghost-talker in the 'burbs had a missing spirit guide and was neglecting his duties, spending all his time with some new living chick, which must be *you*."

I didn't miss the indictment and jealousy all jammed in that one word.

"Did you try to claim Will?" I asked tightly.

She ignored me. "But no one ever said that the living chick was a talker like he is." I could hear the frown in her voice as she tried to match pieces of gossip with the facts as she knew them. "Of course, nobody said you'd look like this either. All weird and . . . glowy in the middle." Her tone held equal parts distaste and fascination.

Glowy? Did I look different to her, not like other living people? Whatever. I dismissed her words, though I recognized on some level that what she was saying was important somehow. But I wasn't about to be distracted, not now.

I closed the distance between us, getting in her face, or where I imagined it would be. "Did you try to claim Will?" I bit each word off. A dim part of my mind, probably the part assigned to reason and logic, pointed out that if she had claimed him, she wouldn't be here. But the majority of me just didn't care.

She gave an exasperated sigh, which I felt against my cheek. "Yeah, but whatever. Like I said, it didn't work."

If I'd thought about it, I would have realized that keeping my mouth shut was the better option, but I was beyond that. A horrible surge of fear and fury overtook me. It didn't matter that her attempt had failed. It might have worked. And then she, this girl who I didn't even know, would have been linked to Will, taking my place. God only knew whether she would have protected him or helped him or just left him to flounder. Frankly, she seemed more concerned with herself than with anyone else. He needed someone to look out for him, not take advantage. And what about me? Would he have just left me behind? I was already alone, stuck in this body and not able to help him like I could before. If it had worked, if she had claimed him, would he have even thought twice? I didn't know what she looked like, but she didn't *sound* stepsister ugly.

And what if she tried again with him . . . and it worked? Then what? I would be replaced, and Will wouldn't look to me for help anymore, wouldn't look to me for anything. Wouldn't smile at me, wouldn't hold my hand. I'd be worse than useless to him; I might as well not exist.

A yawning chasm opened inside me, and this primal sense of possessiveness welled up, spilling over until I could hear the blood rushing past my ears, pulsing with my racing heartbeat, something I'd never experienced before. Not with Chris, not with anyone.

I reached into the haze, feeling my hand sink in and connect with what felt like a shoulder. Well, that was one question answered. Evidently, ghosts had physicality around me, just as they did around Will. I shoved the girl back a step. "Will is mine," I said fiercely. "Got it? So leave him the hell alone."

And that's when the cold breeze, the one I'd been half expecting only moments ago, swept through the room, blowing my hair back and freezing her in place, like oil trapped in ice. I'm not sure which of us was more shocked. Especially because I couldn't see her expression.

Holy shit. Somehow, I was still Will's spirit guide. I didn't show up at his side at my time of death anymore, but it seemed my other capabilities were present and accounted for.

My first reaction was an internal leap of joy. I still had a purpose, and I didn't have to be all self-sacrificing and try to convince Will to find a new spirit guide—*not* this chick—so he could be safe.

But that emotion wore off quickly, because, as usual, without Will actually present, my spirit-guide defense capabilities were limited both in duration and strength.

The blurry spot in front of me wavered and shimmered. Then she sucked in an audible breath. "You froze me!" She sounded horrified.

Get out, Alona. Get out now. My overdeveloped sense of self-preservation, slightly rusty from not having been used much in the last month or so, kicked in with a vengeance.

I started to back up toward the door, my heart pounding. I'd blown it. She had had no idea who I was, and I'd just handed it to her. If she put the pieces together, all the consequences I'd ducked would be landing solidly back on my head. And now she was pissed, on top of it.

She followed me. "Will Killian's spirit guide should be the only one with that power," she said suspiciously, and I wished desperately that I could see her face. "But she's gone. Unless she's not."

The ghost lunged forward suddenly, her outstretched arms flashing in the mist, and I stumbled out of her way, but my left foot tangled in the corner of Misty's quilt. I felt my balance shift, and I knew I was going down.

My backside hit the ground with a teeth-jarring impact, and she was right there, standing over me. Her hand locked on to my arm, and in that second, I could see her clearly. Long red hair hung over her shoulder, a pink bikini top showed through her cutoff Señor Frog's T-shirt. A spring-break bunny. One who should have been wearing a tankini or one-piece. Much more flattering to her modest, at best, chest.

Holy crap. This was Spring Break Girl. She was exactly as Will had described her.

Her brown eyes widened, and I wondered if she could see me, too. Not Ally. Me, Alona.

"You didn't disappear," she accused. "You just found a better deal."

I weighed my options. Continue lying, or fall back on the bravado that had served me plenty well in the past? She wanted something; that much was clear. And, as I knew all too well, people who wanted something, anything, were vulnerable to machinations that made them believe they might actually get it.

So, easy choice. Time to change it up. The truth, the whole truth, and nothing but . . . well, as much of the truth as would help me.

I straightened up as best I could, ignoring the nervous fluttering of the heart in my borrowed body. Mind over matter. "Yeah, I did," I said simply, calmly, as if this were no different than someone confronting me in the hall at school on something I'd reportedly said. Public, teary outbursts had been rare, but still something I'd grown to expect, on occasion. The person with the cooler head—me—always won. So that was it—I just had to stay calm.

I pried at her fingers on my arm. "You mind?"

She released me, ending my ability to see her clearly, and sank to the floor next to me, or at least, that's what it looked like. The blurry space she occupied hovered above the floor in the vague shape of a person. "How did you do it?" she asked.

I ignored her. "Who are you?"

"Erin," she said impatiently. "Did you kill someone?"

My mouth fell open. "What?"

"I thought about that. Like, maybe I could slip in as the other spirit was leaving, but since the only people we might actually be able to hurt would be ghost-talkers who would see us coming . . ." She heaved a disappointed sigh, as if she were talking about not being able to get concert tickets instead of, you know, murdering someone.

"No, I didn't kill anyone!" I struggled to my feet. "What is wrong with you?" I demanded. So much for staying calm.

She rose with me, and I caught a glimpse of flashing dark eyes. "What's wrong with me? What's wrong with any of us? We were cut off before our prime! Right before things started getting good. I want to feel the wind on my skin again. I want to go swimming in the ocean."

"Yeah, because there's a lot of that happening in *Illinois*," I muttered.

She ignored me. "I want that first kiss with a new guy again. I want to dance and feel the music pulsing in my chest. I want to be alive and to know it, you know?" She sounded wistful.

I might have felt sorry for her except for the fact that she was obviously crazy with a capital *K*, and—unless I missed my guess—mad powerful. You couldn't go around haunting people (for reasons I was still unclear about) and thinking about killing others without a serious store of energy to draw upon. Negative activities and thoughts like that would have caused a major drain and wiped out most spirits in the process, but not her, obviously.

"I want to be alive . . . like you," she added, her voice taking on a darker edge.

This girl is going to kill me to get what she wants. It couldn't have been clearer than if she'd said it out loud. "We need Will. He has to be here," I said, trying to sound as though I didn't care, even though I could feel myself trembling. It was a stall tactic, yeah, but I didn't want to be alone in this anymore. "There's this whole ceremony and everything. . . ."

"He can't do anything," she said dismissively. "And even if he could, he's a total straight-edge, believe it or not." She snorted. "He knew about you and didn't even tell me." She sounded hurt.

I clamped down on the panic threatening to overtake me, and made another effort to sound reasonable. "Seriously, Will is the only one who can—"

"No, you're going to show me how." She grasped my arm, tighter than before. It hurt, and I flinched away from her. Which was a mistake. Something inside me shifted, and I felt loose in my own skin—well, my borrowed skin.

Erin inhaled sharply. I could see her again, thanks to her grip on me, so it was not hard to follow her gaze and figure out what she was looking at. She was staring at her hand on my forearm, her eyes almost buggy with surprise.

And with good cause. Her hand was sinking into my— no, Lily's—flesh.

Oh, no. No, no, no. A cold stab of fear shot through me. I knew where this was going.

I jerked back from her, but all that did was pull her with me, her hand now embedded in Lily's arm. Just as mine had once been.

I reached up with my free hand and shoved her shoulder as the expression on her face changed from surprise to glowing delight. "You don't understand," I said through gritted teeth, struggling to put distance between us. "It's a circuit. We need each other. I can't survive without her, and she can't live without me." I vividly remembered Lily's blue face and her gasping for air when the Order had tried to separate us. It had been one of the most horrible things I'd ever seen.

"So? Now she won't be able to live without *me*," Erin said, leaning into me, her jaw jutting out stubbornly.

It couldn't be that simple, could it? Like swapping out one battery for another? Either way, I didn't want to find out like *this*.

I tugged at her arm, trying to pull her out, but she wouldn't budge, and I could feel myself slipping aside. No, being shoved aside.

My breath caught in panic, but I shook my head. No freaking way was I giving up this easily.

"Get off of me," I said, tugging at her arm even harder.

But Erin just laughed. "You've had your turn."

Bitch.

Since I couldn't pull her away, I did my best to keep her from moving closer. If I refused to retreat, she couldn't take over, right? I tried to calm my thoughts and focus on my breathing, imagining the seamless bond holding Lily and me together. Her hands were my hands, her arms were my arms, her lungs were my—

There was a sudden lurch, and my vision—our vision?— skewed, went blurry.

Not like this, please, I begged whoever might be listening.

"Stop," I panted, out of breath from the struggle. And only then did I realize I could feel my chest moving separately within Lily's. We were coming apart.

"Oh, my God!" Misty stood in the doorway, her hand over her mouth, her eyes wide with horror. "Are you okay?"

Of course she couldn't see Erin; only my . . . Lily's body on the floor, jerking back and forth as the two of us fought for control. I tried to answer, to tell her to call for help, but no words would come out.

No, please!

Erin grimaced and forced herself forward, leaning down, and there was an odd slipping feeling followed by a claustrophobic moment of blackness.

And then I was standing over Lily's body on the ground with Misty kneeling next to her, shouting for Leanne. Erin was nowhere in sight.

A horrible chill rushed over me, my whole body quaking with it, and I couldn't breathe. I had just enough time to look down and see a transparent version of myself in the white shirt and red gym shorts I'd wondered if I'd ever see again. Then darkness flickered at the edges of my vision before swelling up to consume everything in sight. And I was gone.

❧ 10 ❧

Will

The outside of Misty's house looked the same as it had an hour before. The yard and plants thriving almost to the point of being overgrown, Misty's Jeep in the driveway, the house itself quiet and still.

For whatever reason, the tightness in my chest eased slightly at the sight, which was dumb because it wasn't like there would be flames shooting through the roof or anything as a sign of a problem. Any trouble here was going to be on the inside. Deep on the inside.

I pulled into the driveway and parked. If Misty's parents wanted to question me about being here, Alona's presence would be enough of an excuse. I was her ride home, or I could be, in theory.

I left the car and jogged to the front door to knock. Standing there on the porch, waiting, waiting, and waiting for someone to answer, I could feel the tension creeping into my shoulders and up my neck as each precious second ticked away.

Misty yanked open the door just as I raised my hand to knock again.

She looked startled and then frowned. "It's you."

"Yeah, it's me. Ally here?" I started forward without waiting for an answer, as though I were sure she was going to let me in.

And she did, stepping out of the way and gesturing down the hall. "Kitchen," she said, her expression still troubled. She drew in a breath like she was about to say more, but then she just shook her head.

I wanted to ask her about it, could almost feel her wanting to say something else, but I couldn't ignore the sense of urgency propelling me forward.

"Thanks." I hurried past her, then stopped at the sound of a familiar voice laughing and talking. Ally's voice.

She was okay. I let out a slow breath of relief. Maybe Erin hadn't even been here. If she'd managed to figure out who and what Ally was, there was no way she could have forced her way into Lily's body and recovered so quickly. Even as strong as Alona was, it had taken her hours just to be able to speak.

I started forward once more, feeling Misty's frown at my back.

The kitchen was oversized with a huge eat-in area and a big granite island in the middle of it. Sitting at stools behind it, their feet dangling off the rungs, and giggling over something, Ally and Leanne Whitaker had their heads together over a bowl of what appeared to be ice cream with chunks of cookie dough on top.

I stopped again, startled. The last time I'd checked, Alona hadn't been Leanne's biggest fan.

A whisper came from behind me, and I turned, almost involuntarily, to see Misty a step or two behind me, frowning at the two of them.

"Oh, my God." Leanne's sneering voice was unmistakable. "What are *you* doing here?" she demanded, and I turned in time to see her drop her spoon into the bowl with a gooey clank.

Ally looked up from the bowl, and a variety of unreadable expressions passed over her face when she saw me. "He's here for me," she said simply. "Right?"

I nodded slowly. She didn't *seem* angry anymore. "I'm her ride home," I said.

"Except I'm not ready to go yet," Ally said, looking away from me and scooping up another bite of ice cream. "You can leave, and I'll find my own way home."

I bristled at the arrogance in her tone. All right, so she was definitely still angry. Fair enough, so was I. And clearly she was fine, so I didn't need to stick around. "Whatever." I turned and started back toward the hall.

"Nice," Leanne said, presumably to Ally, with an

all-too-familiar cackle, a sound that sent me back to my most miserable days of high school.

Misty, who'd been standing in the doorway behind me, waited until I passed and then followed me out.

"Don't worry, I'm not going to steal anything," I said over my shoulder, not bothering to hide the disgust in my voice.

She made an exasperated noise. "It's not that," she said.

"Yeah, right." I kept going.

"Hey." She caught my sleeve, and I turned, surprised.

Misty glanced over her shoulder in the direction of the kitchen before facing me with a worried expression. "Something happened," she whispered quickly. "She's pretending everything's fine, but it was like a seizure or something."

I froze. "What do you mean?"

She gave an impatient huff. "I mean, I left her upstairs to deal with, you know, the ghost."

I nodded, waving my hand for her to hurry up and get to the point.

"And when I came back to see how it was going, she was on the floor," she finished, her blue eyes wide in the dimly lit hall.

I relaxed a little. "Ally still has trouble with walking sometimes. The accident—"

"Dude, no. This wasn't just a fall. She was . . . I don't know, writhing on the floor or something." Misty wrung her hands together, obviously upset.

I considered what it must have taken to convince her to

come after me and try to tell me something was wrong, and dread seeped into my gut.

"Was she, uh, talking to someone before? I mean, someone you couldn't see?"

She nodded rapidly. "She sent me out of the room, so I couldn't hear what she was saying, but I definitely heard her talking."

So unless Alona had decided to put on a show for Misty's benefit, there had been a ghost here. What were the odds it had been anyone other than Erin?

Not good.

And she'd done what? Attacked Alona? It wouldn't have been impossible—Alona was definitely capable of provoking someone to the point of violence, particularly someone like Erin, who already seemed a little unhinged. But then where had Erin gone? Why wasn't she still here pestering us? And why hadn't Alona mentioned it?

Unless, of course, she couldn't. I felt sick suddenly. If Erin had taken over Lily's body and kicked Alona out, that would account for Misty's seeing what had appeared to be a seizure—two spirits fighting over one body.

But if Erin had won that battle, how could she have recovered so quickly? That would have taken serious power, beyond what even Alona had demonstrated. Then again, I already knew Erin was no slouch in the power department— she could change her appearance on a whim. None of the other ghosts I'd ever met could do that, not even Mrs. Ruiz, who'd very thoroughly kicked my ass.

Plus, it occurred to me now, I had no idea how much Lily's comatose state might have slowed Alona down when she took over. But Erin wouldn't have had that issue.

So . . . was it possible she'd taken Lily's body with fewer side effects? I definitely couldn't rule it out. Ice coated my insides at the idea.

"All right, let's keep this between us," I said to Misty. "I'm going to try to get her to go home with me." I had to know for sure who was occupying Lily's body, and this was not the place for that conversation.

She nodded.

"She might not like that, but it's important," I added. The last thing I needed was Misty calling the police because I was trying to bodily remove someone from her home who did not want to go.

"Okay," she said hesitantly.

I wished she sounded more confident, but I didn't have time to convince her further.

I strode back into the kitchen with Misty at my heels.

Leanne groaned. "You again."

I ignored her. "You know, I should just leave you here," I said to Ally. "But I promised your mom I'd bring you home." That was a big lie. Mrs. Turner wouldn't even speak to me, let alone take promises from me. And Alona would know that and would call me on it . . . maybe.

I waited, holding my breath for her response.

But Ally didn't even look up. "I said I'm fine."

Which *could* mean it wasn't Alona . . . or just that Alona

was still mad at me and more concerned about what her friends thought than about what Mrs. Turner thought. It was in line with who she'd been when she was alive, the identity she might be attempting to reclaim in part now with her makeover.

I needed a litmus test, something that would prove beyond a shadow of a doubt who I was dealing with. The only test I could think of would draw on the secret of Alona's messed-up home life and really piss her off, but I had to know.

"Come on, I'll take you to get a burger on the way. And Sam was over last night. He left a couple beers in the fridge we could probably snag, if we stop by my house." I kept my tone as light and normal-sounding as possible, which wasn't very. Every word sounded clunky to my ears, like it screamed, "Lie!" But that didn't matter because it wasn't my reaction that I was looking for.

The real Alona would have glared at me with her lip curling in disgust at the suggestion. But this one . . . she perked up and looked at me with interest for the first time. "Beer?"

My heart sank. Erin. It had to be. No way was that Alona, not with her alcoholic mother. That was one thing Alona had never compromised on, no matter who was watching or listening. She did not drink.

But dead party girl Erin (her Señor Frog's T-shirt was a big clue) wouldn't have known that. And a beer probably did sound good to her after so many months or years of (dead) sobriety.

So, if Erin was occupying Lily's body, where was Alona? Gone for good? I swallowed hard, pushing that thought away. I had to find out what had happened.

"Dude, why are you still here?" Leanne asked with a huff. "She said no."

"Leanne," Misty murmured from behind me. "Stay out of it."

But it was too late. The damage was done. "No, thanks, I'm good here." Erin returned her attention to the ice cream.

Panic surged in me, and I fought to keep my expression blank. The urge to cross the room and shake Erin for answers was overwhelming. But I had to keep calm. Freaking out on her was not an option, nor was leaving her here. She might take off for parts unknown, and then I'd never know what had happened.

Think, think. I forced myself to look at things from Erin's perspective. She had to be worried about people figuring out she wasn't who she claimed to be, much as Alona had been. It was probably the main reason she didn't want to leave with me. I could use that. "Okay, then call your mom and make sure it's cool if you stay," I said.

Erin shrugged and kept eating her ice cream. She knew that the more people who were involved, the greater the chance she'd mess up.

"What is he, your babysitter?" Leanne snorted.

"Fine, I'll call her and tell her to come get you." I pulled my phone out, and that got Erin's attention. She glared at me.

"I'm just looking out for you." I forced myself to project something resembling sincerity.

"All right. Let's go." She heaved a sigh and set her spoon down on the counter. "But a burger and beer first. You promised." Easy to see where Erin's priorities were. Not to mention, if she was at all worried about encountering Lily's mom, making stops along the way would give her an opportunity to slip away from me before I could get her home.

She slipped down off the stool to the floor, where she swayed unsteadily, like the room was moving around her.

Out of habit, I lurched forward to catch her arm, expecting her to throw herself backward to avoid my help or glare at me.

But instead, she placed her arm through mine, leaning on me for balance, as if that was what we always did. Which, of course, would be what she'd have thought, based on what she'd seen yesterday at Malachi's.

She waved at Leanne, who smiled with that hint of a smirk I'd seen countless times before upon encountering her in the hallway.

"See ya, *chica*. Don't forget what we talked about." Leanne pointed her spoon at Ally, who nodded.

I was afraid to ask what that was about. Erin and Leanne conspiring—the very idea was nightmare-inducing.

I led her toward the door to the hall, where she shocked the hell out of me by letting go and launching herself at Misty for a hug. Misty looked equally startled by the gesture. She hadn't even had time to unfold her arms, and they were now pinned in between the two of them.

"Just know that Alona is in a better place, okay?" she said, her words muffled against the taller girl's shoulder.

I froze. Had the light come for Alona when Erin had evicted her? Was that what she was saying? Or was this more of her playing the role of Ally, saying what she thought Ally the ghost-talker would say?

Misty looked at me over the top of Ally's head, her face stunned and pale, albeit for different reasons. She nodded. "Yeah, okay," she said, and cleared her throat.

Ally pulled back, reaching for my arm before I could offer it. Playing a role in this parody made me feel ill, but I had no choice but to follow through until I could get her out of here.

I led her down the hall to the front door and out onto the porch, where she carefully made her way down the steps, clutching my arm with one hand and the railing with the other. She was definitely not moving as smoothly as Alona had been, so there were side effects of her taking over this body.

"I'm starving," she announced, when we reached the bottom. "Hurry up."

"You were just eating ice cream," I said tightly. With raw cookie dough on top, seemingly without a care in the world about fat grams or any of the other stuff Alona usually complained about. That should have been my first clue, I realized. Not to mention the fact she'd been sharing a bowl without freaking out about Leanne's germs.

"But I didn't get to finish," she noted with a pout, as I led her to the car and helped her in.

"We're going to get something right now," I promised, with absolutely no intention of doing so.

"A cheeseburger *with* fries," she said, still sulking. "And the beer, don't forget the beer."

So, definitely not Alona. "Right, fine." I slammed her door shut, the wheels turning in my brain. I'd gotten the impostor out of Misty's; step one complete. But now what?

I opened the driver's-side door and slid behind the wheel. My brain was buzzing with anxiety and too many questions. Was it better to confront her immediately or try to play along a little longer? She obviously wanted me to believe she was Alona. And where was Alona? Oh, God, if she was gone for good . . .

I dared a glance from the corner of my eye to find Ally— no, it was Erin, and I had to remember that—staring down at her hands in an admiring manner, as though pleased with the manicure . . . or, you know, just that she had a physical form that could *have* a manicure.

Shit. I had to play this carefully. She was possessing Lily's body, and I couldn't make her get out. It was like having a built-in hostage. She could theoretically hurt "herself" (a.k.a. Lily) at any time or threaten to do so to keep me in line.

I started the car and backed out of the driveway, on to the street.

Okay, think. I can't keep her in the car forever. Taking her to the Turners' was out of the question. And I couldn't exactly lock her up at my house.

God, when had things gotten so complicated?

Edmund. Maybe Malachi/Edmund would have some-thing to say about this. It was his freaking sister, after all.

"I screwed up, didn't I?" she asked, just as I realized the silence had dragged on for a few seconds too long. She turned to face me, her eyes glittering with a hardness that had never been there with Lily or Alona.

I shivered, seeing something alien behind such a familiar face.

"What was it, the fries or the beer?" she asked, still not sounding too concerned about her cover being blown.

No point in further pretending, I guess. "Both," I said.

She gave an annoyed sigh. "I should have known. She was probably counting calories."

And her mother was, until recently, a raging, out-of-control alcoholic, not that that was any of her business. "Erin, right?"

She nodded, pleased.

"Where is Alona?" I asked tightly.

She laughed. "Gone. Vanished," she proclaimed, sound-ing way too self-satisfied.

I winced, even though I'd been expecting that. "Permanently?"

"How should I know?" she asked, sounding annoyed.

"What did you do?" I demanded.

She heaved an exasperated sigh. "I don't see how it mat-ters now."

"It matters," I said, trying to keep my voice level.

"Is this about the ceremony?" she asked with a frown.

The what? I stopped the words from coming out just in time. A ceremony? There was no ceremony. At least, none that Alona had mentioned to me. "How do you know about that?" I asked instead, trying to weasel more information out of her without giving anything away.

She shrugged. "Alona said something about needing you there for a ceremony, but I figured she was just trying to stall me, keep me out."

Oh. My chest ached. That was exactly what Alona must have been trying to do. And even though I hadn't known what was going on, I still felt like I'd failed her.

"Like that's even fair," Erin scoffed. "She had her turn."

"So you ambushed her instead?" I muttered.

"What?" she asked.

I shook my head, feeling the tension creaking in the back of my neck. "Just tell me what happened."

She shrugged again. "I tried to claim her at first, as my ghost-talker, but that didn't work any better with her than it did with you." She rolled her eyes. "But once I figured out she was your spirit guide, it wasn't that hard to put it all together. Then when I grabbed her, this body sort of pulled me in and forced her out."

Wait, Alona was still my spirit guide? That would explain why Erin hadn't been able to make the connection with either of us. We were still connected to each other. Or, at least, we had been up until an hour or so ago. And I'd just left her there.

I shook my head, pushing those thoughts, and the fear

squeezing my chest, aside. If anyone could have survived all of this, it was Alona. Maybe another spirit taking over Lily's body would have been enough to save her. If Lily's body didn't need her anymore, maybe that would give her more energy to sustain herself. Maybe.

She smoothed her hands down her body in an utterly creepy manner. "Must have been nice having it all in one package, huh?" She grinned and elbowed me, none too gently, in the ribs. "A spirit guide in a tight, living body. All the perks."

I grimaced and shifted away from her. She made it sound so gross. It wasn't like that, had never been like that. We hadn't even known that Alona was still my spirit guide after she took over Lily's body. But I doubted Erin would believe me, and I didn't want to waste my breath explaining something she'd never understand. So weird the way Erin changed everything about Lily into something creepy and threatening, in a way that Alona had not. It said something about how much the soul or spirit in charge mattered. "What do you want?" I asked.

Erin laughed, and I shuddered.

"What do I want?" she repeated. "Nothing more than I've got right here, baby," she said, slapping her thighs. "It's a little beat up, sure, but nothing I can't work around." She sounded delighted. "I'm going to live it up." She winked at me like this was all no big deal. Like she hadn't potentially sentenced Alona to a more permanent form of death. "Now, are we going to get burgers or what?" she demanded.

I drove on autopilot, steering the car toward Krekel's, Alona's favorite burger place, and thinking furiously. I needed a plan. One thing was for sure: I couldn't let her out into the world like this. God only knew what Erin would get up to if left to her own devices, and she was, for all intents and purposes, Lily. Around here, someone would eventually recognize her, and that would be bad. Not to mention her parents, who would be worried sick about her. And what if Alona wasn't gone and she needed Lily's body back? The Order had said the two of them had become dependent on each other. Lily seemed to be doing okay with Erin in Alona's place, but Alona didn't have that same option.

Locking Erin up, at least until I had a better grasp of the situation, seemed to be the only logical solution, as much as I hated the idea. But where? Maybe Edmund/Malachi would have an idea.

I looked over at Erin, her arm on the rest between us. She was weakened by her transition into Lily's body; I could probably drag her along pretty easily. But some of what I was thinking must have shown on my face.

"Oh, no." She snatched her arm back and scooted away from me. "I've already wasted too many years watching and not living. You're not going to do that to me again. You try to lock me up somewhere and I'll scream until someone calls the cops." Her chin jutted out in determination, pushing aside any doubts I might have had that she would do less than she claimed. And the Turners, when they got wind of it, as they surely would, would probably press charges against me, thus eliminating any chance I had of fixing this mess.

"In fact," she said, "I think you can let me out here." She nodded at the red stoplight we were approaching.

"Here?" I asked, incredulous. "We're not even close to anything, and she can't . . . you can't walk—"

"We'll manage," she said, already tugging at her seat belt.

"Erin, wait," I said, fighting desperation. "What about Edmund? I know he'll want to see you and—"

"Right," she scoffed. "Like I'm going to waste any of my time on him."

"He's your brother," I argued.

"Fat lot of good that did either of us," she muttered. She yanked at the handle and shoved the door open as soon as we reached a stop.

I lurched across the car to grab her, but she slipped away. Then she surprised me, ducking her head back in and mashing her mouth against mine in a rough parody of a kiss.

I jerked back, hard enough that my elbow banged into the steering wheel.

"I would have expected better from you," she said in mock disappointment before slamming the door shut.

The light turned green, and someone behind me honked and held it, loud and obnoxious. But I refused to move. "Get back in the car, Erin," I shouted. I felt my face burning, imagining what this must look like to the other drivers. *No, I'm not some jerk threatening his girlfriend. I'm trying to keep a ghost from kidnapping a body that doesn't belong to her.*

"Stalking is illegal, Will," she warned loudly, her voice

muffled through the closed door but clear to anyone who had their windows rolled down. Her gaze darted to the cars behind me, a tiny smirk playing on her lips as someone else added his horn to the mix.

"Erin!" I shouted again, as a truck from somewhere behind me whipped into the turn lane and zoomed around me. A squad car coming from the other direction slowed down, the officer staring at me through his window.

Shit. "Get back in the car. Please!" I tried one more time.

Watching me through narrowed eyes, Erin took a deep breath and started to scream.

Out of choices, and expecting the sound of sirens any second, I straightened up behind the wheel and hit the gas.

Hating myself and Erin, I watched her become a smaller and smaller figure in the rearview mirror, like I might never see her again, and feeling half relieved and half freaked at the idea.

I doubled back around the block as soon as I could, but the neighborhood had streets that curved oddly, and unexpected culs-de-sac.

By the time I got back to the intersection, she was gone, of course. Either she was hiding somewhere, or she'd hitched a ride with a stranger.

God, she was going to end up dead in a ditch somewhere, and it would be all my fault.

The light was red (again), and while waiting for it to change, I rested my head on the steering wheel, wishing for things to be different, wishing for Alona, wishing I could go back to the days when my biggest problems were Principal Brewster and getting through class without any ghosts noticing me. That had been a vacation compared to all of this. A really, really sucky vacation, but a vacation, nonetheless. I didn't need Alona to tell me I was in over my head with this body and soul stuff and sinking fast. But I wanted her here, more than anything.

I shook my head. I had to get her back. I had an idea about how to do that, thanks to something Erin had said. But just one. And if it didn't work . . .

I clenched the wheel. No, it *had* to work. That was all there was to it. Because I didn't know how to live with any other outcome. And if it didn't work, Alona wouldn't live at all.

✿ 11 ✿

Will

I broke speed limits retracing familiar streets and flying past landmarks on my way toward Groundsboro High.

This was my one and only brilliant idea: if Alona was still my guide, as Erin had said, and she was back in spirit form, I might be able to "call" her to me. Theoretically, I could call her from anywhere, but the dead who meet their ends violently/unnaturally are always drawn to the places of their death. Calling her from that location might provide enough added pull to drag her back from wherever she'd vanished. It might have even been better to try it at the time of her death, but there was no way I could make myself wait almost a whole day for 7:03 a.m. to roll around again.

Despite my best efforts to focus on the positive, my mind

created images of me sitting on the curb next to the spot of pavement where she'd died and calling her . . . only to have nothing happen.

I shook my head, pushing that thought away. No, she was strong. She had to be okay. She'd survived this long. She'd been sent back from the light, for God's sake. That couldn't have happened only for things to end this way. That couldn't be right. It didn't make sense.

A tiny voice in my head reminded me that in addition to being unfair, life could also be nonsensical. Messed up. Like my dad killing himself without first giving us the slightest hint that that day would be different than any other. In some ways, I'd thought it would have been better if he'd tried to warn us, even if we'd missed it initially. Then at least maybe it would have seemed more logical. Or maybe it would have simply made my mom and me feel worse for not under-standing what he was trying to say.

Either way, one day he was just gone. So quickly it seemed like the air should have rushed in to fill the vacuum where he'd once stood, brushed his teeth, slept. . . .

I couldn't lose somebody else like that, without even the chance to say good-bye. Not again. Not her.

"Come on, Alona, don't do this to me, please," I muttered, and then stopped, clamping my mouth shut in the fear that those words somehow counted as a call.

But if they had, the passenger seat next to me remained empty. And my heart sank a little further.

I made myself focus on the road ahead of me, dimly

aware of the refrain—*please, please, please, please*—pulsing through me and ticking off the seconds.

The school finally rose up in the distance, and I pulled to a hard stop by the fenced-off tennis courts, the Dodge's tires screeching on the overheated asphalt.

I jammed the gearshift into park and flung the door open, stumbling out in my hurry. The kids on the tennis court—a couple of boys, too young even to be freshmen, it seemed—stopped hitting the ball around to watch me run.

The trouble was, it had been four months since Alona had died. There was no longer any sign of the violence that had occurred, the life that had ended somewhere here on the double yellow lines.

Was it here, closer to the corner, or farther down the street? Suddenly I wasn't sure, and I found myself pacing back and forth in the middle of the road, desperate to get this right.

A passing car honked at me.

"Hey, are you okay?" one of the kids shouted.

I ignored it all, aware that my eyes were stinging with tears only when a drop rolled off my chin and splattered on the yellow painted line that I was studying so intently.

I swiped a hand over my face. *Stay calm. She's fine. Erin took over Lily's body, so she's the one caught in the cycle now. Alona should be fine.* The ache in my chest told me even I didn't believe this.

The Order had said the two of them would become dependent on each other. After a month in Lily's body, did

Alona have enough energy to survive on her own anymore?

That was the question, and there was truly only one way to find out. I took a deep breath, forcing it past the lump in my throat. I had nothing to lose by trying, except all hope of her ever coming back. If she didn't answer now, I'd keep calling her; but the odds that her energy level in this situation would improve with time were slim to none.

Another car swerved around me, with the driver honking and shouting through his rolled-down window.

All right, enough delaying, I told myself. Time to try this before someone actually stops and tries to pull me out of the way. Or calls the police.

But I felt like I was ripping away a bandage long before the wound was healed.

I finally picked a place as close to exact as I remembered it and shut my eyes.

I pictured Alona as I'd seen her that first time after her death. Stalking the grounds in the red gym shorts and white shirt she'd died in, her face flushed with fury and hurt at the people she'd once called her friends turning on her, only days after her death. The way she pushed me to deal with Principal Brewster, helping me until I could manage him on my own, more or less. The silk of her hair catching on my fingertips when we were behind the bushes at the Gibley Mansion. How she refused to accept pity or help unless she had no choice. Just this morning when she'd stood in front of me in her new clothes with the new look she'd created, tilting her head up toward me with that vulnerable smile.

It occurred to me for the first time that while she hadn't said so, she'd been looking for my opinion. My approval . . . No, my appreciation.

She didn't need it. She wasn't like that. But that didn't mean she wouldn't have liked to have it. Spirit or no, she was still human. And all I'd been worried about had been my own too-strong reaction and what that meant for *me*.

I concentrated harder, funneling my fear and anger at myself into force behind my thoughts. I *willed* her to appear.

"You're my spirit guide," I said through clenched teeth. "You *have* to come when I call, and I'm calling. Get here. Please?"

That last word sounded dangerously close to begging, and I didn't care. It wasn't for Alona, but for whoever else might be listening. God. The light. Someone was running things, and I needed whoever that was to hear me.

Please don't do this. Don't send her to me and then take her away. Please don't. Just don't. Please. I need her.

I kept repeating those words over and over again, distantly aware of the kids resuming their game and another car or two passing me.

But I didn't stop until I felt a strange shift in the air, like the world had moved around me, water flowing around a rock.

I opened my eyes, and Alona—a beginning outline of her, anyway—stood a few feet in front of me, looking around with a startled expression.

I let out a breath I hadn't realized I'd been holding. *Thank God.*

But that brief moment of dizzying relief quickly dissipated, replaced by a growing sense of panic. She wasn't filling in the way she should have. I could still see through her. For the first time, she actually looked like a traditional ghost, at least the way they were most often depicted on television and in movies.

No, no. Not good. Her energy was low enough that she couldn't even fully appear.

"Say something nice!" I shouted at her, fighting the urge to grab her and hold on. I wasn't sure what would happen, what I would do, if my hands passed through her.

Her lips moved to form words, but no sound emerged, and her eyes widened. She knew something was wrong. She looked down at herself, her blond hair sliding forward over her shoulder as she took in the extent of her nonexistence. And when she lifted her head to face me, tears sparkled in her eyes. She took a deep breath and straightened her shoulders before raising her hand slowly and turning it palm out. Stop . . . or good-bye.

"No!" I moved closer to her, within touching distance. "You have to do something." I'd never felt more helpless in my life. I couldn't do anything to help her. Then a flash of brilliance—or utter idiocy—struck. "Claim me again." A stronger tie to me, one with a firmly held position smack in between the living and the dead, might help, even if it was only reinforcing a connection that already existed. I refused to blink, my eyes burning with the effort, as though my gaze would hold her here. "Claim me again," I repeated, hearing the plea in my voice and praying she could, too.

Her gaze met mine and held it as she said the words. I still couldn't hear her, but I caught a few of the words on her lips. "Will Killian." And then last, so slowly that there was no doubt what she was saying. "Mine." Tears slipped down her face, and I knew that no matter what differences there were between us, this wasn't the way either of us wanted it to end.

She closed her eyes and repeated the words over and over again, just as I had earlier.

The air around her wavered, like when you open the door to a car that's been closed up for hours on a hot summer day. And then suddenly she was there . . . fully there.

I reached out for her hand at the same time she grabbed for mine. We moved toward each other, narrowly avoiding banging heads in our hurry. She wrapped her arms around me, and I buried my face against the side of her warm neck and in her hair. I could feel her trembling . . . or maybe it was me.

"It's okay. You're okay," I murmured against her skin, but I wasn't sure which one of us I was talking to. Maybe both of us.

"You're right. I think he's crazy," I heard one of the tennis court kids declare loudly in a tone that suggested a great debate had been resolved. And for once in my life, I did not care in the least.

❦ 12 ❧

Alona

Will would not stop looking at me.

And it wasn't the hey-you're-so-attractive kind of looking that I was used to, once upon a time. That would have been fine. No, this was more like compulsively-checking-every-five-seconds-to-see-if-you're-still-here-and-not-slowly-disappearing-before-my-very-eyes kind of looking. Which was a little disconcerting.

"Are you sure you're okay?" he asked for the twelfth time in fifteen minutes, with another sidelong glance at me in the passenger seat. Once we'd managed to disentangle ourselves from our stance in the middle of the road, he'd led me back to the Dodge with a tight grip on my hand. His eyes were red. He'd been crying. So had I. Though neither of us was talking about that.

"Stop asking me that," I said, trying to sound as snappish as I would have normally. But I couldn't blame him, for the staring or the asking. I kept checking my hands and feet to make sure they were actually there and not see-through. In the grand scheme of things, I hadn't been gone for all that long. I'd disappeared for hours before, after the emotional turmoil of learning my mom was tossing my stuff and my dad was having a new baby. But I'd never, *never* come back as faintly as I had this time.

I'd shouted and he couldn't hear me. I could see it in the panic on his face. I was going, going, gone—like falling off the side of cliff in the movies—until I managed to find a foothold and stop myself. But who knew how long it would last? That bit of rock or vine always gives out, doesn't it? The only question was when.

Even now I could feel the ebb and flow of energy in a way that I had not since right before the light showed up to take me away from Will's hospital room a few months ago.

I took a deep breath, trying to ignore the lighter, floatier, *disconnected* feeling that came with being outside of Lily's body. Like I might drift away at any second. I hated it. When Will let go of my hand to drive, it had taken every ounce of my considerable self-possession not to scoot closer (it wasn't like I needed a seat belt to keep me alive if we crashed) and grab hold of his arm or a fistful of his (awful) T-shirt, as if he were an anchor keeping me here. But when it came down to it, that wouldn't stop me from disappearing, and I couldn't stand the idea of slowly losing the feel of him until there was nothing.

So I kept my hands to myself and stayed on my side of the car.

"If you want, I can take you home . . . to my house . . . or the Turners'," he offered, with another cautious look at me. "And you can rest if you—"

"I'm dead, not sick," I said sharply. "Remember?" Like either of us needed any greater reminder than what had just happened.

He flinched, actually hunching his shoulders like I'd hit him. But pretending otherwise, particularly now, wasn't going to do us any good. It was kind of pointless, wasn't it? I felt tears welling up again and forced myself to look away from him, out the side window.

"So that's it? With Erin, I mean?" I asked, my voice rougher than normal. I hoped he wouldn't notice or call me on the abrupt subject change. He'd filled me in on what I'd missed, though most of it I'd already pieced together on my own. "She made off with Lily's body." *That little bitch.* "To go party, eat hamburgers, and drink beer or something?"

We were on our way to check at Krekel's now, stopping at every liquor store along the way (thanks, Mom, for that bit of knowledge) for a quick peek around the parking lot. She couldn't buy beer—not looking like Lily, who barely seemed as old as she was—but given what I knew of Erin, and what Will had told me, she probably had her fair share of experience with "hey, dude"-ing it from older guys.

Will nodded wearily.

I resisted the urge to shout *I told you so.* He'd come down so hard on me about how I was doing as "Lily," and I'd tried to warn him that someone else might be worse. But now was not the time to interject that bit of retaliatory wisdom . . . even if it was the truth.

"You can say it," he said, reading my thoughts. He looked away from the road to raise an eyebrow at me in challenge. I shrugged. "It's not as much fun if you're expecting it." He cracked a smile. "I bet."

"So . . . *if* we find her, then what?" I asked, forcing the words out past my fear of speaking them. They implied there was something beyond this moment, which I wasn't sure there would be for me, and I didn't want to tempt fate or God or the light or whoever had come up with *this* masterful plan. I squelched the surge of anger rising up from my gut, but with limited success. I was so tired of being tossed around like someone's doll . . . or a chess piece. First I'm stuck here, then I'm not, and then I'm sent back—maybe to save Lily—and then definitely not. What the hell? And now I was supposed to just sit here and, what, wait with Will for whatever energy I had left to disappear? That SUCKED. Beyond the telling of it, frankly.

Will rubbed his hand over his face. "I don't know." He sounded tired, defeated. I realized he was out of his depth as well; not what he'd signed up for, either. Right about now, he probably wished he was out ghost-busting with Mina somewhere.

I reached out hesitantly and touched his shoulder. And this time, when he glanced over at me, his expression was different, with a warmth that shone through his weariness and worry. Unable to resist, I scooted closer to lean against him, and he put his arm around my shoulders, resting his cheek momentarily against the top of my head.

"We'll figure this out," he said, sounding more certain. "If we can't find her, we'll go after her brother. He'll know what she's going to try, where she'll want to go." He paused. "Crap. I just left him there. I told him I'd be right back," he said, almost to himself.

"What?" I asked, confused.

"I was talking to Malachi when I figured out you might be in trouble." He shook his head. "Doesn't matter. We'll work it out. We'll find Erin and evict her, and then . . ." His voice trailed off.

Yeah, the and-then part was the tricky bit.

"Will." I sat up slowly and his arm slid off my shoulders. "We need to talk."

He eyed me warily. "What is there to talk about? If you're still upset about this morning"—he hesitated—"you were right. I should have handled that better. You just . . . the changes took me by surprise."

I sighed. Some things between us might have grown and shifted, but this was the same—I was still the more pragmatic one.

I took a breath and forced myself to take on a matter-of-fact tone. "You need to accept that this might be the end. That this"—I waved down at my solid-for-the-moment form—"is a temporary stay of the inevitable."

"No," he said without even looking at me, like that was all there was to it. He'd declared it and so it would be. Right.

I shook my head, exasperated. "You know what the Order

said: Lily and I are dependent upon each other. I wasn't even supposed to have survived without Lily for this long."

He lifted a shoulder in a stiff shrug. "And you'll be fine as soon as we find her again and—"

"If we can find her. If I have the strength to kick Erin out. If I can keep her out," I said wearily. "Have you thought about that? What's to stop her from taking Lily back, assuming I can even boot her in the first place? How many times do you think I can go through that and survive?"

He didn't respond.

"And more important, what gives me the right? More than Erin, I mean." The first time, I had done it to save Lily. But this wouldn't be about that. It would be about saving my skin, metaphorically, and I wasn't sure I could do that. It didn't feel right.

Will glanced over at me with a reproving frown. "You were sent back here to help me. Maybe Lily, too."

Crap. It was, I supposed, time to come clean. I leaned my head back against the seat. "About that . . ." I hesitated. "You know, it's not exactly like there was a big booming voice in the sky giving me directions or anything."

His frown deepened. "Uh-huh."

I shifted uncomfortably. I shouldn't have waited this long to tell him. But when it happened, when I first came back, he was still mostly that guy who was kind of annoying and weird, but cute. And then, somewhere along the way, things had changed, and he became somebody I needed in my life for more than practical reasons, and telling the truth sort of became impossible. "I don't really remember anything,"

I said quickly. "I remember feeling safe and warm and at peace, but . . . that's pretty much it."

"Until you got sent back," he said.

I grimaced.

"Right?" he pressed.

"I woke up in your room that first morning and saw your graduation gown hanging on your closet door and kind of freaked," I admitted. It hadn't taken a lot to figure out that time—a lot of time—had passed. I'd actually come back on the morning after Will's birthday—I'd found the left-over cake and a small pile of unwrapped presents on the kitchen table. And I knew Will's birthday was at the end of May. Then there were the trees outside, much greener than I remembered, and the air, much warmer and closer to summer.

"I needed some time to think," I said. "So I took off for a few days, trying to get things clear in my head." At Misty's, I learned exactly how long I'd been gone: almost a whole month! That was also where I'd discovered Leanne's plot to humiliate Ben at graduation. "At the time, all I could think about was getting back to the light, and I only knew of one way to do that." Which was to do exactly what I'd done to get there in the first place—help Will Killian.

"So . . . I told you I'd been sent back to help you," I said, wincing in anticipation of his response. Oh, this was so not going to be good.

"You lied," he said tightly, his knuckles turning white as he gripped the steering wheel.

"I . . . made a logical leap based on presumed facts,"

I argued, even though I could hear exactly how weak that sounded. "You needed help, and suddenly I was back. It seemed logical that the two things were related."

He pulled abruptly off the road and into an abandoned gas station and jammed the gear shift into park before turning to face me, his cheeks flushed. "You lied! Worse, you told me what you thought I would believe."

"Which doesn't mean it couldn't still be the truth," I said, resisting the urge to shrink back into my seat at the sound of the hurt and pain in his voice. He would not make me feel bad about a choice I'd made before I really knew him.

"Oh, my God, Alona." He scrubbed his face with his hands.

"Well, what did you want me to do?" I demanded. "Say, 'I don't remember anything'? You would have thought I was hiding something."

He shook his head. "Don't make this about me. It's all about you and getting rejected. You can't stand the idea that someone, somewhere, turned you down."

Ouch. That stung.

I sat up straight. "Has the flip side of this occurred to you yet?" I asked, starting to get angry. "That I stuck with you and helped you even though it wasn't a mandate from God, or the light, or whatever?"

He was silent.

"No, I didn't think so," I snapped, flopping back in my seat.

"You did it because it benefited you." He gave me a dark look.

"And you, too," I pointed out quickly. "But whatever. That's the past. I'm trying to do the right thing here and now." I flipped my hair behind my shoulders, and for a moment, I was surprised when it actually stayed back. I guess I'd gotten more used to being Ally than I'd realized. "I'm telling the truth today when I didn't have to." That was a big deal. To me, at least. Why didn't he get that?

He snorted. "Do you want a parade?"

His words landed as a heavier-than-expected blow, and I flinched. It wasn't like him to be quite this sarcastic. And I was *trying* to change, couldn't he see that? I forced myself to keep going, not to snap at him. "My *point*," I said, emphasizing that I had one, "is I don't have the right to be 'Ally' any more than Erin has to be . . ."—I frowned—"well, whatever she's calling herself."

I imagined Mrs. Turner trying to adjust to another name for her daughter and felt a surprising pang. She'd made my life as Ally more of a pain than it had to be, but only because she actually cared. Now she'd have to deal with Erin's version of Lily. And that wasn't fair at all to her. It was weird. If Mrs. Turner had been like my mom—out of it and only concerned about herself—then my pretending to be Ally would have been easier, and I probably wouldn't have cared half as much. But maybe some things are better when they're more difficult, I don't know.

"Even if we find Erin and get her out, I wasn't . . . sent

here to do anything. To be Ally." It killed me to say that out loud. To admit that I didn't know why I was back, that maybe there wasn't even a reason. But I couldn't let Will continue operating under that lie.

"The point is," he said, mocking me, but with real anger threaded through his tone, "is that Erin doesn't give a crap what people call her as long as she's doing whatever it means to be alive. Her definition of it, anyway."

I shuddered, imagining what that might be. It was like rental-car syndrome, only worse. That limo for prom? No one cared what happened on the inside, because it wasn't like it was *our* car.

"So forget about the reason you were sent back, or all the reasons you weren't—"

I flinched at the venom in that last word.

"—and just help me find Erin and Lily," he said. "Then we'll worry about what to do next, and who has the right to do what."

And how to deal with you . . . He didn't say it, but I could hear it nonetheless. Great. I'd be looking forward to that. Maybe I could disappear first.

"All right," I said finally. I could help—or try, at least. If only to spare the Turners another call to the hospital . . . or jail.

He nodded curtly and put the car back in drive without another word.

Well, at least there wasn't any more crying. Guess I'd fixed that.

❧ 13 ❧

Will

She lied. She freaking *lied* about the light. Did Alona have no limits? No moral boundaries? *Jesus.*

I focused on the road, all too aware of the silence between us. Even though I hadn't done anything wrong, I got the distinct sense that Alona was upset with me, which was rich. It was never her fault, always somebody else's. In this case, maybe the light was to blame because she hadn't received specific directions and had felt forced to make something up. Whatever.

I shook my head in disgust.

And yet, in spite of myself, I couldn't help imagining what it must have been like for her to find herself back here that first morning, without any information, any guidance on why or what to do next.

Anyone would have been terrified, wondering if they'd done something wrong or if there'd been a mistake or if this was some kind of punishment from on high. After all, who gets sent back from the light ever, let alone after almost a month?

And Alona, always with control issues, would have been even worse. She'd spent most of her living years trying to contain everything, to keep her life—her mother's condition and her father's complete lack of willingness to get involved—from imploding. Variables that were beyond her ability to influence ate at her, worried her until she'd done everything she could to manage them and create contingency plans. I knew this girl, probably better than she knew herself.

Still, that didn't make what she'd done right.

In fact, it made it sting more. She'd been lying to me, not just when she'd met up with me after graduation on her bench, but also when we were kissing outside the Gibley Mansion last month, and when she'd held my hand in the car yesterday. She'd been lying, if only by omission, that whole time. I didn't know what to do with that. She couldn't have found another time, an early point in our . . . whatever it was we had . . . to tell me the truth? Had she really not trusted me until today?

Don't get me wrong: I knew, logically speaking, that she'd had plenty of reasons not to trust me, and that it was a significant change for her to tell me a truth she found personally humiliating, even now, when she knew I'd probably be angry.

But I guess I just thought we were well past that point. And it hurt and made me feel a little off balance to learn I was wrong.

I pulled into the parking lot of Krekel's and found a space.

Alona cleared her throat. "So, what's the plan?" She was trying to sound normal.

"We'll take a look around, talk to some people." I shrugged, avoiding her gaze. "See if they've seen her." My fear was that even if Erin had actually come here, she was already long gone and no one would remember anything.

"I'll handle the looking, you take the talking," Alona said with a nod.

"You think?" I muttered. Given that no one else could hear her, it was the only option that made any kind of sense. And no, it wasn't the most mature response ever. Sue me. I was still struggling with the bomb she'd just dropped on me.

She stiffened. "Hey, you know what? I said I'm sorry, and if that's not good enough—"

"Actually, you didn't," I said, biting off the words.

She stopped, frowning, her head cocked to one side as if she were mentally replaying our earlier conversation. "No, I'm pretty sure I—"

I just looked at her.

"Oh." She stared down at her hands for a long moment before glancing up at me. "Okay, well . . . I'm sorry," she said defiantly, chin jutting out in challenge, daring me to . . . what, gloat? Like that was at all what I felt like doing in this situation.

"Fine, whatever. Let's just do this." I reached for the door handle.

"It's not . . . I wouldn't do the same thing now, okay?" she said quietly. "I just—"

"Didn't trust me," I said, my mouth tight.

"Didn't know you," she corrected. "And now I do." She met my gaze without flinching.

The steadiness in her clear green eyes reassured me that she meant what she said, and some of the anger and uncertainty bubbling in my chest melted away. But not all of it. How was I supposed to know if we were really on the same page? That she wouldn't, at some point, reveal some new level of duplicity? Maybe it was my turn not to trust.

I sighed and shoved open the door. "Let's focus on one thing at a time for now."

She nodded and followed me out, but not before I caught the flash of hurt in her expression. I supposed she probably wanted something more for one of her rare apologies, and maybe she had a point, but this was as much as I could manage at the moment.

"Be subtle," I said as we started for the restaurant. "Remember, if you could see her, she can probably see you, and she'll know what you're after."

Alona nodded, but I got the sense her mind wasn't entirely focused on the task at hand.

"And if you start to feel . . ." I hesitated, not sure what to say.

"Less than myself?" she asked, her lips twisting into a wry smile.

"Don't even talk to her, just come find me."

She nodded again.

I felt my heart pounding harder than normal as we walked into Krekel's, which was packed with the late lunch/early, early dinner crowd, and past a family that seemed to consist solely of screaming children and some people our age that I didn't recognize. They were just out living their normal lives, blissfully unaware of everything happening beneath the surface.

It took only about ten minutes to determine what I'd feared was reality. Erin/Lily wasn't here, and no one seemed to have seen her. So she hadn't come here, or she'd slipped in and out without anyone noticing. Either way, we had no way of knowing where she was now or even where to start looking.

"They have security cameras," Alona pointed out, once we were back in the parking lot heading toward the car.

"Yeah, and how do we explain why we need to see what's on them, without getting the police involved?" I wanted to avoid that for as long as possible. If I could get things back to some semblance of normality before the Turners found out something was amiss, all the better. "And even if we could, the cameras won't tell us where she went from here."

"So now what?" she asked. "Check every tattoo parlor, strip club, and doughnut shop between here and the Indiana border?"

I stopped in the process of pulling my keys from my pocket and stared at her. "Strip clubs? Really?" I asked.

She shrugged. "Closest thing to a party at two in the afternoon, probably, right?"

"I have no idea." I tilted my head to one side, regarding her with curiosity. "Do you?"

"You wish," she snapped, clearly offended.

In spite of everything, I almost smiled. "We're going to Malachi's," I said, unlocking the car.

Alona made a face. "That place is so gross," she muttered. "Seriously, a few hundred bucks more a month and he could have a place that *doesn't* look like a front for a Russian mail-order-bride service."

"Better office space isn't exactly his top priority," I said, opening the driver's-side door for her to scoot across the seat. She could have opened her door, but with all the people in the parking lot, it didn't seem like a good idea. I hoped she wouldn't fight me on it.

"What does that mean?" she asked with a frown, climbing in without complaint.

I followed her in and slammed the door shut. "It means Malachi has other ways of attracting business."

I waited until I'd backed out of the space in the crowded lot and got us on the road to Malachi's before sharing everything he'd told me about his sister's death, my dad's visit, and their unusual method for obtaining new customers.

"That's what she meant by Misty being just business," she said, more to herself than to me. "So they're haunting people to make money, and they picked Misty because of me, because I was her best friend and I died?"

I nodded. "And because they thought her family probably had enough money to make it worthwhile."

"Son of a bitch," she whispered. Then she straightened up. "Malachi . . . *Edmund's* not going to have to worry about his sister being dead anymore, because I'm going to make sure he joins her."

And that was pretty much how I felt about it, too.

But when we got to Malachi's storefront, it was as abandoned and locked up as when I'd been there earlier, and this time, the back looked the same. No van, no boxes, no Edmund.

The jerk had taken off. Evidently he'd gotten tired of waiting around for Erin. Or maybe he thought that she'd catch up to him if she could, and if not, well, then, that wouldn't be so bad, either.

"Shit."

Alona raised her eyebrows at me. "What's wrong?"

"I don't know his last name," I explained through clenched teeth. "I have no other way to track him down. I don't even know for sure if Edmund is really his first name. It's not like I asked for ID."

She rolled her eyes. "Oh, for heaven's sake, don't be such a whiner." She marched past me toward the back door.

"What are you—"

She disappeared inside before I could finish the question.

With a sigh, I moved closer to the door so she could shove it open for me, which she did a second later, almost clipping me in the face.

"I hope there isn't an alarm," I said.

"Here?" she asked incredulously. "Please. Like anyone

would *want* anything in this place." She stepped back, making space for me to walk into the dim back rooms of Malachi's office. Only the buzzing fluorescent fixture above the sink in the kitchen was on.

"He took everything with him," I pointed out. "He was packing up to leave town, remember?"

She shook her head mockingly. "How would you survive without me?"

I stiffened.

She grimaced and waved the words away. "Never mind. . . . I didn't mean . . ." She took a deep breath and flipped her hair back behind her shoulders, a pale gleam of gold in the dim light. "People are never good about getting rid of everything. Tamara Lindt got outed on that thing with the student teacher because she lent her phone to someone without deleting all the evidence."

Tamara Lindt. That had been a scandal from way back in sophomore year. Even I'd been aware of it, which was saying something. She and this slimy d-bag college senior on assignment from EIU had had a thing in the equipment room . . . during school lunches. He'd been using her, from what I'd heard afterward, while "dating" several other girls on campus at the same time. Someone started a rumor that spread like, well, a juicy rumor, and it eventually got him kicked out of school, ours and his. Tamara had never seemed particularly grateful, but she wasn't spectacularly bright, as I recalled. The biggest question had always been who had found out and how.

Huh. "Text messages?" I guessed.

Alona grinned. "Left herself logged in to Facebook. Her inbox was full of his sleaze."

I knew it.

She moved deeper into the room, fumbling for the light switch and waiting for me to catch up so she could turn it on. "We'll find something. Trust me."

But Edmund, if that was his name, was much better than Tamara "Daddy Issues" Lindt, because he'd taken every scrap of paper with him. Even the garbage cans were empty. Probably a wise choice when running a semiscam.

Except for a disturbingly wrinkled apple in the minifridge, there was no sign that anyone had even been here recently.

"Here," Alona called faintly from the waiting room.

I poked my head through the door to find her crouching next to a stack of chairs. "What?" I asked.

"The chairs and stuff are rented." She pointed at something on the bottom of a chair. "There's a label with a company name and phone number."

"So?"

She stood up. "So," she said with exaggerated patience, "you need information about Malachi, like his real name. They'll have it with his credit card info. Unless he's running that kind of scam, too." She frowned. "Let's hope not."

Oh, Lord.

"And how do you suggest we get that information? Break in? We don't even know where that place is!" I did not especially treasure the idea of spending the rest of the day finding this place and then waiting for everyone to leave so we could get in, while Erin ran around town doing whatever she wanted.

"We could," she said with a shrug. "But calling and asking them is a lot easier."

"They're not just going to give us his personal information," I said in disbelief.

"Phone. Gimme." She held her hand out.

"They're not going to be able to hear you," I reminded her. I crossed the room, digging my phone from my pocket.

She pursed her lips. "This would be so much easier if I could do this myself." She scowled at me and she flickered. Her edges went soft for a second, and I could almost see through her.

I caught my breath. "Alona . . ."

Her eyes snapped shut, and she furrowed her brow in concentration, murmuring positive comments in a whisper I could barely hear, let alone understand.

But apparently it was the thought that counted and not the volume, because after a second, she stabilized, becoming fully solid once again.

"Are you all right? Do you need me to—"

She shook her head and held up her hand to cut me off.

Okay, evidently we weren't discussing this issue.

After taking a deep breath, she straightened her shoulders. Then she snatched the phone from my hand, consulted the number on the bottom of the chair, and started dialing.

"Call them and say . . ." She paused, clearly thinking. "Tell them you're the landlord and all this furniture is supposed to be cleared out. You need the tenant's contact information, all of it. And if you can't get ahold of him, or someone's not over here in the next ten minutes, you're going to throw it all out."

And we had to hope the rental place was farther than ten minutes away, I supposed. "Wait. If I'm the landlord, why wouldn't I have his contact information already?"

But it was too late. She shoved the phone into my hand, and it was ringing.

I glared at her.

"They're not going to think that far ahead," she said quickly. "And if they do, hang up."

"Remember how much you hate the idea of jail and germs," I said in a low tone.

"Jail? For what, impersonating a slumlord?" She sniffed. "Doubt it."

"Hello?" a female voice said in my ear.

"Uh, hi," I said, feeling ridiculous.

"Just be angry. Really angry!" Alona hovered at my elbow, coaching, which I ignored; but I did try to sound stern and landlordish, though I hadn't a clue what that might actually sound like.

As it turned out the bored receptionist probably would have given me Malachi's social security number, blood type, and anything else I asked, to avoid having to actually do work or walk away from FarmVille, or whatever was holding her attention.

"His real name is Edmund Harris," I said to Alona after I'd hung up. "And his home address is in Decatur. Four twenty-two Sycamore, Apartment B. I can't believe that worked."

"Me either," she said, shaking her head. "You were a *terrible* landlord."

I rolled my eyes. "Let's go."

The apartment was empty. Dents in the dingy brown carpeting showed where the furniture had been. A cheap plywood entertainment center still remained in the corner, heavily listing to one side.

"Oh, my God, it's like that part in *Empire Strikes Back* where they can never get into light speed," Alona said with a disgusted sigh.

I stared at her.

Catching sight of me, she scowled. "What?

"Nothing. I just . . ." I tried to find the words. "Alona Dare making a *Star Wars* reference. I never thought I'd live to see the day."

She arched an eyebrow at me. "At least one of us did." She crossed the small room to the tiny hallway, which presumably led to a kitchen and bathroom. "Besides, it's only because you made me watch it, like, a hundred times," she called back, her voice sounding hollow in the empty space.

"It's a classic, and it was twice," I said, following her to a minikitchen. If I stood with my arms outstretched, I probably could have touched both walls. "And only because you fell asleep in the middle the first time."

She shrugged dismissively. "The Dagobah stuff was so boring. No Han Solo."

She looked around the room at the cabinet doors hanging open and sighed. "There's nothing here."

I should have figured that. He had, after all, been packing up to leave town.

"All right," she said in the tone of someone done messing around. "Phone." She held her hand out.

I pulled my phone from my pocket but held on to it. "Who are you—who am *I* calling?" I asked cautiously. I'd saved the number the rental company receptionist had given me for Edmund, but I didn't think calling was a good idea. "Malachi . . . Edmund, whatever, he's not going to be thrilled to hear from us." In fact, I was afraid calling him might make him bolt farther than he already had.

Alona shook her head. "I'm not calling anyone." She peered with a grimace into an open drawer. "We're going to—"

Before she could finish explaining her plan, my phone rang, echoing loudly in the empty apartment and startling both of us.

I looked at the number. *Uh-oh.* I felt a renewed surge of panic. "Uh, Al, did you have your phone on you when Erin—"

"No. Mrs. Turner still has it confiscated," she said, bumping the drawer shut with her hip and moving closer to me. "Why?"

I held up my phone and showed her the words LILY'S CELL flashing on the screen. "Someone's noticed you're not where you're supposed to be."

Her eyes widened. "Answer it!" She reached for the phone.

I lifted it over my head, away from her grasping hand. "No way; it has to be the Turners," I said. If Mrs. Turner had dropped Ally off at Misty's this morning, it wouldn't have taken much for her to connect the dots. Mrs. Turner had probably called Misty, and Misty had told them about their newly recovered daughter leaving with the guy Mrs. Turner hated most. Great.

"Exactly. You have to tell them I'm okay." She crossed her arms and glared at me. Interesting that she cared so much about them now, when all she'd talked about before was how difficult it was to be around them.

"Except I don't actually know if *you* are okay. The version of you that they know, anyway. And they might get a call about *you*—*her*—being very *not* okay at any time." I didn't know much about our legal system, but vouching for the safety of a girl who later turned up hurt or in jail or something struck me as a particularly bad idea.

She bit her lip.

There was a *loooong* gap between the final ring and the voice-mail signal, and even the happy little chime sounded angry.

"Shit," I muttered.

"Are you going to listen to it?" she asked, seeming more anxious than I would have imagined.

"No," I said, stuffing the phone back into my pocket. No sense in confirming things were as bad as, or worse than, I figured they already were.

"They're going to be worried," she mumbled, sounding annoyed; but she wouldn't look at me, focusing instead on a splotch of something on the chipped and fading tile floor and kicking at it with the tip of her gym shoe. After all this time, she couldn't fool me. If she was annoyed at anyone, it was at herself for caring.

"I know." I looped an arm over her shoulders and pulled her toward me. She didn't resist. What was it about family that had such an immense hold on you, even if it wasn't your own, even if they didn't understand who you really were?

And suddenly, pieces of what I knew about Edmund Harris connected in a new way. I turned away from Alona and started for the hallway.

Alona followed me. "Where are you going?"

"I know where Malachi, Edmund, whatever his name is—I know where he went," I said over my shoulder. It's where I would have gone if I'd been in his situation, or what I knew of it, anyway. But I wasn't sure how long he would stay.

"Where?" Alona persisted.

I picked up speed, feeling like every second that passed was vital and one we could never get back.

"Home."

❧ 14 ❧

Alona

*E*xcept, as it turned out, Will meant *his* home, at least as a first stop.

"I can't believe you don't have Internet on your phone." I flopped back in the passenger seat of the Dodge. We needed more information about Edmund—like another address—and without the ability to look it up on the go, which had been my plan, returning to his house and his computer was the fastest option.

"Do you know how much that costs every month?" he demanded.

Actually, I didn't. When I'd been alive (the first time), I hadn't worried about it, and I hadn't yet regained phone privileges in my new reality, obviously. I thought about the message sitting in his voice mail from Mrs. Turner and flinched again.

"You have to promise me that no matter what happens, you're going to try to talk to the Turners, to tell them none of it was their fault," I said quietly. Mr. Turner was barely over feeling guilty for the first time something bad had happened to Lily, and I knew Mrs. Turner would probably blame herself—after she got done blaming Will for being a bad influence or something. And after yesterday's blowup, Tyler would probably take on his share of responsibility, too, if something happened to his sister. Or if she simply never came home. God, we needed to find this Erin chick . . . and soon. "It's important, okay? You need to promise me you'll talk to them."

Will frowned at me and tightened his grip on the wheel until his knuckles went white. "Stop it. Stop acting like you're not going to be fine."

Did he think I hadn't noticed when I'd gone all see-through back there? I opened my mouth to point that out, but what good would it have done? He was still angry, and right now it seemed he was determined that I would be sticking around, if only so he could yell at me some more.

The car bumped up over the curb into the driveway, taking out a portion of the dried-out yard with it.

"Wait here." Will unbuckled his seat belt and got out, leaving the car running.

"Yeah, right," I said. I switched off the engine, snagged the keys before he got too far away, and scrambled after him.

He caught a glimpse of me following him and sighed heavily. "Do you ever listen?" he asked.

"When someone's trying to tell me what to do? Uh, no. Besides, who died and made you the boss of me?"

He shot me an unhappy look as he rounded the corner.

"Oh, touchy, touchy," I muttered. "Like I'm going to just sit out there while you waste time online," I said in a louder voice. In truth, I didn't want to be by myself at the moment. It felt like if Will wasn't there to glare at me, I might slip away. And while I'd accepted that was a possibility, I . . . I didn't particularly want to be alone if/when it happened. Besides, it wasn't like we'd be disturbing anyone. His mom's car wasn't in the driveway.

"I think you're confusing me with you, Miss I Have Nine Thousand Friends on Facebook," he said darkly, yanking open the screen door and reaching for the doorknob. Then he stopped, flummoxed momentarily by the locked door.

"Oh, ouch, seriously wounding me there." I dangled the keys over his shoulder, and he snapped them away without so much as a thank-you. "Between the two of us, who do you think has better research skills? I would have graduated with honors."

"At least *I* graduated," he muttered, stabbing the key in and unlocking the door.

I sucked in a breath. "I think *dying* was a little outside my control, thank you very much."

"If you say so." He shrugged, but I saw the corner of his mouth turn up in a faint smile. So maybe I wasn't the only one taking comfort in the familiar nature of our exchange.

He shoved the door open, and I followed him into the

kitchen, where he stopped short and I nearly bumped into him.

"Not now," he said under his breath, seemingly to himself.

"What's wrong?" I asked.

He turned with a grimace and held his hands up in the classic stop position.

Ooookay. I listened for a second; it didn't take me long to identify the sound of voices, lots of voices, coming from the back of the house. What the hell?

Before I could ask him, even in a whisper, what was going on, an unfamiliar face appeared in the doorway to the hall. "You're here," she exclaimed at Will. Then, when she caught sight of me, her eyes widened. "You found her!"

Uh-oh.

She disappeared from the doorway, and I heard her yell, "They're here!"

Within seconds, the kitchen was flooded with spirits, many of whom I didn't recognize, all jabbering at once. They flowed in, surrounding Will and me individually, cutting us off from each other.

"Why didn't you tell me it was this bad?" I shouted at him over the clamor.

"What were you going to do? We didn't know you were still my spirit guide," he shouted back. "And it wasn't this bad . . . until now."

Fabulous. Well, that was helpful. I straightened my shoulders, tossed my hair back, and started to wade my way through to Will, or at least to the last place I'd seen him. The kitchen wasn't that big.

Of course, most of the spirits were too agitated to pay attention to what I was doing. They kept pulling at me, trying to stop me so they could explain, beg, plead, whatever. Though I couldn't see Will, I could only imagine it was worse for him.

The last straw came when someone actually grabbed hold of my arm and yanked until I stumbled back.

Not. Cool. I pulled my arm free with a vicious tug that sent my attacker—a soccer mom circa the 1980s, based on her wardrobe and her pink-and-purple-braided headband— *eesh*—sprawling forward.

I sidestepped her face-plant, but barely. "Enough already!" I shouted.

The room quieted immediately, faces whipping around toward me. Through a gap I could see Will's pale face. They'd cornered him against the door to the basement.

I took a deep breath to reinstate my claim on him, to tell them they had to go through me to get to him. That would shut them up and make them go away . . . or at least freeze them in place.

Before I could say anything, though, I heard Will.

"You heard her. Out, now!" He stepped away from the basement door and pointed to the nearest exterior wall.

Shock rippled through me. I stared at him, but he refused to look in my direction, splotches of red rising in his pale cheeks. He focused instead on the spirits in front of him, some of whom were already starting to protest.

He shook his head and spoke over them. "Who else do you have to help you? No one. So don't piss me off!"

I gaped at him. This was exactly what I'd been after him to do from the beginning. Take control, own his power. It's what I would have done. If you can't get rid of a feature in your life that is less than desirable, make it work for you. But I'd never expected he'd actually follow through on it.

It took a few moments for his words to take full effect. But then some of the ghosts started drifting out the back door. Others moved through the wall that Will had indicated.

"We will be back to help you," he said to those who lingered. "Just not today. We're already on task for someone else. You wouldn't want us to stop if we were working on your behalf."

Points to him for not framing that as a question.

With a few more reassurances and warnings from Will, the rest of the crowd slowly dissipated.

"You did it," I said, when the kitchen was empty except for the two of us. I couldn't quite keep the note of disbelief from my voice.

He shrugged, but he looked pleased, if a little stunned by his own accomplishment. "I wasn't sure what would happen to you if you tried to stop them. I didn't want to risk it." He turned and walked down the hall to his room.

I stayed put. He didn't want to risk it, but why? Because he didn't want me to be gone? Or because he still needed me to try to stop Erin? Both? It shouldn't have bothered me that I wasn't sure which his answer would have been had I been brave enough to ask. But it did.

Especially because he'd just proved, in no uncertain terms, that he no longer needed me as much as he used to, if at all.

This was a good thing, I told myself. Will needed to be able to take care of himself. That's what I wanted for him.

Except . . . what about what I wanted for me?

Honestly, I wasn't sure what I wanted. I didn't want to disappear for forever, that was for sure. But I didn't know if I had a choice in the matter. If I was lucky, the light might come for me before that happened. That would be okay, except I'd sort of gotten invested in what was happening here. I couldn't imagine being happy or at peace, not knowing what happened to Will or the Turners. And returning to life as Ally Turner . . . was that even an option? Did I want it to be?

I rubbed my forehead, pushing at the dull ache starting there. God. Who said being dead was easy? Dying had only been the start of my troubles.

With the details about Edmund that we had now, thanks to Will's questionable landlord performance, it didn't take long to find the information that we needed online. We tracked down his parents' names from his sister's obituary and then their address from a white-pages search. Easy peasy.

Ted and Althea Harris lived on the outskirts of Peoria. A couple of hours away at most. And Will was convinced from the conversation he'd had with Edmund that that was where he was headed.

"He only left because of Erin," he said, once we were back in the car. "If he thinks she's gone, even temporarily, he'll go back. At least to let them know he's okay. Trust me." He signaled to turn on to the highway.

I made a face. "Maybe." I wasn't convinced that we knew Edmund half as well as Will thought we did. But then again, not much of this situation made sense to me, so what did I know?

I flipped through the pages we'd printed, looking for the article on Erin's death again. "How weird is it that he can only see one ghost?" I asked, more to myself than to Will, but he answered anyway.

"On a scale of one to ten? Fifteen." He shook his head. The Dodge started to tremble as he pushed it to its maximum speed, which was still less than the legal limit on the highway. "I think it has to do with the twin thing."

"What, some kind of psychic twin connection or something?" I asked, trying not to scoff. I was, after all, a spirit communicating with him based on a similar sort of premise.

"Maybe." Will hesitated. "I don't think he's really a ghost-talker, at least not in the way we understand it. He said that Erin doesn't have physicality around him. She can't touch him."

"That is so weird." I shivered. I didn't like her. And not only because she was hella powerful and a bully. She was operating outside the principles that I knew guided our little shared space between the living and the dead. Did. Not. Like. It made me feel unsettled. "The Order never mentioned anything like this?" Will's near conversion was still a bit of a sore spot with me.

"No," he said, his mouth tight.

"Really? Because I would have thought they'd be all over this, recruiting twins so they could kill one off and—"

"If you recall, I only spent about twenty-four hours in their favor. I didn't exactly have time for the full initiation and tour."

Huh. Perhaps I was not the only one feeling a bit sensitive about that whole ordeal. Or maybe Will was thinking how having them as an ally—which we didn't—would have been pretty useful right about now. Up to a point, like the one in which they would probably let Lily die and box both me *and* Erin.

Whatever. I shrugged and returned to browsing our printouts. I finally located the page I was looking for at the bottom of the stack, behind our MapQuest directions.

It wasn't her official obituary—that was a different page. This was the blurb that had appeared in the *Peoria Journal Star*'s Web site archives with details about her accident. I'd read it once over Will's shoulder but wanted to review it again. According to the article, Erin had been at a spring break–themed Halloween party at a fraternity at ISU. She'd had too much to drink and had tumbled off the roof of a porch in the middle of—dear God—a limbo contest. Apparently, any other day she might have walked away with a few scrapes and bruises—the porch wasn't that high up—but the frat brothers had just laid paving stones to make a walkway in the yard, right where she fell.

In reading it again, I was struck once more by how . . . ordinary, albeit sad, Erin Harris's death had been. Aside from the limbo part. That was just kind of ironic, I suppose. Death by limbo and you end up in limbo?

I suppose not all of us can be so fortunate as to have a bus provide us with a dramatic exit from the living world. Ha-ha. But aside from her being a twin, nothing about Erin's demise had been particularly surprising. That, in combination with the fact that she didn't seem to have any specific unfinished business to address, was . . . odd. I grant you that most spirits with sudden access to a body will take advantage of the opportunity to live wild and free. But that she had been aiming for that even before she got hold of Lily? I wouldn't have thought that was a strong enough reason for her to be stuck here. I mean, who doesn't wish they had more time alive? Who wouldn't wish to have a few more days of Krispy Kremes and shopping? But if that was the only requirement, this in-between place would be a lot more crowded.

No, we had to be missing something.

"Was there anything else Edmund said about—" I began.

Will's phone rang, and we both jumped.

Keeping one hand on the wheel, Will leaned back to reach into his pocket for his phone, and I felt the teeniest return of lust, despite everything that was going on. He looked in control and lean and strong . . . *Hello.*

The sensation wasn't nearly as powerful as it had been when I'd been Ally, but it was enough to make me wish Will and I were on better terms and not in such a hurry. I mean, if these were my last hours, why not make them fun, at least?

He glanced up from his phone, and some of what I was thinking must have shown on my face. He hesitated, faint color rising in his cheeks, and said, "It's my mom."

And there went that moment. . . . "Don't answer it," I warned. "She's probably—"

He ignored me, clicking the speakerphone button. "Mom?"

"—talked to Mrs. Turner," I said with a sigh.

"Will, where are you?" Will's mom sounded like she was in full panic mode, in a way I hadn't heard since first meeting—well, seeing—her a few months ago.

"What's wrong?" he asked.

"Is Lily Turner with you?" Her voice was tight with worry.

"I told you," I said in a singsong voice.

He glared at me.

I shrugged.

"No," he said to his mom.

"Do you know where she is? Corine Taylor seems to think you do." I heard her breath catch, as if she were close to tears. "William, she's talking about trying to get the police to issue an AMBER Alert. Lily's underage, and with her medical issues . . ."

Will shot me an alarmed look. "Mom, she's not with me. I did give her a ride this morning, but she asked to be let out about a block away from Misty Evans's house. I have no idea where she is now." A succinct description of our problem, if nothing else.

Will's mom took a deep breath. "Okay, I knew there had to be an explanation. Just come home and we'll talk to Corine."

Oh. In spite of myself, I couldn't help but feel a flicker of intrigue. I turned to face Will. *Now, this is going to be interesting.* Not just in an academic sense but also in a making-the-wrong-choice-here-could-really-screw-us kind of way. Will rarely, if ever, defied his mother. He dodged, he avoided, he fibbed—but out-and-out refused? No way. Back when I first started talking to him, a few days after I'd died, he'd almost let himself end up in a mental institution because he wanted to avoid outing himself as a ghost-talker to his mother and upsetting her.

Which, in my opinion, was crazier than talking to dead people ever could be.

So which would win out? His super-over-the-top loyalty to his mother or his responsibility as a ghost-talker?

I resisted the urge to hum the theme from *Jeopardy!* A) because it wasn't really appropriate, and B) because I already knew the answer. His mom always came first. I couldn't blame him, no matter how much it frustrated me at times. After his dad killed himself, they'd had only each other.

Will's head sagged for a second before he straightened up and took a deep breath. "Mom, I'm sorry. I can't."

My mouth fell open, and I swear, I got chills. He'd actually done it. He'd told his mom no. Somewhere along the line, Will Killian had grown a mother-proof spine.

"I'm in the middle of something important right now,"

he continued, "and I can't walk away." The determined set of his jaw spoke volumes. He wasn't backing down on this one. Color me stunned.

On the other end of the phone, his mother seemed as flabbergasted as I was. "Will . . . I don't . . . You need to understand. This is serious."

"I know. And I do understand," he said. "But I have to do this."

"Honey—" she began.

"Tell Mrs. Turner to call the police. That's fine. Lily is not with me, and they should be looking for her." He looked to me for confirmation, and I shrugged. At least if they caught her and brought her home, we would eventually find out about it and be able to try to fix this. Maybe. Of course, in the meantime, Erin would wreak havoc within the Turner household, the very idea of which made me flinch. Blah. There was no good solution here.

"I love you, and I'll be home as soon as I can," Will said, and hung up before his mom had a chance to respond.

"She's just going to call back," I pointed out, unable to resist.

He pushed the button to turn the ringer off and held the phone up to show me the volume symbol with the line through it. "Satisfied?"

"Yeah, actually," I said, seeing him through new eyes. Who was this guy, this new assertive version of Will? And why did he have to show up just as I was leaving?

❧ 15 ❧

Will

Edmund Harris's parents lived on a quiet street in a middle-class neighborhood on the north side of Peoria. At seven thirty, the sun was setting, but kids were still out playing in the yards, occasionally chasing balls, dogs, and one another into the street. I slowed down, ignoring the urge to hurry to the Harris driveway. If we were this close, a few more seconds weren't going to matter.

At least, I hoped not.

I glanced out the window to check house numbers again—we were looking for 1414 and were currently passing 1398—and noticed Alona watching me again. She had her head tipped to one side, blond hair tumbling down over her arm, and she was studying me.

"What?" I asked, resisting the urge to wipe my face.

She shook her head, as if waking herself from a zone-out. "Nothing," she said quickly, but her cheeks were pinker than normal.

I frowned. "Uh-huh."

She lifted her chin with a haughty sniff. "I was trying to figure out why my presence hasn't influenced you more, particularly your wardrobe."

In spite of myself, I looked down at my dark jeans and T-shirt. "My shirt is gray," I pointed out. "You've expanded my fashion horizons dramatically. I wear three colors now."

She rolled her eyes, but I caught a glimpse of a smile before she looked away. Nice. In spite of everything, I still liked making her smile. It didn't happen all that often.

"Hey." I sat up straighter behind the wheel, staring at a house down the street on the right. I nudged her shoulder. "That has to be it." I pointed to the perfectly ordinary two-story red house, my heart beating a little faster.

"It doesn't look like the family home of a criminal mastermind," Alona said. "Not nearly lair-y enough. And where is the moat?"

"Funny," I said. But I knew I was right. An all-too familiar battered van sat in the driveway. "He's here." I nodded toward the vehicle as we approached, and I slowed down.

"No," Alona said sharply. "Don't stop."

"What?"

"Do you actually pay attention to any of the movies you

watch?" She gave me an exasperated look. "We don't want to spook him."

"You would be the expert on that," I muttered.

She stuck her tongue out at me. "Ha-ha. Keep going," she said.

And much as I didn't like to admit it, she probably had a point. The subtle approach was definitely better with this guy.

I drove past the house, which was dark with no signs of life, and pulled to the curb about four houses down, where the street curved and would partially hide us from view.

"We still have to walk to the front door," I said, unbuckling my seat belt, "unless you're planning some kind of ninja stealth attack." I opened the door and got out.

She slid out after me, shaking her head. "Don't be ridiculous. We don't have to sneak up to the house. It was the car that would have attracted attention." Alona stood and stretched her arms over her head, and I could have sworn I heard her joints pop. "Think about it. You notice when someone pulls into your driveway. But do you pay attention to people out walking around? No," she answered for me. "Especially not here." She nodded to the residents walking their dogs, chasing their kids, and watering their lawns.

She was right again. I raised my eyebrows at her in question.

"I spent years hiding my mom from people," she said with a shrug. "The only ones who ever caught me by surprise were the neighbors when they walked over."

Once again I felt a twinge of sympathy for her for the life she'd lived before. No wonder she was so concerned about the Turners. They'd actually been concerned about her in return. Well, what they knew of her.

I felt the last of my anger toward her evaporate. Yes, she'd lied about the light, but lying to protect herself was her primary defense mechanism. Should it have surprised me, then, that in a moment of fear and confusion she'd exaggerated to make sure things worked out to her benefit? And she was trying to change, trying to trust. That was huge for her.

She also maybe had a point in that it had been a little naive of me to assume that she'd been given specific instructions. Nothing about the afterlife, or at least my experience with it, worked quite that precisely. The only thing that seemed to have any definitive impact in the in-between place was action. Certain things a spirit did or said to get closure or resolution would bring the light. Being nasty would— eventually, depending on the spirit's strength—make you gone.

So . . . if the light hadn't wanted Alona to be Ally, perceiving it as a selfish move, maybe she would have disappeared already? She would have just depleted her energy and vanished, leaving Lily's body as it had been before.

Maybe.

Except Erin was currently holding that position, without, as far as I knew, any ill effects. And the light surely couldn't have intended for Erin to do what she did, right?

My head hurt just thinking about it. And somewhere

in this whole debate, there had to be an element of that free-will thing, points for making the unselfish choice or something, but was it the selfish or unselfish choice for Alona to be Ally? I didn't know. I couldn't figure out how the system worked. And maybe that was the point. If you aren't sure how it works, it's a lot harder to game it. Okay, maybe. But it made me long for the days when I'd thought it operated as my dad had first told me. Simple. Exact. Which, in retrospect, struck me as the kind of explanation you gave a little kid when you weren't capable of or didn't want to give a more detailed and accurate answer. You know, thunder is just two clouds bumping into each other, and that sort of thing.

"Hello?" Alona waved a hand in front of my face. "What's the plan?"

I slammed my door and put aside the deep philosophical ponderings to consider her question, which was far more relevant to the moment.

If Edmund had actually been able to see ghosts, it might have been easier to send Alona ahead through the walls for the element of surprise. But since he couldn't, I wasn't sure that ringing the doorbell wouldn't be equally effective.

After a moment, I shrugged. "We see if he's home and try to talk to him." Actually, more like plead with him to help us, but I couldn't see any point in being that specific with Alona right now. Maybe it wouldn't come to that.

I started down the street, and she followed.

"That's it?" she asked, when she caught up, skepticism heavy in her voice.

"What were *you* thinking? Hot pokers and broken glass?" I moved to the edge of the sidewalk, forcing Alona into the grass, to let a neighbor with schnauzer pass. He stared at me, the crazy unknown guy in his neighborhood talking to himself. I forced a smile and nodded at him. *Whatever, dude. You can think what you like.*

"We're not trying to break him. We want his help," I whispered to Alona, once the schnauzer guy had passed and we'd moved back to the center of the sidewalk.

"If everything you said is true, I think we might have better luck with the pokers and glass," she said grimly. "He doesn't want his sister back. And if we can find her and kick her out of Lily, that's exactly what will happen. She'll end up right back at his side."

I shook my head. "I think it's more complicated than that. If he wanted her gone, all he had to do was have my dad call in the Order. But he didn't. And when he thought I was one of them, he was packing up and leaving town to protect her." I hesitated, going more from a gut sense than from anything Edmund or Erin had said to me. "There's more to it, whatever happened between them." Which was going to make dealing with them much trickier.

And that wasn't the only thing. Approaching the house from this direction, I saw something I'd missed before. In the yard, under the shade of a huge maple tree, was a fairly discreet real estate sign. What was less discreet, however, was a giant foreclosure notice plastered diagonally across it.

I stopped. "Crap."

"What?" Alona asked, but then she followed my gaze. "Oh." She shrugged. "So? His van is here. He has to be here."

Yes, but in what kind of state? Probably not one prone to helping us. He'd been gone from his family for five years—thanks to the ghost we were trying to shove back in his direction—and in that time they'd evidently lost their home.

I sighed. "Come on. Let's go."

We made our way toward the house, dodging neighbors and their small children alike.

Up close, the home had a distinctly abandoned look and feel to it. The grass was longer than it should have been. The windows didn't have any blinds or curtains, creating the look of hopeless eyes gazing back at us. And through the windows, we could see dark squares on the walls where pictures or paintings had been. The rooms, at least the ones I could see, were empty—no furniture visible.

I took a side trip to the driveway to check out the van. It was definitely Edmund's. Even if I hadn't recognized its battered appearance, the box full of half-melted purple candles on the passenger seat was a dead giveaway. But he wasn't in it.

"His?" Alona asked.

"Yeah."

"Still want to walk up and ring the bell?" She rested her hands on her hips, as if this plan had sucked the whole time instead of just the last ten minutes.

"No," I admitted. If Edmund was inside, he certainly wasn't going to be running to answer the door, that was for sure. "You want to—"

I didn't even have to finish before she'd turned on her heel and marched up the porch stairs to the front door and then through it.

Suddenly, with her absence, I felt more conspicuous hanging around this house that was not mine, like someone was going to start pointing and shouting at me. Which was ridiculous. From the perspective of the living residents here, I'd been alone the whole time. It was just, I guess, that I hadn't felt it until now.

I ducked my head and tried to look like I belonged here, trying to ignore the uneasy feeling growing in my chest.

Was this going to be what it was like if/when Alona vanished for good? Me, lurking around places alone, feeling even more like a freak just for being by myself in this mess? What if we couldn't find a way to get Erin out . . . or if Alona was right and she was no longer strong enough to keep the physical form of Ally going? Or, if she simply chose not to? In the end, it was Alona's decision, in the *best-*case scenario. Would she really intentionally choose to live as someone else, knowing it would be forever and that the person she'd been before would be gone for good?

I could safely say the Alona I'd first met would have chosen disappearing over life as Lily—or even Ally—Turner, and I certainly hadn't made the prospect of changing her mind any easier by being so hard on her changes to Lily's appearance and the way she was handling her second chance at "life."

I wanted her to stay, definitely. But when it came down to

it, I didn't want her to be miserable just because I would miss her if she were gone, because my life was better—although, okay, more complicated and sometimes more stressful, too—with her around.

No. I pushed those negative thoughts away. We couldn't have come this far together for her to just . . . not be here anymore. We'd figure it out. We had to.

"Hey."

I looked up to see Alona leaning out through the still-closed door, her hair hanging forward over her shoulders.

"It's unlocked already. And you should probably get in here." Her mouth was curved downward in distaste or worry, or maybe both.

Uh-oh.

Then she pulled back inside the house, leaving me no choice but to follow.

The house had that clean but closed-up smell that I associated with the first day of school after summer break. Floor wax and disuse, I guess.

I was standing in a small foyer, with what was probably the living room to my left—the spacing of dents in the whitish carpet indicating that a sofa and chairs had once lived there. A long, narrow hallway led to a kitchen, and an open stairway to the second floor was to my right.

"Up here," Alona said from a landing midway up the steps. Her expression did not look any less grim than it had moments before, and I wanted to ask why, but that would have meant giving up any element of surprise, which I didn't want to do yet. Getting through the door without a racket—the stupid real estate lockbox on the door had rattled with every movement—had been tough enough. If Edmund was still unaware that I was here, I wanted to keep it that way for at least a little while longer.

I followed Alona up the stairs as quietly as possible to an open area at the top that also looked like it had once held furniture. Three more empty rooms branched off from this space—probably bedrooms—but I didn't have to go any farther to find Edmund . . . or smell him.

He was sitting on the floor, leaning against a small section of wall between two bedroom doors. The fumes pouring off him, and the whiskey bottle clutched in his hand, made my eyes water even from ten feet away. That explained Alona's reaction, at least. She was probably experiencing flashbacks of her mom.

"Hey," Edmund said with a goofy grin, lifting his bottle in greeting. "What are you doing here? It's me, Ed." Like I'd somehow managed to forget him in the last eight hours.

Alona rolled her eyes.

"I messed up, man," he continued before I could respond. "I left because of Erin, and everything went to shit." He waved the half-empty bottle around, the contents sloshing. "The neighbors said my mom got depressed, my dad lost his job, and now . . . they're gone. Kicked out of their *own* house." He shook his head glumly. "No one knows where they went. And even if they did, they aren't going to tell *me*, the crazy son who caused so much trouble and made everybody's property values bottom out."

I shook my head, not sure I'd gotten the gist of what he was saying through his muddled speech. What did property values have to do with anything?

I moved closer and knelt down next to him, breathing through my mouth and forcing myself to be patient, when all I really wanted to do was shake him. "It's not your fault. You were doing what you had to do to survive, and I'm sure they'd understand that if they knew. And we can help you find them, eventually. But first I need you to tell me—"

"Nah, man, you don't get it." His head flopped from side to side in a poor imitation of voluntary movement. "I was there. I could have stopped it."

Except that made no sense. The whole point was that he hadn't been here, and that's why everything had fallen apart. Evidently, he'd already gotten to the part of this drunken excursion where he'd lost his grip on reality. Wonderful.

Alona frowned and knelt next to me. "At the party? On the roof?"

"What are you talking about?" I asked her.

"Ask him," she insisted and nudged me hard in the ribs when I hesitated.

I glared at her, but repeated after her dutifully, "At the party? On the roof?"

Ed looked up, his gaze glassy, but it was, at least, direct eye contact for the first time in this conversation.

He leaned forward with a sudden intensity in his expression, and I edged back slightly in case that was his I'm-going-to-throw-up-right-here-and-now face. "No," he whispered, like he was revealing some big secret.

I glanced over at Alona—it was my turn to roll my eyes at her—but she wasn't paying attention to me. "Where were you?" she asked Ed.

With a sigh, I repeated the question aloud, not waiting for her to jab me with her elbow again. My ribs still ached from the last time.

"On campus. In my dorm room," he said in that same hushed voice, and tears spilled over from his watering eyes down his cheeks. "She wanted me to go with her to that stupid costume party, expand our social horizons, whatever that means. She was nervous about going alone."

And then it clicked. He wasn't talking about his parents; he was talking about his sister and her death.

Alona gave me a triumphant look.

"We fought about it, and she went alone. I was just so tired of doing everything together." He thumped his head back against the wall, and the bottle in his slack grip tipped. If he hadn't already drunk more than half, the whiskey would have spilled out onto the carpet. "The same college, the same dorm, the same major in Econ. And she was changing, becoming this person I didn't know. Contact lenses, different hairstyle—"

"How about just a hairstyle in general?" Alona muttered, eyeing the out-of-control curls on the top of Ed's head.

"—ditching her jeans and sweatshirts for clothes like the sorority girls were wearing, hanging out with dickhead frat guys . . . and she wanted me to change, too. Telling me who to talk to, what to wear. Nothing all that different from what she'd always done, but suddenly I was just sick of it. I didn't like who she was becoming—all fake and plasticky—and I didn't want to be a part of it. But if she reinvented herself without me, then who was I, you know?" He let go of the bottle to scrub at his face, and liquor flowed out, staining the carpet. "I was . . . It was confusing. I was trying to work it out, figure out what to do. So I told her no that night, probably for the first time ever. She was pissed, but I thought, It's only one night—no big deal. Instead, it was everything." He drew his knees up to his chest and rested his forehead on them. "It was just a stupid party," he said, his voice muffled.

I'd told Alona that, for the moment, we only had to worry about finding Erin. But I realized now that having Ed tell us where Erin might want to hang out wouldn't be enough. Not with all of this guilt hanging around, binding the two of them together. Ed's unfinished business with someone who was essentially the other half of himself was the real problem. Without him, there was no way we were going to reach any kind of resolution, even once we managed to find Erin.

I made an executive decision. "You need to come with us. We need your help with Erin."

He squinted at me. "You keep saying *we*."

"My spirit guide, Alona, is here," I said.

"Was that really necessary?" she muttered.

"For real? Hey, Alona." Ed waved at a point well above where she knelt on the floor next to me.

She rolled her eyes.

He wiped his face and sat up straighter. "What do you need my help with? Is Erin okay?"

Alona sighed. "I wouldn't if I were you," she said to me. "It's only going to make things worse."

I ignored her. "It's kind of a long story," I said to Ed. "But the gist of it is that Erin has sort of taken a body that doesn't belong to her, and we need your help to fix that."

He lurched forward, once again making me wonder about the vomit potential of the moment. "A body?" He frowned. "She's possessing someone? Is that even possible?"

"Seriously," Alona said, "do you ever listen to me?" She pushed herself to her feet and stalked away.

"Kind of," I said to Ed. "Like I said, it's complicated. We need you to help us find her and get her out, back here where she belongs."

He struggled to focus, rubbing his eyes. "But she's in a body? Like, she's alive?"

Oh, crap.

"Told you," Alona singsonged from somewhere behind me.

I refused to look at her. "Not exactly," I said to Ed, struggling to keep on topic. "The point is, the body doesn't belong to her. We need to get her back here as a spirit, so she can resolve her issues and move on to the light. That's what you want, isn't it?"

"Is she happy?" he asked.

I thought of Erin gleefully smashing her mouth against mine. *Happy* would be one way to describe her. *Ecstatic* might be more accurate. But that didn't change the fact that what she'd done wasn't right. She was in this only for herself. She didn't care who got hurt—Alona, Lily, Lily's family . . .

"I don't think you understand," I began.

"No, *you* don't understand. I *owe* her." He pounded his fist against his leg. "What happened was my fault. I could have stopped her from going, or I could have gone with her, like she wanted, and she wouldn't have had so much to drink. Then none of this ever would have happened." He gestured around, obviously including his parents and their financial distress in the mix. "If she's happy now, I'm not going to stop that. At least something decent will come out of this mess."

I stared at him. "Are you not hearing me? She's possessing an innocent person!"

"She's my sister," he said, jabbing an unsteady finger in my direction. "And I killed her."

I stood up and stepped back from him, frustrated. "No, you didn't."

"I might as well have." He stared glumly at the floor.

"Look, it was her decision to go to the party and to drink on the freaking roof or whatever. She died, and she needs to move on. End of story." I raked my hands through my hair, trying to find the words that would click with him, that would make him understand. "Her choices are not your responsibility. And sometimes you have to let people go." As soon as the words were out of my mouth, I knew they were a mistake.

I heard Alona's sharp intake of breath behind me and turned quickly to face her. "I didn't mean you."

She gave me a sad smile. "Why not? The same rules that apply to Erin apply to me, too. That's what I've been trying to tell you."

"It's different," I insisted. "You were sent back for a reason, even if no one spelled out what it was."

"Glad to hear you think so now," she said quietly.

Ed, of course, noticed none of this. He forced a laugh. "Let people go? You keep telling yourself that, man. Let me know how it works out for you in real life."

Damn it. Drunk and ridiculous, Ed had a point.

✤ 16 ✤

Alona

I followed Will down the stairs after he stormed past me. He started pacing the empty living room, back and forth in front of the windows in the rapidly fading squares of sunlight on the carpet.

I leaned against the wall in the foyer and watched. The frustration rolled off him in nearly visible waves, and I felt a pang of sympathy for him. He was doing his best. That being said, I couldn't leave it like this. We couldn't just hang out in an empty house and hope for all of this to resolve itself. I mean, I guess we could have, but not without a lot of the collateral damage we were hoping to avoid. "So, what now?" I asked.

Will stopped to glare at me. "I don't know, okay?" He rubbed his hands over his face. "You were right," he said, his voice muffled. "This was a stupid plan."

He sounded miserable, and it tugged at me in a way I normally would have worked very hard to ignore. Except . . . this was it. The end. In that knowledge, I felt a reassurance and freedom I'd never experienced before.

I straightened up and approached him cautiously, my steps soundless on the carpet. When I touched his shoulder, he jerked his head up, startled.

"It's all right," I said. "It wasn't a stupid plan. There were just more variables than we counted on, is all." Actually, more variables than *he* had counted on. I'd foreseen that Ed might not be as easy to maneuver as Will had thought, and Will might have avoided some of this if he'd listened to me. But I saw no point in bringing that up now and making him feel worse. Hey, look at me, growing as a person.

He laughed bitterly. "You can't fool me. You're gloating on the inside. You tried to tell me, and I wouldn't listen."

That stung. Maybe I wasn't perfect yet, but I was trying. I pulled back from him, but to my surprise, he reached out and enfolded me in his arms, pulling me closer and burying his face against my neck. "I'm sorry. I just want everything to be easier, like it was before," he whispered, his lips moving against my skin.

For some stupid reason, this sparked tears in my eyes. I gave a shaky laugh. "Who doesn't?" I smoothed his hair down; it was softer than it looked and shorter than it had been when I'd first been forced to take real notice of him. The idea that at some point he'd gone out and gotten a haircut without my knowing made my heart ache. He had a life without me, and he would continue to once I was gone.

It was ridiculous to get upset about it, and I knew that, but I couldn't quite stop myself, either.

I blinked a bunch of times, trying to get my emotions under control, and cleared my throat. "You know, it wasn't so great before. I was kind of a bitch sometimes, and you were hiding from everything."

He laughed, and I felt the vibration of it beneath my hand on his back. I would miss this. I would miss him.

"It just seems harder now because we're not used to this," I continued, swallowing the lump in my throat. "Not used to being something other than what we were."

"You are so damned practical," he said with another laugh, one that held more than a little sadness. He leaned back from me without letting go and reached up to touch my face, brushing his thumb across my cheek, maybe to catch a tear that had somehow escaped. "No one would have ever guessed that before, least of all me."

I could see the warmth in his gaze and sense the words rising up inside him, words that not a single person had ever said to me and actually *meant*. My mom loved that she had had someone else to blame. My dad loved that he'd had someone else to clean up his mess. My ex-boyfriend Chris had apparently loved someone else entirely. . . . "Don't," I said quickly, pushing away from him.

He frowned. "Why not?"

Because Will knew me in a way those other people hadn't, and I might have believed him. And that seemed way too dangerous, especially now. I stepped back from him and wiped under my eyes, as though my mascara would run.

"It doesn't change anything," I said in my haughtiest tone.

Which rolled off him like I hadn't said anything. "If things were different . . ." he began.

"But they're not," I reminded him.

"They could be."

He meant being Ally again for good. If we could track Erin down, if it was even possible that that arrangement could last, if I wanted to literally be someone else for the rest of my life . . . if, if, if . . . "Maybe."

He sighed and walked a few steps away before turning back to face me. "What do you want to do?"

"What?" I asked, certain I'd heard him incorrectly.

Will gave me a look that suggested I might have suddenly developed a severe mental impairment. "I'm asking what you want to do," he said slowly.

I stared at him, still not sure if he was being serious. He'd *never* asked me that before. For all that he'd tried to avoid being a ghost-talker, with the implications that went along with it, he'd always had very definite opinions about the right and wrong thing to do in any given situation. And getting him to see things my way had usually required some form of bribery or blackmail.

"We're running out of options, and this isn't working out like I thought." He waved a hand toward the stairs and the second floor, from which loud snores resonated through the empty house. Ed had evidently passed out. Will hesitated, then said, "I'm not going to push you into something that's not you." He forced a laugh. "Literally."

I didn't know what to say. Someone thinking of me first—it was what I always tried to insist on, what I'd manipulated into existence when I could. And here Will was doing it on his own.

"If you want to let it go . . . let everything go, I'll find another way to fix the Erin situation." He grimaced, and I knew he was thinking of the Order. Who knew what it would cost him to enlist their help? But he would do it, if necessary. If I said so.

For a second, some part of me deeply wanted to say, *Forget it all, forget everyone but me.* If these were my last few hours, then why not spend them the way *I* wanted? That was the one advantage of knowing you're about to not exist anymore, a benefit I had not been afforded in my previous death.

We could take the Alona Dare greatest hits tour—visit all the significant places I'd be leaving behind, one last time. My bench outside our school. My former room in my mother's house, which was now as empty as Ed's parents' house. Krispy Kreme. I couldn't actually eat a doughnut, but I would be able to see them and smell them. That would be worth something, wouldn't it?

We could listen to my favorite songs—most of which Will would probably hate—and make out on his bed—which he definitely wouldn't hate and neither would I.

All of that . . . or spend more hours chasing a girl who we might not even be able to find or save. And even if we did manage to save her and I took Lily's body back for good,

I wouldn't be me, not the me from the first eighteen years of my life.

This was not a small decision. But for now, all I had to do was decide to keep trying. And I could do that. Will deserved that much. Not to mention that I, for whatever reason, couldn't stand the idea of seeing the disappointment on his face if I said no. It would definitely put a crimp in any potential make-out plans.

"All right, all right," I said with a sigh. "We keep looking . . . as soon as we find another place to try."

But Will didn't move or burst into ecstatic applause at my decision. Actually, Will and "ecstatic" don't really belong in the same sentence. Ever. Still, his lack of response left something to be desired.

"There's no point in continuing to look," he said warily, "if you're not going to—"

"Don't push me," I snapped. "And I'm not the only one who should be thinking this through." I stepped forward until I was inches from his face. "We're talking permanent here. And that means more than changing hairstyles and trying new makeup. I'd be Ally Turner. I'd go to school as Ally Turner." God save me. "I would *date* as Ally Turner." I poked my finger in his chest with those last words.

He flinched.

"Yeah, that's what I thought." I backed off.

His mouth tightened, and he made an unhappy face. "Let's just do this."

* * *

In the absence of some other, more productive activity, we decided to go back upstairs to retrieve Ed. We would need him, most likely, if we found Erin; and besides, leaving him to sleep it off in his abandoned, bank-owned, child-hood home, only to be awakened by a screaming real estate agent, who would probably call the police, seemed kind of cruel.

Unfortunately, reviving him proved beyond our capacity, even with my skills and experience in that area.

"We're going to have to carry him," I said, out of breath from tugging at Ed's arm to get him to his feet. He kept flopping over like a rag doll.

"Like that's not going to look suspicious." Will was bent in half, hands on his knees, in the same breathless condition. Ed wasn't a particularly big guy, but in his current boneless, drunk condition, our attempt to move him was taking a lot more effort than it would have otherwise. With my mom, I'd often given up and covered her with a blanket where she lay. Way, way easier.

I waved his concern away. "You can pull the car into the driveway, and it'll be dark soon. Unless you've got a better suggestion."

Will shook his head. "No."

"Fine. Get his arms."

He stepped around me to grab Ed's wrists, and I moved to his ankles. "Ready?" I asked.

"Not really," he muttered. "You realize this is technically kidnapping."

I shrugged. "One of our lesser crimes. It's for his own good."

"You can tell that to the police . . . Oh, wait. That's right. You can't." He gave me a sour look.

"Ha-ha." I gripped the cuffs of Ed's worn jeans. "Ready? Lift."

We stumbled toward the stairs with Ed swinging between us, hanging above the carpet by a mere fraction of an inch. "So, did she say anything else to you? Anything besides 'burgers and beer'?" I asked through gritted teeth.

"We've been over this," Will panted, as he backed toward the first step.

"Well, go over it again," I said. I couldn't help feeling that we were missing something. This girl was not that complicated. Yeah, she'd be smart to be hiding, but I was betting she wasn't that smart. She was all about sensations and experiences—new boys to kiss, more chances to dance, more beer to drink. . . . She wasn't going to waste any time finding those things. But she didn't know anyone—or didn't know that she, as Lily, knew anyone. And I couldn't see her seeking out strangers for random experiences; though, maybe . . .

I stopped suddenly as a thought occurred to me, and Will stumbled forward, almost falling on Ed. "Did she kiss you?" I demanded.

Color rose in his already flushed face.

"Son of a bitch," I said and dropped Ed's feet.

"Look, it was no big deal." He set his half of Ed down more carefully at the top of the stairs. "I already knew it wasn't you, and—"

"That's supposed to make me feel better?" I asked, crossing my arms over my chest. I wasn't sure why it bothered me so much. I guess it didn't seem fair that he'd already kissed that mouth—my mouth, sort of—without me present.

"It wasn't like that," he protested. "It didn't count. She jammed her face against mine and—"

"Not helping!"

"Whatever. Can we have this discussion at a later point, like when we're safely in the car?" he asked, grabbing Ed's arms. "Let's get him downstairs before someone decides to come over and find out why his van has been in the driveway for so long."

Reluctantly, I scooped up Ed's feet, but I let Will take more of the weight this time, even though he was going backward. He deserved it.

"Anyway . . ." Will frowned at me like I was the one in the wrong. Please. How could he have let her kiss him knowing she wasn't me?

"I got to the house and Misty opened the door," he said, carefully negotiating his way down the first couple of steps.

It took me a second to realize he was acquiescing to my previous request and going over the events I'd missed at Misty's house.

"She seemed to know something was up with . . . Ally." He shook his head. "But she didn't say anything to me, at least not right away."

"Or maybe not. Maybe she didn't notice anything at all, since evidently we're completely interchangeable in that body anyway," I muttered, feeling the need to be a little nasty.

He looked at me pointedly, and I looked down, past Ed's feet, to see my own, flickering. Sigh. "I realize you are just trying to be helpful." Weak, in terms of a nice thing to say, but it must have worked, as I stopped flickering. For now.

"But then we walked into the kitchen," he continued, "and I saw you . . . well, I thought it was you, all cozied up with Leanne Whitaker, which was weird." He paused, waiting for me to feel my way over the edge of the first step down with my foot. "Even weirder, considering your fixation with germs."

I glared at him as I took the next step. "It's not a fixation. Do you know how many diseases you can get by sharing food?"

"No, but I bet you do," he said under his breath, struggling as he started around the curve in the stairs.

"Fine. Make fun until you . . ." I stopped, pieces clicking together in my brain, creating a horrible new picture. "Wait. Wait a minute."

Will looked up, concerned.

"I was . . ." I grimaced and corrected myself. "She was with Leanne, and Leanne was playing nice?"

He nodded.

My heart sank. "Oh, crap." I dropped Ed's feet, and gravity pulled him toward Will. Will stumbled down another couple of steps, Ed's momentum pushing him backward.

"Hey," he protested. "What are you—"

"I know where Erin is," I said grimly.

❧ 17 ❧

Will

"Y̶ou can't be sure," I said to Alona. But I was beginning to think it might be wishful thinking, rather than a rational argument, that kept me fighting.

With Ed now safely tucked into the backseat of my car—without notice from the neighbors, as far as we could tell—we were heading out of town, but Alona and I were still arguing over her assertion that she knew where Erin was, or, rather, where Erin would be. Shocking, I know.

Alona rolled her eyes. "Oh, please. It's simple deductive reasoning. Leanne wants the biggest train wreck she can find, and Erin is only too happy to oblige." She slumped back in the passenger seat.

To be fair, Alona wasn't particularly thrilled about the

possibility of being right in this instance, either. But she wasn't backing down.

"Leanne asked her to the party, just like she was talking about doing when I heard her, and Erin, in her quest to create her own personal version of Girls Gone Wild, said yes." Alona shook her head. "There's no other way this could have gone down." Though she sounded like maybe she wished there were.

Ben Rogers's back-to-school bash in the woods behind his McMansion was an annual tradition, a final good-bye for the seniors leaving for college, and this year, most likely, one last chance for skeevy Ben to hit on the vulnerable and naive underclassmen girls heading back to Groundsboro High. Yeah, he was *that* guy.

It was also, quite possibly, the worst place in the world for Erin/Lily to be, given everything that had transpired the last time Lily had been at one of Ben's parties. A humiliating and very public breakup with the king of the asshats, Rogers himself, followed by a horrible car accident. It was that accident that had sent her spirit on to the light but, in a quirk of fate, left her body damaged, though still functioning, and open to possession.

Of course, only Alona and I knew that. To the rest of the world, Lily had survived and had recently woken up unexpectedly from a nearly yearlong coma.

Which was exactly why Leanne Whitaker, gossip-monger and instigator galore, might want to engineer this particular disaster-waiting-to-happen. Everyone would be watching, if not openly mocking, the person they thought was Lily Turner, and God only knew what Erin would do in response or retaliation or by just not giving a damn about who she was supposed to be. She'd have no clue what she was walking into.

It might also be the worst conceivable place from which to rescue Lily and/or confront Erin. For Alona, it was okay. None of the partygoers would be able to see her, except for Erin. In fact, because Erin would likely be able see her—and probably deduce our plan from Alona's presence—it would be better if Alona stayed hidden until the last possible second.

But me . . . I'd be the one who'd have to march in there and try to find Erin/Lily and drag her out. Dealing with Ben and his crowd—Alona's former friends—at school was bad enough. Walking into one of their parties, though, struck me as potentially life threatening. We'd all graduated, yeah, but I wasn't stupid enough to think that the lines that had divided us and the labels that identified us had gone away overnight. In terms of social status (and cafeteria seating), this crowd was first-tier—or desperately aspiring second-tier people—and I was off the chart, and not in the good way.

Walking into an event to cause trouble, where I'd be outnumbered, oh, about fifty to one, was not something to take lightly. Especially when Ben and his ilk had shown no compunction in the past about proving their points with their fists.

The thought made me queasy.

"It's a leap, and not one I want to make unless we're sure." In addition to my own desire to survive the ordeal with the least number of broken bones possible, I also didn't want to waste time unnecessarily in the search for Erin/Lily. Alona might not have it to spare.

"You don't know them like I know them," Alona reminded me.

"Thank God for that," I muttered.

She sighed loudly over Ed's drunken snoring in the back. "I can prove it."

I snorted. "Right. How?"

She shrugged. "Call Misty."

I laughed before realizing she was serious. "You want me to call your former best friend, the current commander in chief of the snob patrol, for help? Why would she want to help us on this?" Yeah, she'd tipped me off that something was wrong with "Ally" earlier, but I wasn't sure if her generosity would stretch this far, especially if her friends—well, Leanne, at least—were heading up this scheme.

Alona glared at me, probably for the snob-patrol comment. "Because, as far as she knows, you and your strange friend 'Ally' saved her ass from me, the big, bad, evil spirit haunting her, remember?" She lifted a shoulder. "And she's not that bad."

A far cry from the evil incarnate she'd believed Misty to be only a few months ago.

"Trust me, she'll do it," she said, holding her hand out for my phone.

"What is that, exactly?" I asked, not making a move to give my phone to her.

"She'll tell us for sure whether Erin will be there tonight," she said impatiently.

I turned on to the highway, pointing us toward Decatur and Groundsboro. "And how is she going to do that? It's only eight thirty, and you said his parties don't get going until later."

"Because if Leanne is up to something, she'll brag about it to Misty. That's just the way it works," she said, in a tone that suggested I'd questioned the laws of gravity.

"Fine," I muttered. I pulled my phone from my pocket and slapped it into her palm. At least, that was the plan. What happened, though, was it slipped through her faded and flickering hand to the seat below and then bounced to the floor.

Panic lit up my insides. I swerved to the side of the road, ignoring annoyed honks from the drivers around me, and stopped on the shoulder. "Are you okay?" I asked, hurriedly putting the car in park. Behind us, Ed continued to snore peacefully.

Alona wouldn't look at me, focusing instead on the dashboard. "Just give me a second," she said.

She whispered to herself, too quietly for me to hear over the noise of passing cars, but after a long heart-stopping moment, her physicality returned, shifting her from see-through and kind of blurry to solid once more.

I bent down and retrieved the phone, resisting the urge

to ask once again if she was all right. The truth was, she wasn't, and she wouldn't be. And there was nothing she and I could do about it now, except all that we were already doing.

I silently held the phone out to her, but instead of reaching for it, she turned to stare out the window and rattled off Misty's number. It sent a chill through me, seeing her remove herself from the action, like she'd already given up in some way.

I had to have her repeat the number so I could punch it in, and as the phone started to ring on the other end, I put it on speakerphone.

"Hello?" Misty answered, in the suspicious voice of one who doesn't recognize the number on her caller ID.

"Hi, Misty, it's, uh, Will Killian. From before?" I shifted in my seat and looked at Alona for reassurance.

She waved me on, impatient, but a weak imitation of what it would have been under other circumstances.

"Yeah?" Misty sounded wary.

"I'm sorry to bother you, but I'm looking for my friend, the one who was at your house today?" I wasn't sure whether to call her Lily or Ally.

Misty huffed loudly. "Why are you asking me? She left here with you."

"I know, but—"

"And her mom has been calling over here, all freaked out about her being gone."

Crap. I'd forgotten about that.

"What did you tell her?" I asked. If she'd so much as

hinted to Mrs. Turner that Lily was going to this party . . .

"Same thing I'm going to tell you. She left with you, and I haven't seen her since." Misty's voice rose on a defensive note at the end.

I gave Alona an I-told-you-so look.

Alona shook her head. "She knows, though. She *always* knows. Leanne can't do anything without an audience."

A rustling came through from Misty's side, followed by a loud clatter and a stream of swearwords. "Look, I have to go. I'm trying to get ready and—"

I took a deep breath, banking on Alona knowing these people as well as she claimed to. "Leanne invited her to Ben's party tonight, didn't she?"

Misty sucked in a breath. "How did you know that? How do you even know there's a party?" She made it sound like I'd somehow managed to crack the complicated code surrounding their supersecret elite activities. Like I'd been blind, deaf, and dumb through four years of high school.

I ignored her words and the insult behind them. "Did Lily say she was going?"

She was quiet for a long moment, and I thought we might have lost our connection, but just as I tipped the phone up to check, Misty sighed.

"Look," she said wearily. "I don't want any part in this. This last year has been hard enough—"

Alona gave me a satisfied nod. "Told you."

"Just tell me what happened," I said to Misty.

"Leanne invited her over to pregame and to go to Ben's

party together. But I don't know if the girl's actually going. I mean, everyone's going to be there, including Ben. And they're going to make fun of her. She has to know that." Misty hesitated. "She'd have to be stupid . . . or crazy."

Neither of which we could rule out in this situation.

"Thanks, Misty." I moved to hang up.

"Wait," she said quickly. "You're not actually going to *go* to the party, are you?"

I didn't say anything; better not to give anyone forewarning. Maybe I'd be able to get in and get Erin/Lily out without notice.

"Listen, I appreciate everything you did," she said in a rush. "It helps me to know Alona is at peace."

Next to me, the girl in question rolled her eyes.

"But you have to know that going to Ben's tonight . . . that's a bad idea." She sounded almost worried. "Like, a *really* bad idea."

I grimaced. "Thanks, I'll keep that in mind," I said, and disconnected.

Unfortunately, bad ideas, really bad ideas, were the only ones we had.

❦ 18 ❧

Alona

Once we were back in Groundsboro, I gave Will directions to Ben's place, though he didn't seem to need them. It made sense, I suppose. Small town, relatively small school, and Ben's parties were the stuff of such fervent gossip that you didn't need to have actually attended one to know how to find their official sponsored location.

Not to mention the fact that about a mile from Ben's actual house we had to pass THE tree, the one Will would recognize all too well, the very same one that had gotten us into this mess. Well, that may be a slight exaggeration. This particular situation was, I suppose, more my fault for taking Lily's body than the tree's for simply existing for Lily to crash into. But still.

I stared at the tree as we drove by. It seemed like it should bear some mark of its significance—if not some other-worldly celestial glow or a giant flashing arrow over the top of it, maybe massive damage left from the crash—a sign that something tragic and important had occurred there.

But there was no glow or arrow, and if there was damage, I couldn't see it in the dark. It was just a big old tree. A flash of bark bleached white in the sweep of our headlights, and then it was gone, lost to the shadows as we made the curve Lily had missed.

"You okay?" Will asked. "You're quiet. It's kind of freaking me out."

I stuck my tongue out at him, even though he probably couldn't see that in the dim light from the dashboard. I was too tired to make more of an effort. It felt like it was taking everything I had to keep myself together . . . literally. "Just thinking."

"Why start now?"

I punched his shoulder lightly.

"It's going to be fine." He held his hand out to me.

Sure, as long our two definitions of that word were not wildly different, which I wasn't so certain of at this moment.

But I took his hand anyway, lacing my fingers between his and enjoying the sensation of security and warmth while it lasted, however long that would be.

The closer we got to Ben's house, the number of cars parked on both sides of the street, in shitty attempts at parallel parking, increased, and I could hear the distant thump of music even over the sound of the engine.

Despite everything, and I do mean everything, some part of me reacted to the familiar stimuli, and my heartbeat kicked up a notch in anxiety and anticipation. Like this was somehow permanently encoded as part of my identity. And maybe that wasn't far from the truth. Ben's parties had been as much of my school life as cheerleading or classes. I'd been going since seventh grade, though those early parties were more "seven minutes in heaven" and spiked Sprite than sexual misconduct and full-on keggers.

I'd looked forward to them with equal parts eagerness and dread. I mean, hey, who doesn't love a party? Except it was another couple of hours to be on my guard, another chance for my carefully constructed sham of a life to tumble down around me if I said or did the wrong thing, showed weakness, spoke to someone I should have ignored, or drank too much or too little.

Point of fact, I didn't drink at all. Which only added another layer of complication, actually, seeing as that was not the norm. It was another thing that had to be, if not covered up, at least not openly acknowledged so as to avoid questions. It occurred to me now, thinking about all of this, how very little of my life had been real.

It had, however, been exhausting.

And yet I remembered laughing with Misty in the kitchen at finding a chip shaped like a more-than-generous representation of the male anatomy—a silly, stupid moment, but fun—and the brief feeling of safety that came from being surrounded by my friends and followers, people I thought cared about me.

Well, I'd learned better since then, but that hadn't made the memories go away—just tainted them with a longing and nostalgia for a time that hadn't really existed.

"You're going to have to turn around to find a place to park," I said. "It's full this close to the house, and nobody's leaving yet."

"The driveway's empty," he pointed out, cocking his head toward the sweeping brick driveway. The drive was large enough for three cars across and probably four rows deep, and it had a huge circular turnaround at the far end. Ben's dad was a car dealer; what can I say?

"Yeah, Ben's rules. Something about making it less obvious where the party is being held or something." Like his neighbors weren't all too aware of that already. I suspected his dad must have bribed them. How much would it have cost for a dealer to give away a car or two, anyway?

Will's lip curled, and he cranked the wheel hard to the right, sending the car into the driveway. Then he pulled all the way up to the four-car garage and a ridiculous stone fountain they had in the center of the turnaround.

"Yeah, that's good," I said. "Subtle."

He gave a sulky shrug. Will did not like Ben. I didn't blame him, but now was not the time.

"Can you just be less of a guy right now and focus?" I let go of his hand—making myself do so swiftly and without the reluctance I felt—and reached for the door. Everyone was already at the back of the house; nobody to freak out over a door opening by itself.

Will caught my arm. "Wait, where are you going?"

"Duh. Someone has to make sure Erin's actually here before we go charging in."

"But if she sees you—"

I raised my eyebrows. "As opposed to the dozens or more who will definitely see you?"

Will released my arm with a sigh and slumped back in his seat. "Just . . . be careful."

He looked so dejected and worried I couldn't resist. I let go of the door and slid across the seat. I leaned over him, bracing myself with one hand on the center armrest and the other on his door. I was only a couple of inches from his face before he figured out what I was up to.

He sucked in a sharp breath in anticipation, and warmth spread through me. Nice that I could still provoke that reaction.

I brushed his mouth lightly with mine, focusing on the details. His familiar clean-boy-and-laundry scent and the soft friction of his lips beneath mine.

Will surprised me then, leaning forward into the kiss and lifting his hand to the back of my head to hold me closer. His mouth moved fiercely over mine, and it was like he was pouring all the words he couldn't say, all the complications we couldn't unsnarl, all his frustration and fear, into this one moment.

And I couldn't think, caught up in the taste of him, the

feel of his heat inches from me, but I couldn't touch him, not without falling . . . and I really, really wanted to. Both touch and fall.

My arms started to shake . . . No, wait, scratch that—all of me was shaking. But I didn't care. I wanted to stay here forever.

Then Ed coughed and mumbled something in his sleep from the backseat, startling both of us. I'd forgotten he was there.

I leaned back away from Will, my breathing all uneven and my heart pounding, and slowly eased back into my seat. I caught myself wondering what it would have been like to be Ally during the kiss. It had been intense as it was, but I *felt* so much more when I was her. I shivered.

Will watched me retreat with a warmth in his gaze that suggested I wasn't the only one who'd lost track of time, place, and circumstances.

I bit my lip, which felt puffy and tingly; I was so tempted to stay.

But for how long? That thought alone was enough to dump a metaphorical bucket of cold water on my overheated emotions.

I looked away from Will and fumbled for the door. "I'll be right back."

"Promise?" he asked as I climbed out.

I didn't know what to say, caught between what I wanted and what I could control. So I didn't say anything at all.

* * *

A long-established piece of wisdom from Ben's soirees was that it wasn't a party until someone was barfing in the bushes. Specifically, Mrs. Rogers's rhododendrons. Fortunately, Katee Goode was filling that role quite admirably—and kind of impressively—when I came around the corner.

Such a sophomore. I shook my head in disgust and started to walk around her, and then stopped with a sudden realization.

Katee was a *junior* now. School was starting up again in a couple of weeks. Everyone was moving on, getting older. Everyone except me.

I looked at the back of her blond head—plainly visible in the bright moonlight—bobbing above the greenery, and felt a sharp pang of envy. Katee would, in theory, put in another two years at Groundsboro and move on to college and then the rest of her life, where this moment would be a distant memory. She had her whole life ahead of her. I did not.

I felt my nails dig into my palms as I clenched my hands in fists. I, who'd never envied anybody anything—except maybe Lily for her family—envied the girl upchucking in the underbrush? No way.

It was pathetic.

Anyone dumb enough to come here and get that wasted, especially alone—a very sophomore, third-tier move—did not deserve to be envied.

Maybe. Maybe not. But it didn't change how I felt.

I sighed and kept walking.

Ben's backyard looked like it had at all the other parties

I'd attended here. The food—chips of assorted varieties in plastic bowls, and pizza that was already mostly gone—was laid out on several card tables.

The keg was probably just inside the tree line at the back of the property, based on the steady flow of red-cup-carrying partyers coming and going from that general direction.

Most people had gathered on the open grass between the deck and the woods, dancing, talking in small clusters, and generally stumbling around. The outdoor floodlights were on, and someone, Ben probably, had stabbed the ground with those tacky bamboo torches at varying intervals throughout the yard. The flickering flames cast wild shadows across the faces of those standing near them. Music thumped hard from huge speakers near the deck—someone's iPod was plugged in, churning through a party mix that was mostly bass and nothing recognizable at that volume.

I spotted my friends—former friends, actually—sprinkled throughout the yard. Misty and Chris didn't seem to be here yet—no surprise there, as Misty was always late for everything. But Ashleigh Hicks and Jennifer Meyer were dancing together near the deck in a manner probably intended to be provocative. Unfortunately, it came off more like creepy and awkward, given their matching outfits (as always) of short navy skirts and blue-and-white-striped shirts and their wildly disparate body types. Jennifer was a good five inches taller than Ashleigh. Also, they looked kind of like slutty sailors from the 1970s.

Jeff Parker, the intended audience for said sexy dancing,

was paying no attention, his head bent over his guitar, and an adorable underclassman girl standing next to him, asking about the guitar or playing or something. Ha, good for him. I'd always liked Jeff—he was less likely to participate in our bullshit. At least he hadn't openly mocked me after my death. Unlike some people . . .

Miles Stevens stood off to one side, watching. He was spiffily dressed as usual, in a long-sleeved dress shirt and khakis, despite the lingering August heat. I couldn't be sure from this distance, but I was willing to bet that, thanks to me, his nerdwear was now designer.

And Leanne was next to Miles, staring out at the crowd with him and likely whispering catty comments in his ear. But where was Erin/Lily? I didn't see her near them.

My heart sank. Maybe she wasn't here after all. She'd be near Leanne, the only person she knew, wouldn't she?

I moved closer for a better look, skirting the edge of the crowd and weaving my way through the tiki torches. It wasn't until I was within a few feet of Leanne that I realized she wasn't watching the crowd in general but was focused quite intently on someone or something. Her eyes were bright with spite and amusement . . . not to mention something that looked an awful lot like loathing.

And she wasn't the only one watching whatever or whoever it was. In fact, a good majority of the people on this side of the party appeared to be enjoying the same spectacle, pointing and giggling and whispering and . . .

Oh, God. I froze, afraid to turn around. Only one

person made Leanne's eyes glow with hatred like that—Ben Rogers. Ben and Leanne had hooked up freshman year, and when he'd dumped her, she'd never quite gotten over it. Any chance she could find to cause chaos for him—and get a laugh from it—would be an opportunity she'd take. But his presence alone wouldn't have been enough to trigger much notice from Leanne or the partygoers. It was, after all, his party. Of course he would be here. Most likely surrounded by whatever drunken or stupid girls he could find . . .

And suddenly I was terrified that I knew exactly who one of them would be.

Let's be clear: I never expected the Erin/Lily-at-Ben's-party scenario to be *good*. I had heard enough from Erin to know that if she was here, she was looking for debauchery at its finest. Or worst. Whatever. Combine that with people thinking she was Lily and remembering what had gone down at the last party she'd attended, and we were already in uncharted levels of nasty.

But I have to confess, when I finally convinced myself to turn around and see what everyone else was seeing just fifteen feet from me, I never expected it to be *this* bad. Erin/Lily was wrapped around Ben Rogers like he was a stripper pole. Dark lipstick—*not* a flattering color or the one I'd picked out for Ally—was smeared across her face; her top bore a huge wet spot from beer she must have spilled down the front of it; and she had grass stains on her jeans from where she'd probably fallen. She was also somehow missing a shoe. But that wasn't the worst part. No. The worst—*oh, sweet Lord*—was her sticking her tongue so far down Ben's throat I half expected it to be poking through the back of his head.

And all of it while wearing MY face and MY body. Well, a face and a body I still thought of as my own; I'd seen them in the mirror every day for over a month.

I gagged first—oh, so many germs; I couldn't even think about what was living in Ben Rogers's mouth—and then a flash of fury swept over me, burning everything away, including common sense.

The smart thing would have been to turn around before Erin noticed me, go back to the car to talk it over with Will, and come up with some kind of plan to get her out of here . . . or at least away from everyone else.

Right.

"You stupid bitch." The words flew out of my mouth in a shriek, like I had no control, and in that moment, I didn't. So much for doing the smart thing.

Erin heard me, even over the music, and looked around, dazed and startled. But she still kept her hold on Ben.

Unacceptable.

My vision blurry with rage, I threw myself past Leanne and collided with Erin/Lily, hard. She needed to learn. You do not mess with me. Any version of me. Past, present, or possible.

❧ 19 ❧

Will

Ed woke up with a snort seconds after Alona slammed the door shut. The two events were probably not unrelated.

It seemed to take him a few seconds to orient himself in the world again. In the rearview mirror, I watched as he sat up slowly, one hand holding his head and the other reaching out to touch the roof of the car, as if he wasn't sure it was real.

He belched in that alarming fashion that often precedes major stomach evacuation. "Where am I?" he whispered, more to himself than me.

I turned in my seat to get a better look at him. "About to get kicked out of my car if you're thinking about puking."

He squinted at me. "Hey, I know you." He gave me a

wobbly, still-drunk smile. "You're that kid who sees ghosts. Lots and lots of ghosts . . ." His smile faded as more details returned to him. "You were at my parents' house." He cocked his head to one side. "But they weren't there. The place was empty. . . ." He sniffed loudly.

I shifted uncomfortably. "Yeah, look, I'm sorry about—"

"Where are we?" Still holding his head, he leaned forward to stare out the windshield, most likely at the brick monstrosity that was Ben's house.

I took a deep breath. Of course Alona would not be here for this conversation. She was much better at being . . . well, blunt. That was probably the nicest term for it. Insensitive, occasionally mean, brutally honest—those were probably more accurate. And exactly what we needed in this situation. "We're trying to find your sister."

"Erin is here?"

"Maybe." I glanced back toward the side of the house, where Alona had disappeared. By now she'd reached the party and was probably searching. Given the chaos that Ben's parties were reported to induce, it might take her a few minutes to determine whether Erin was there and then to report back. "We're trying to find out."

He rubbed a hand over his face. "You said . . . you said she had a body." He sounded vulnerable and uncertain, like he wasn't sure if he was remembering correctly, or like he was afraid that he'd somehow incorporated an unrelated drunken dream into reality.

I grimaced. *And here we go* . . . "Yeah, she took the body

of a friend of mine." True, regardless of circumstance. "And we need your help to get her out."

"No," he said, as firmly as before. "If what you're saying is true, then I—"

"Yeah, yeah, you owe her, it's all your fault. Got it," I said impatiently. "We covered that. But you need to listen to me." I twisted around in my seat to face him, hoping that would help him understand the gravity of the situation. "It's not just your life that this is messing with. There is a whole family affected by her actions. Whether she gives a shit about them or not." Alona, to her credit, had done her best to keep that in mind, at least.

He shook his head and opened his mouth to speak, but I cut him off. "And here's the truth: you have got to own up to this, man. If you want to believe it's your fault because you let her go to the party alone, fine."

He winced.

"But neither one of you is moving on until you deal. She is here because of you. Because *you* are keeping her here." That was, in fact, a guess on my part. But it made sense. The two of them had been so tied together in life, it would follow that it would also be the case in death.

He looked up sharply.

"Yeah, you." Based on my admittedly limited interactions with Erin, she didn't seem to have a specific reason for sticking around, other than to live more—and what ghost wouldn't want that? And frankly, Edmund could *see* her, when he'd had no previous capacity to do so. That had to mean something, didn't it?

Once again, it would have been so much easier if this job came with labels and a how-to manual; but no matter what, in this situation, I had to go with my instincts and hope they were enough. Even if Alona didn't want to be—or couldn't be—Ally again, I couldn't leave Erin in Lily's body. I just . . . couldn't.

"It's better than her not existing," Ed muttered.

I took a deep breath, struggling to hang on to my patience. For most people, this was new territory, and Ed didn't have the advantage of years of seeing ghosts and the in-between world. "It was an accident, a horrible accident. But there's nothing you can do to change that now."

He shook his head.

"There was nothing you could have done, even if you'd been there," I said, getting exasperated. "They said it was a freak thing. The drop off the porch roof was only about eight feet into bushes and stuff. She probably would have survived if they hadn't put that walkway in, like, that afternoon."

Ed looked up. "What?" He seemed paler suddenly, even in the dim light.

Finally I was getting to him. "She fell off the porch roof," I repeated. "And she probably would have been okay, maybe a broken bone or two, except there were these paving stones piled up from them putting in a walkway earlier that afternoon. She hit her head just right, apparently."

Ed flopped back into his seat with a dazed expression. Apparently this was news to him. Not all that surprising, I supposed, given that he probably hadn't been prone to reading articles about her accident back when it had happened.

Maybe knowing there was nothing he could have done was all he'd needed.

Encouraged, I tried to return to my original point, the one I'd attempted to make way back at Ed's parents' house. "If you can let her go, it will be better for both of you. It's true that, to you, she wouldn't exist anymore. But this is not the end. At least, it doesn't have to be."

He turned his head and stared out the window, but at least he wasn't arguing. That was an improvement.

"You can't let her run you, man. It's bad for both of you. You'll still be alive, but you'll be a shadow of what you're supposed to be." I knew that from experience, always living in fear of the ghosts cornering me. Having Alona as my spirit guide had helped, but until today, when I'd finally stood up to the dead on my own, I hadn't realized how much it had weighed on me. I felt freer than I had in . . . well, forever.

I was about to launch into my the-light-exists-and-it-is-awesome speech when the music from the party paused, a three-second gap between songs, and I heard shrieking from somewhere behind the house. It was loud enough for me to hear it clearly even in the car, but not distinct enough to understand the words.

I did, however, recognize the voice and the note of outrage in it. *Alona.*

My chest contracted in fear. She was in trouble. "Crap." I scrambled out of the car without waiting to see if Ed followed.

* * *

As should be obvious to just about anyone by now, I've never been to one of Rogers's shindigs, nor have I ever had the desire to attend.

Still, it kind of surprised me, after rounding the corner at a run, to find it so . . . ordinary, at first glance. Nobody was snorting cocaine off anybody else's chest. That I could see. Instead, the yard was filled with intoxicated people hanging out, eating chips, and listening to really crappy music. It could have been a night from the old days of me and my few friends hanging out, except it was outside, with about a hundred more people, and, well, our music hadn't sucked.

It was kind of a letdown after all the hype, frankly.

Then, of course, I noticed that, despite the so-called music, no one was dancing. Most everyone was crowded around the open space between the deck and the woods, watching something.

I bet I knew what, too. The shrieking had stopped, but I could hear the occasional shouted word or grunt. Definitely Alona and Erin.

I lowered my head and started to shove my way through the crowd.

"She's having a seizure or something," someone whispered as I passed.

"Get her off me. Do something!" Lily's husky voice held an uncharacteristic whine, and she sounded out of breath.

"No, dude. She's, like, crazy or something," another genius declared.

I elbowed through the last layer of my former classmates

and tormentors and arrived to find, pretty much as I'd expected, Alona and Erin/Lily grappling for position and rolling around on the ground. To the crowd, though, it looked simply like Lily was throwing herself around for no reason.

Leanne Whitaker stood off to one side, doubled over with laughter. Some of Alona's former cheerleading cronies looked vaguely concerned . . . or maybe vague was how they looked all the time. Ben watched impassively, like it was something on television that was maybe a little annoying but mostly boring.

Asshole.

None of them could see Alona, of course, but they could see a girl in obvious distress of some kind. And not a one of them had made a move to help.

Erin as Lily already looked fairly messed up, her lipstick smeared everywhere and her clothes dirty. But Alona was in worse shape, her body shifting between solid and see-through, like someone caught in the transporter beams on one of those old *Star Trek* episodes.

Jesus.

I darted forward and grabbed Alona's shoulder. She was, for the moment, on top. "Hey, stop it!"

She twisted to look up at me, startled but with fury still stamped across her features, like she might lash out at me for interrupting.

"Look at yourself," I whispered to her.

She glanced down and stiffened in shock.

Erin/Lily laid her head on the ground and laughed with the abandon that comes with relief and total drunkenness. "Tol' you," she slurred.

Fabulous.

Alona looked back at me with panic.

"Just stay calm," I told her, trying to follow my own advice. Clearly, our original plan was blown to hell. And now I didn't know if Alona had enough strength to continue existing, let alone routing Erin from Lily's body. I never should have let her go in ahead of me.

At the moment, I was torn between the urge to grab Alona and haul her out of there to someplace safe—which, of course, was an illusion in this situation, given that the threat of disappearing was not something that could be escaped by changing location—and kneeling down to help hold Erin so Alona could try to transfer in right then and there, if she wanted.

But as it turns out, I didn't get a chance to do either.

"Will Kill?" Ben asked in disbelief and disgust from behind me.

I froze. *Shit.*

I forced myself to turn in his direction. I didn't want him coming at my blind side.

He stumbled a step or two toward me, and I had to fight the urge to move back. "Who invited you?" he demanded.

It didn't take much imagination to see Ben as a mean drunk.

"Stay calm," Alona murmured. "He's wasted."

Oh, good, so he wouldn't even feel it if I managed to hit him.

My heart pounding, I held my hands up. I was so very outnumbered here. It was worse than even that one time I'd gone into the first-tier section to talk to Alona. Add alcohol and I wasn't sure what the results would be this time. Worse than a black eye, that was for sure. "I'm just here to get my friend."

Ben snorted. "Should have known, crazy attracts crazy."

Absurdly, someone in the crowd actually did that *ooooh* sound, as though Ben had come up with some kind of magnificent burn instead of pretty much making up a nonsensical statement that contained only the insult of calling me crazy, which everyone had already assumed anyway. Whatever.

Alona yelped suddenly, and I turned to see that Erin/Lily had taken advantage of our distraction and scrambled out from underneath Alona and was running for the woods, her bad leg slowing her down only slightly.

If she got away now, we might never be able to find her again. I lurched after her, but Ben grabbed my arm.

"Where do you think you're going, man? We're having a conversation."

Alona rose to her feet unsteadily, still flickering. I yanked my arm free of Ben's grasp and focused on her.

She tipped her head to one side to look at me, her hair gleaming in the torchlight and her eyes bright with unshed tears. She reached out and touched my face, her fingers alternating between warm and solid, and cold and barely there.

And I knew this was good-bye.

I shook my head mutely, tears welling. "Don't."

"Are you going to cry, Will Kill?" Ben demanded.

She leaned in to me, pressed her cheek against mine, and whispered, "Be careful," then slipped away before I could grab her.

"No!" I started after her, but Ben stepped around to block me. I caught a glimpse of her passage through the crowd, people moving involuntarily away from a strange cold spot near them. But then she was gone, beyond the reach of the lights, and into the shadow of the woods.

"We're not done talking about how you crashed my party, freak," Ben said, giving me a shove. Others behind him—ambitious juniors, the new seniors now—circled in anticipation, beer fueling their need to prove something.

Suddenly I was weary. Tired of all this stupid posturing and bullshit when more important things—life-and-death matters—were going on.

I sighed. "Look, high school is over. And if you weren't such a dickhead, you'd know that. We're just people now, okay? All of us. And you're not any better than—"

That's when he punched me. Hard.

❧ 20 ❧

Alona

It hurt more than I'd thought, leaving Will behind. I didn't want to do this alone. I didn't want to die again . . . alone.

I shoved those thoughts away, forcing myself to focus on the task at hand. Finding Erin.

Fortunately, even in the dark, it wasn't that difficult. The moonlight was pretty bright . . . and she was crashing through the underbrush like a lovesick elephant.

"It's called grace, and maybe a little coordination," I muttered when I heard her hit the ground with a thud.

I paused for a second to catch my breath—it would take her longer to get back up and going again—and leaned forward, my hands on my knees. Unfortunately, I could see right through my lower half to the tree behind me, down to the detail on the bark.

With effort, I tried to shift to thinking happy thoughts. Mrs. Turner lighting up at the prospect of a shopping trip with her daughter. Will smiling at me. Will's hand in mine. The way he would argue with me, not afraid to push back.

So many of them were related to Will and the last few months. Well, it kind of made sense. I hadn't really lived until after I'd died, in some ways.

But this time, focusing on the positive didn't seem to make any difference. I could still see through me. Which meant this was it.

I took a deep breath, feeling surprisingly calm at the idea. But there was one more thing I had to take care of.

I rallied my flagging strength and pushed myself forward to where I'd last heard Erin.

As expected, she was just picking herself up off the ground.

I folded my arms across my chest, hoping it made me look more imposing, which is, frankly, a tough feat when you're mostly invisible. "Erin."

She spun around, startled, and nearly fell down again.

Good grief.

"What are you doing here?" she asked, wobbling until she regained her balance.

Evidently she hadn't heard me following her amid all the noise she was making. Shocking.

I huffed impatiently. "You know why I'm here."

She laughed, swaying. How much had she had to drink?

"Nope, not yet," she declared. "Not done with my turn

yet." She swiped her hands down her front, succeeding in removing some dead leaves and twigs.

I stalked toward her, closing the distance between us. "This isn't a game."

She stepped back warily. "Maybe not to you."

"It shouldn't be to you either, stupid." Oops, there I went being negative again. Guess it didn't matter now. "Where do you think you're going to go?"

She glanced over her shoulder, deeper into the woods. "There's got to be a through street or a highway or something . . . eventually."

"Not like that." I rolled my eyes. "I mean, you've been hanging around in the in-between for five years. How much longer do you think it will last? Another five years? Five days? All I can tell you is it won't be forever, and it's way less now that you're blowing through energy carrying her around." I nodded toward her appropriated body.

"You're lying."

"Nope, I'm not. I was in there once, remember? And look at me now." I gestured down at the vague outline of my body.

Her eyes narrowed. "You're only saying that because you want me out so you can take over again."

"You honestly think I'm going to be able to do much of anything like this?" It pained me to admit that to her.

Her smug look returned. "Then I guess we're done here." But then she hiccuped, destroying what I'm sure she imagined was a triumphant moment.

I sighed. "Not even. Look, the girl whose body you're wearing, she has a family."

"So?"

"So . . ." I resisted the urge to add "you jerk," because I wanted to have the time to finish the conversation. "She's not a plaything. She's a real person with people who care about her. You can't just waltz around as her, doing whatever you want. They're worried about her. Thinking she's run off or been kidnapped or something."

In fact, the image of Mrs. Turner hunched by the phone waiting for news, as she'd once sat by Lily's bedside, waiting for her daughter to show some sign of life, killed me. I hated that I wouldn't get to thank her, however indirectly, for all she'd done for me, even though she believed it was for her daughter. She . . . cared. Really cared. And it was, well, a nice experience, if an unfamiliar one.

Erin waved a dismissive hand. "Like you bothered with that when you were her."

I gritted my teeth. "I did, actually."

"Why?" she asked, sounding genuinely surprised. "What's the point?"

"The point is that in death, just like in life, not everything is about you!" The words exploded out of my mouth before I had time to consider them, and when I did . . . I found I believed them.

Huh.

"Everyone is struggling in their own way," I said, trying to find the words to convince her, to make her understand.

"Whether you can see it or not. If you can't make things better, you have an obligation to try, at least, not to make them suck more. Got it?"

"Who says?" she demanded. "God or something?"

"I don't know," I said wearily. I could feel my energy fading, whispering in my ear that I should stop fighting and lie down. "How about human decency?"

Erin opened her mouth to protest, but I held up my hand. "All I'm saying is your choices will come back on you. Trust me." I sat down at the base of the nearest tree and leaned against the trunk, feeling a small measure of relief.

Erin eyed me with a frown. "But I didn't get my chance," she said in a small voice.

"Yeah. You did," I said. "And you blew it by limboing a little too close to the edge. Sucks to be you."

She glared at me.

"But the point is that if you're determined to stick with this . . . with her"—I gestured at her body—"you still have the opportunity to do the right thing for someone else. A family who never did anything to you, who never cost you any portion of your life."

She grimaced.

Yeah. Having a corporeal form was way less of a party when you had to think of other people's feelings. *Ha. Welcome to my world.*

"Erin?"

She looked up startled, and I turned around to see Ed, the moonlight reflecting sharply off his glasses, stumbling through the brush toward us. Great.

"Ed? What are you doing here?" She took a step toward him and then remembered my presence and held her ground, perhaps afraid I'd take a swipe at her ankle when she walked by. And . . . who knows? I might have, if I could've summoned the effort.

He stopped a few feet away, putting me in between them, and cocked his head to one side. "Is that really you in there?"

"How did you find me?" she asked, unfolding her arms and then refolding them, as if she didn't know quite what to do with her body in this situation.

I could imagine. She was a twin, probably used to looking at Ed and seeing some version of herself. Not anymore. He towered over her.

"I followed you from the party," he said, studying her as if he wasn't sure what he was seeing.

She sighed. "When you bashed your head on the coffee table because I was chasing you—"

"—you told Mom it was the dog," he said grimly.

"Satisfied?" she asked with a smirk.

"What is . . . What are you doing?" He frowned.

She brushed herself off again. "Like it? It's a new look."

I groaned. "Were you even listening to anything I said?" I demanded.

She scowled at me and then returned her attention to her brother. "Well?"

"Who is she?" he asked finally, nodding at her body.

She jerked back, obviously not expecting that question. "What?"

"I mean, who is it?" he asked, sounding exhausted, like he'd been having this conversation, or some type of it, for years.

"It's . . . it's me." She gave a nervous laugh. "We covered that already, remember?"

He didn't say anything.

"Oh, come on, Eddie, don't be such a pain. What's the big deal? This is good for all of us," she said pleadingly. "I can have the life I missed out on, and you don't have to blame yourself anymore. I'm making things better, for both of us."

So, clearly, nothing I'd said had stuck with her.

"So this is your solution, to take what you want, just like always?" His voice was deceptively calm, but even I could hear the thread of anger running beneath the surface.

Apparently, so could Erin. "I don't have to listen to this." She turned away, pointing her nose up in indignation, but she stumbled and fell again when she tried to stalk off.

"I am sorry," Ed said in a clear, calm, angry tone.

She looked over her shoulder at him, her eyes wide with panic.

"I should have gone with you," he said, "if only to keep you from hurting yourself."

"What are you doing? Stop it. We don't talk about this." She scrambled to her feet. "We never talk about this!" She sounded outraged and maybe a little afraid.

"But the truth is, I was tired of always doing what you

said, and I was starting to think for myself. And you knew it." He advanced on her, drawing even with me. "You were losing control over me, and you wanted to punish me for it."

"No." She shook her head. "It was an accident!" Despite the anger in her voice, Erin was crying. I could hear her sniffling. I sympathized. I didn't know what Erin was like, but Lily was a crier, for sure. In that body, there was no way around it. Angry, happy, sad, surprised, Lily would sob through it all.

"It wasn't. Want to know how I know?" Ed demanded. "You're afraid of heights," he continued without waiting for an answer. "I could never figure out why you were on that roof in the first place. The only reason you would have gone up there was to prove something. I thought it was to those other people, the frat guys and whoever, but they wouldn't have known what it meant for you to do that, would they? But I did."

"It was an accident," she repeated. "I slipped and—"

"No." Ed shook his head vehemently. "This is just like all those other times: Cub Scouts, the science fair, prom. I wasn't playing along, so you did whatever you thought it would take. A few bumps and bruises from a tumble off a roof, and you knew I'd make damned sure you didn't go to another party alone, even if it meant sitting in a corner all night while you ran around talking to people."

Holy crap. Erin had done this to herself? By accident, it sounded like, but still . . . that was hard-core.

"You didn't mean to kill yourself," Ed continued, "but—"

"Of course not!" she shouted, her fists clenched at her sides. "It's your fault that I'm like this." She gestured down at herself, and I had to assume she meant being dead rather than being in Lily's body. The latter was all on her. "If you'd come with me, the way I'd asked you, the way you were supposed to, then none of this would have happened. But oh, no, Edmund always has to be difficult. Never mind what I'm trying to do for us."

"I didn't want to be somebody new, talking about keg stands and frat parties. I liked who we were," he said.

"We were losers!" she snapped. "I was trying to make us better, but you're so selfish—"

"As selfish as hurting yourself to get other people to do what you want?" he demanded.

She threw her hands up in frustration. "Like I had a choice!"

"There is always a choice!" he shouted back at her. Then he stopped, visibly making an effort to calm himself. "You made yours, and I'm making mine. You have owned me for the last five years. You let me torture myself with guilt for something *you* did. But I'm done. This is *my* life, and I want to live it."

Uh-oh. I could sense some kind of change looming, like a charge in the air around us. I would have spoken up in warning, but suddenly it felt like too much effort. I didn't bother to look down to check the progress of my disappearance. It wasn't like it was going to be getting any better, right?

Erin seemed to sense the shift, too. She looked truly

scared for the first time, and stepped toward her twin, her hands out in a placating gesture. "Eddie, wait, listen. It wasn't like that."

He looked at her in a cool, evaluating way that actually made me feel a little sympathy for her. "I'm sorry you're dead, and I'm sure I'll miss you . . . eventually."

Oh, ouch.

She flinched.

He took a deep breath and tilted his face toward the dark sky above us. "I'm letting her go. She doesn't need to be here for me anymore," he declared.

A chill slid over my skin at his words. He and Will must have had another chat after I'd left the car.

"Edmund!" Erin shrieked, her hands flying up over her head as if to fend off some invisible force from above.

But nothing happened. At first.

Then her eyes rolled back, and she collapsed . . . or, rather, Lily's body fell to the ground. And standing above it was the whisper-thin outline of Erin in her original form, barely visible in the bright moonlight. The pink of her bikini was a mere hint of color in her rapidly fading appearance.

He'd released her, completed his unfinished business with her, and now she was disappearing, her energy depleted from possessing Lily's body.

What was left of Erin, more shadow than person, stepped toward her brother, but he looked away.

She glanced around wildly until she spotted me. *Help me,* she mouthed.

I shook my head, which felt like it weighed about thirty pounds. I could have told her to try to claim her brother, as I'd reclaimed Will, but I wasn't sure it would work. Same with trying a barrage of positive thoughts and comments. Eventually she'd have ended up right where I was . . . vanishing for good.

"This is it." I forced the words out. "Last chance. One more opportunity to make the right choice."

She rolled her eyes.

I made a frustrated noise. "You don't get it. You go this way and there's nothing else. Gone for good."

Erin's eyes widened.

"So, don't be a dumbass," I said wearily. But to be honest, I thought this was a bit of a long shot. After all, I was disappearing, too—a little slower, thanks to my connection with Will, but it was still happening. And the light hadn't come for me. What were the odds that it would come for her, even if she did manage to pull the stick out of her butt and say the right thing to her brother?

We were both screwed, most likely. But if she could make Ed's existence slightly better before she went, that could only help.

She shifted her attention to her twin, who still was not looking at her.

I'm sorry. I could see the words flash across her mouth, but of course he couldn't hear them. He didn't even glance—didn't see her making the effort.

And that finally seemed to spark a sense of panic in her.

She flailed her arms around in front of him, her lips moving in a rapid stream of words.

But her brother remained oblivious, half turned away from her.

"Oh, come on," I said to him, knowing he couldn't hear me, but unable to resist the urge to say *something*. "Look at her." It would have been one thing for her to try and fail anyway, but for her to try and have him not even be aware of it? That wasn't fair to either of them.

She stopped jumping around and shouting, then, to stare at him, her focus almost palpable.

Yeah, like that was going to work.

But to my surprise, after only a few seconds, he turned swiftly, almost as if he didn't realize he was moving until it was too late to stop, and their gazes locked. For the first time, I recognized clear similarities between them.

He was older now, of course, so they looked more like regular siblings than twins. But their hair color, the shape of their faces . . . I could see it now.

I'm sorry. I didn't mean to . . . She mouthed the words, slowly and distinctly, but her gaze conveyed desperation.

The cynic in me kind of thought this probably had way more to do with her panic over her own state than with some intense desire to make everything right with her brother.

But then she reached out to touch his arm, even though that wasn't possible, and I felt a strange kind of pressure in the air, like a bubble pushing us outward. Then, a very familiar warmth and brightness began to spill from above.

No. No way. My gut twisted in shock and disappointment. *Son of a bitch.* She *gets light?*

Erin stepped back in surprise, her body tensed as if she were about to bolt. But I saw it the moment that rush of warmth washed over her. Her appearance solidified, taking on the glow of the light, and she relaxed with a smile, virtually swimming in her newly found peace and acceptance. And I wished I could hit her.

Squinting into the light, Ed held his hand up over his eyes, tears leaving bright tracks down his cheeks.

I was pretty sure I was crying, too, though more out of fury and bitterness. I was being left behind again. Even after everything I'd done. *Quelle surprise.*

Ed watched the unnatural brightness slowly pouring down, like honey from a jar, and he stepped forward quickly, as though he might try to go with. "Erin!"

But she held her hand out to stop him and gave him an all-knowing, peaceful smile, one that suggested she'd reached some new insight on her life (and death) in those few seconds. Or maybe just being in the light made everything else seem less important by comparison. I didn't know—most of my memories of my time in the light were gone.

As I watched, Erin waved good-bye to her brother.

Ed seemed to be barely holding it together, based on the way his shoulders were shaking, but he managed to wave back.

Then I looked on with wholehearted envy as Erin stepped back fully into the light, her face tilted up to bask in the warmth I barely remembered.

Her form grew brighter until it blended with the light and vanished.

Choking on sobs, Ed turned and fled, leaving me alone with Lily's crumpled body.

I sighed. Or tried to. No noise came out. I felt a spike of panic. It seemed I was only seconds behind Erin on her previous path to disappearance, and the light sure as hell wasn't going to appear over my head to beam *me* up at the last second.

Except . . .

The light hadn't retreated yet, I realized with a start. Unlike my previous encounters with it, the light was lingering, a golden and welcoming column only a few feet away. Like it was waiting for something.

For me? Hope pulsed through me. Was it even possible?

I was afraid to move, like if I did anything to attract its attention, it might vanish . . . again.

With trepidation, I dragged myself a few inches forward, testing; but to my surprise, it didn't pull back.

If anything, it moved closer . . . or perhaps it simply expanded until the outer edge reached me.

I felt its warmth and strength seeping into me, and I almost cried out with relief. I looked down and saw my body returning, filling in and becoming solid again, only this time with a glow that I recognized as part of the light.

Pushing myself to crawl again, I discovered it was easier than before, like I might be able to stand soon and walk into the light.

After a few feet, I paused to listen, trying to identify a new sound that was still somehow familiar. Harsh, raspy, uneven.

I looked over and found myself next to Lily's body. She was flipped over on her side, her arm dangling limply, and without Erin, she was, as expected, dying. That new sound was her struggling for breath.

I froze even in the outer reaches of that eternal warmth, uncertain what to do. Without me, Lily would die. No question. But I was being offered the chance I'd been waiting for. The light was here. For me, this time.

I craved the light like the air I'd once needed to breathe, as Lily still did, and this close to it, I felt it pulling at me as if it were a home I'd never known and yet missed desperately.

But I was being offered a choice here, wasn't I? And there had to be a reason for that. . . . Right?

Maybe. I sat back on my knees in frustration.

It was always about choices, just like I'd told Erin. But how was I supposed to know what the right one was in this scenario?

I got the sense that this choice—to stay or go—might have been one I'd struggled with before. It held a vague and misty sense of familiarity that surrounded everything I remembered—or didn't—about the light. Was it possible that I hadn't been *sent* back but had *chosen* to come back, of my own free will? I'd never understood why I couldn't remember the peace of being in the light. I'd thought maybe the removal of those memories was part of the punishment that sent me back to the living. But if I'd chosen to return, then maybe not remembering the light—and the bliss I'd likely experienced while there—was actually a kindness.

But even if that was what had happened before, it didn't help me now, faced with *this* decision.

"Fan-freaking-tastic," I muttered. "Like you can't give me a hint here? Like that would kill you?"

But the light remained warm, welcoming, and silent; and the girl next to me continued dying.

I sighed. "Of course not. That might actually make this easier." I wished I could talk to Will one last time before . . . well, just before.

❦ 21 ❦

Will

"**H**ey! Are you really this stupid?" A female voice demanded from somewhere nearby.

For a second, from my position on the ground, with my face buried in the grass and dirt and blood, I thought it was Alona speaking to me. And while I agreed that getting whaled on wasn't the smartest thing I'd ever done, it wasn't like I could stop it. I'd gotten in a few good swings, but not enough. Not nearly enough. Again, that's what happened when you were outnumbered sixteen to one.

"Hey!" she said again, and the pummeling paused momentarily.

"He's gate-crashing," Ben said, out of breath. *Sorry that beating the crap out of me winded you so badly, dude. I* wanted to crawl away, but everything ached too much to move. Breathing hurt. I settled for turning my head so I could at least see what was coming next. My new world-view showed me Misty Evans standing above me, a red cup clenched in her hand, and her boyfriend, Chris Zebrowski, at her side. Misty was my defender? That didn't make any sense. But she had stopped Ben, temporarily at least, which struck me (no pun intended) as a good thing regardless.

"He came after that other freak, that Lily girl." Ben's voice held a chilling amount of contempt, like he'd never once thought of Lily with affection.

"Apparently, you didn't think she was all that freaky a few minutes ago," Misty snapped, and a few people tittered.

Oh. Oh, no, Erin, what did you do? If she'd been all over Ben, that, at least, would have explained Alona's deviation from the plan and her no-holds-barred attack on Erin.

"What do you want, Evans?" Ben swiped the back of his hand at the blood dripping from his nose. Yeah, I'd done that. I might have felt pride, if I had been capable of feeling more than anything but hurt and kind of broken.

"How about starting college without a criminal record?" she demanded. "Do you remember what happened the last time that chick got into trouble at one of your parties? Cops everywhere."

A murmur spread through the crowd, as though this was the first time they'd considered the possibility of law-enforcement intervention. Dumbasses. Just because Ben was invincible on school grounds didn't mean the same concept applied here.

"And beating *him* up is going to help how?" Misty continued, in that same pushy tone I recognized from Alona. "You're just making it worse for yourself. All he has to do is tell the police he came in to get her and you attacked him."

The crowd murmur grew louder, and Ben, ever the experienced host, looked around and saw his party on the brink of breaking up in a panic. He shook his head and spat on the ground next to me in disgust. "Whatever." He kicked at my leg, but since he lacked most of his previous force, it was more for show than anything else. "Get her and get out."

He turned and walked away. "We're not going to let them spoil our party!" he shouted to his audience. "Time to tap a fresh one!"

A celebratory cry went up from those standing around me, and the crowd began to dissipate, without anyone giving me a second glance, let alone checking to see if I was okay. The show was over, and I had all the significance of a discarded prop.

Above me, Misty gave Chris a gentle shove to follow Ben, but instead of going along with him, as I expected, she paused for a quick second and scanned me from head to toe, like she was checking for broken bones poking out.

"Thanks," I managed to mumble. Misty had saved my ass. I could maybe see now why Alona had stuck by her, even after Misty did what she had done with Chris.

For a long moment she didn't respond, and then she

nodded at me. It was barely noticeable—in case anyone was watching, obviously—but it was there. Then she strolled away, beer cup in hand and shrieking a high-pitched greeting to one of her fellow cheerleaders across the yard.

In Misty's mind, we were even now. Fair enough.

I rolled to my side and the pain made me catch my breath, but I pushed myself up to my knees and then slowly to my feet. Taking stock, I could feel countless bruises and scrapes, and from the sharp pain on my left side every time I inhaled and exhaled, I was betting on cracked ribs. I could, however, still breathe, so probably not a punctured lung or anything.

Goody. Yay me.

I raised my gaze to the tree line in the distance, attempting to steel myself for the walk to find Alona and Erin, wherever they'd disappeared to (and with Alona's situation I could only pray that wasn't literally the case) and froze when I got a good look at the woods.

The light—bright, warm, and glorious—reached above the treetops in a gleaming column. It had come for someone. Erin . . . or Alona?

Or both?

Would Alona be gone before I even got a chance to say good-bye? A real good-bye? One last kiss and the chance to tell her that she'd made my life better even as she'd made me crazy? That we were better together than I would ever be by myself, but that because of her, I would be okay? Not great, but okay, and I owed that all to her?

No. I *needed* to see her one last time.

My eyes hot and stinging, I pressed my hand against my ribs in an attempt to keep them from being jostled, and took off in a limping run.

I'd barely crossed into the woods and passed a few drunken couples who hadn't bothered to retreat to Ben's house for one-on-one time when Ed came charging out and nearly slammed into me.

"What are you doing?" I asked, astonished to see him out here. I hadn't seen him leave the car after me, but he must have.

He was crying, his glasses clutched in his hand. "She's gone."

My heart plunged toward my stomach. "Alona?"

He frowned at me, his forehead crinkling. "Who?"

Before I could answer, he shook his head. "No, Erin. She . . . the light . . . it was so bright, and she just . . . went into it." He sounded awed and sad all at the same time.

Normally, I would have stayed with him, tried to talk him through it. The first time you see the light, especially if it's not coming for you, it's a bit of a mind-blowing experience. But I couldn't this time, not now.

I shoved past him and kept going.

"Hey, are you okay?" he called after me. "You don't look so good."

I ignored him and focused on the column of light in the near distance. It grew brighter the deeper I went into the woods. But I couldn't tell if that was because I was getting closer or if the trees were blocking out the competing light from Ben's house.

And then it was gone. Like someone overhead had flipped off a gigantic switch.

I stumbled to a stop, blinded by the sudden darkness.

"No, no, no." I could hear the broken words in my croaking voice, but they sounded like they were coming from someone else.

When my sight returned, I started forward in the direction of where I thought the light had been, but everything looked the same in the dark. Trees. Everywhere.

"Ally!" I shouted. It was the only name I could safely use for her with so many people nearby, and one I'd come to associate with her, anyway.

No response, and though I'd half expected that, it didn't prevent me from feeling that socked-in-the-stomach sensation, with which I was all too recently familiar.

I kept going, searching blindly for something, anything, when the moonlight caught a pale shape on the ground about ten feet ahead of me.

Oh, no.

I raced forward, ignoring my ribs, my brain shouting at me to hurry, even though some part of me knew it was already too late. Whatever had happened had happened. And there was nothing I could do to change it.

I slipped in the dead leaves and half slid, half fell into place next to her.

Gathering her up in my arms, I caught the overwhelming

scent of beer, but also the fainter scent of the sweet-smelling shampoo she used, both as Ally and Alona. Lily's body was still breathing, I could tell, but there were no signs of life other than that. Alona was gone, and it was over.

So . . . that was it. Tears spilled down my cheeks, warm, wet, and stinging my various cuts and scrapes, but I didn't care.

I lifted her up, holding her closer, her face pressed against my shoulder. "I'm sorry. I should have been here. I didn't mean for you to be alone. . . ."

"You know, I went to a lot of trouble to stick around," she said quietly, her voice muffled against me.

I jumped a little at the sound, and then started to laugh and cry at the same time, feeling ridiculous but unable to stop. "You're here."

"It would be nice if you didn't suffocate me right away," she continued, sounding exhausted.

I tipped her head away from my shoulder, so I could see her face. "Are you okay?"

"Tired. Really tired, but okay. Nothing a gallon of mouthwash and a full decontamination shower won't fix."

She lifted her head slowly, like it was an effort, and it probably was. I kept my hand behind her neck to help support it.

She touched my cheek gently, and I winced. "What happened to you?" she asked.

"Ben was feeling artistic. Wanted to rearrange my face." I searched her eyes, looking for signs that she was as okay as she claimed to be. Lipstick was still smeared across her mouth, and I used the side of my thumb to rub it away. She'd hate it as soon as she saw it was messed up.

She smiled. "Funny guy. But there's good news."

"What's that?"

"You look good in bloodred, too, I guess."

I rolled my eyes. "Oh, you're a riot."

"I try," she said with a modest shrug.

Then it was all too much, and her eyes went bright and shiny with tears, and she looked away. "I thought . . ." she began in a trembling voice.

"I know." I held her tighter, ignoring the pain in my ribs and various bumps and bruises. None of that seemed important at the moment.

"The light," I said. "Did you . . ."

"Yeah," she said softly. "I could have gone. It was giving me the choice. Like last time."

That was news to me, and, dim as it was here in the woods, there must have been enough light for her to read that in my expression.

"Yeah, I didn't know, either," she said, looking down. "Didn't remember. Not until it was here and I was on the edges of it."

"You didn't stay for me." I hesitated. "Did you?" As flattering as that would be, I didn't want it on my conscience.

She laughed, actually snorted. "Please. Who do you think I am?" She sat up straighter, seeming to grow stronger the longer we sat here. "I stayed because I could," she said simply. "Because I could have been done, but I don't think I am. Not yet."

I wasn't sure what that meant, exactly, but right now, I didn't care. She was here.

"But," she said, carefully avoiding my gaze, "your continued presence may have been a perk that I considered."

I tucked her hair behind her shoulder, where it wouldn't stay because of her new haircut. "I think, uh, I might be in love with you," I said, my voice sounding gruff and awkward even to my own ears. Strange after everything we'd been through together that this would be so difficult to say, but it was. I couldn't even look at her, focused instead on that errant strand of hair. "Is that going to be a problem?" I asked stiffly when she didn't respond.

She laughed. "Probably. Probably lots of problems. But"—she put her hands on my shoulders when I tried to pull away—"we'll figure them out. I'm not going anywhere." She wrapped her arms around my neck and held on tightly.

It would take more time and patience for her to get to the point where she was comfortable enough to *say* that she loved me, but I knew in that moment that she did.

I leaned back to look at her, seeing only her, this girl who was Ally but also Alona, and who bore a resemblance to a friend I'd once had but was someone new. Someone I could live without, but didn't want to.

I eased closer, drawn in by the desire to cement this moment in reality, in touch and taste.

She pulled away slightly, her hand covering her mouth

like she had garlic breath. "Do you have any idea who Erin was kissing?"

"Yeah, so we'll brush our teeth really, really thoroughly afterward," I said, bumping her nose with mine gently. I wasn't going to let *anyone* spoil this moment.

She lowered her hand slightly. "And burn our tooth-brushes?" she persisted.

"I'll buy you a case of new ones," I promised, my lips moving against her cheek.

She nodded and lowered her hand the rest of the way.

I brushed my mouth against hers. She shivered, and her hands swept up to touch my hair and urge me closer. They were chaste kisses, in deference to the night we'd both had, but electric in their potential. I could feel the future in them. A future I never thought I'd have, and one I wanted more than anything.

❧ 22 ❧

Ally

Will was waiting for me in the pickup/drop-off area in front of school when I walked out at the end of my first day. At the sight of him, I stopped dead, blinking in the super-bright afternoon sun, not sure if I was seeing what I wanted or what was actually there.

It had been two weeks since I'd last seen him. When Will brought me home to the very worried, very angry Turners, I'd explained that he'd tracked me down at a party and driven me home. They were doubtful, but I insisted, and they eventually thanked him, albeit reluctantly.

Then they'd taken turns hugging me until I couldn't breathe . . . and grounded me for a freaking month. No visitors, no phone, and no INTERNET.

Fun.

It had almost been enough to make me look forward to going back to school. Actually, no. It hadn't.

Will had kept his distance for the last couple of weeks—trying to respect the Turners' wishes, he'd said, on the few whispered phone calls I'd managed to make.

Okay, yeah, fine, I got it, but I missed him—more than I was willing to admit. And it was enough to make me start worrying. We'd already been through more than two people should go through in *multiple* lifetimes, which was not surprising, considering the circumstances. What if, after time to think away from the heat of the moment, he'd reconsidered?

I wasn't sure I could blame him. It wouldn't change my choice to stay as Ally—it couldn't, really, anyway—but it would hurt. A lot.

So I'd been obsessing on what I would say, how I would play it—particularly with the other item I had on my agenda—when I saw him again, not expecting it to be for another couple of weeks. Which was why I wondered, upon seeing him waiting for me outside school, if he were a figment of my imagination.

But he didn't shimmer into nothingness or morph into someone else. It was definitely Will. He was leaning against the Dodge, his hands in his pockets, watching everyone warily, as though expecting someone to proclaim there'd been a mistake and try to drag him back into the building.

I started toward him, and when he saw me, his tension seemed to ease, and he straightened up with a smile that made my heart—yes, mine, because it *was* for all intents and purposes now, even if I hadn't been born with it, and making further distinctions at this point seemed ridiculous—give an extra-hard thump.

I had to check the urge to run at him. First, because running? Still not my thing with a bum leg, though that was getting better with time and physical therapy. Second, because, hello, it was better to play it cool, even now . . . just in case.

"What are you doing here?" I asked, approaching at what I hoped was a reasonable pace but was probably still too fast, and trying not to grin too hard. So much for playing it cool.

He said he loved me. This is the guy who knows me and LOVES me. The words ran in a constant giddy refrain in my head. I tried to ignore them.

He shrugged, looking a little smug. "Got permission from the Turners to pick you up today. Told you playing by the rules would work." He stepped to one side and opened the door for me.

I scowled at him as I climbed in. "*I'm* the one who taught *you* that."

He laughed. "Yeah, well, you're still grounded for now, so I have to have you home in half an hour." He slammed the door and walked around to get in on the driver's side.

"What about Tyler?" I asked with a frown when Will slid in behind the wheel. I didn't want to abandon him at school with no word as to where I'd gone or what he should do. Not now that he and I had reached a tenuous truce with each other over the last couple of weeks. I think he still wasn't sure what to do with me, how to match who I was now with the sister he'd known before. But he was trying; we both were. And he'd found my knowledge of the inner workings of high school fascinating and at least somewhat valuable. He'd asked me to help him pick out something to wear today. Thank God.

"Mrs. Turner said she'd let him know to catch the bus without you," Will said.

Tyler probably wouldn't be happy about that, but right at this moment, I didn't care. Half an hour alone with Will after two weeks of virtually no contact was worth it. Plus, I only lived eight minutes from school. Six, if he drove quickly. Whatever would we do with remaining twenty-four minutes? I could think of something.

My heart started pounding harder in anticipation.

But Will made no move toward me. Just started the car up, like he was going to drive me home. Really?

"So, how'd it go today?" he asked.

I slumped in my seat. "It's my second first day of senior year. How do you think it went?" Thank God they'd allowed me to test out of the remainder of "my" junior year. Everyone was amazed at how well I'd done on the exams. Frankly, so was I, considering I'd learned most of the material a year and a half ago or more. But I'd been beyond motivated. Two more years of high school? *Unacceptable.* One was going to be bad enough.

"Any problems with ghosts?"

How funny that *he* should be asking *me* that. Though he'd apparently been managing well enough without me over the last couple of weeks. As I'd always sort of suspected, once he'd let the spirits know in no uncertain terms that he was in charge, instead of the other way around, things had gotten better for him.

"Nothing I couldn't handle," I said. I could see spirits now, more than ever. My "vision" had come in fully after I'd returned to Lily's body the second time. The light had passed over us before vanishing, and it was like some final connection had been made. I was now just as much a ghost-talker as Will.

"Good." He signaled to join the line of cars waiting to exit the parking lot.

Seriously? He was actually going to take me home now?

"You're awfully quiet over there. I feel as though I might get to complete a sentence."

I glared at him. "Oh, shut it."

"That's better," he said cheerfully.

Since there clearly wasn't going to be any kissing at the moment—and why the hell not?—I thought I might as well freak him out all at once. Get it over with.

I thought of the folder full of paperwork I'd been carrying around in my bag for the last week or so, mentally flipping through the potential opening arguments I'd created. During my grounding, I'd had a lot of time to think about things. Future stuff. Will was going to Richmond Community College for his Gen Eds, and he would have his own apartment next semester. I couldn't help but shiver at the idea of a place that would be ours. Well, his, but more ours than his mom's or Sam's—now that Will's mom would be moving in there—or my home with the Turners.

We needed a plan. At least, I did—that was how I worked best. It was up to him, I guess, if he wanted to be a part of it.

"So . . . I've been thinking about the business possibilities of our gift," I said carefully. "If you look at the ratio of people who need—"

"You want us to make money off people?" He pulled out of the line abruptly and drove to the edge of the parking lot, not far from the burner row, where he'd once parked.

"No, I want us to *help* people. And charge accordingly," I snapped. I had this speech all worked out, if he'd just let me finish it. I took a deep breath. "Look, doctors don't work for free, right? And they're saving lives. We're helping people complete theirs."

He opened his mouth to speak, but I cut him off. "No tricks, no funny business. If we can't reach the spirit they want, then we don't take them on. Period." I wasn't in this to cheat people. But I wanted a way to help them without trying to have a regular job, where, most of the time, I'd have to ignore the spirits I was supposed to be assisting. "We'll keep doing some pro bono stuff, helping spirits without living relatives or friends to pay us, because that's just what we do. But if you look at the profit Ed was making without being able to see other ghosts, you'll see it's possible, especially with two of us." I dug into my bag for the folder and handed it to Will. I'd created a spreadsheet using the data I'd gotten from Ed. He'd made contact once he found his parents. He was living with them in Springfield.

"I see Ed found you, too," Will said dryly. We'd given Ed a ride to the bus station that night after the party and shared some of our story with him. Well, we had had to tell him something when he saw me and knew I wasn't his sister. We'd made quite the impression, I guess, and he wanted to stay in touch.

"For the first year or so I'd have to work for you," I said. Will raised his eyebrows.

"In name only," I added swiftly, giving him a sour look. "As, like, an intern or something, until I'm eighteen . . . again." So annoying! "After that, we'd have to restructure, probably as an LLP." I paused. "Think of it sort of like a private detective agency, only with ghosts instead of guns and without a license. For now."

He didn't say anything, and I rushed to fill the silence. "We're not going to be able to have the normal lives everybody else does, but so what? Why not use it to our advantage? You can major in whatever you want. I'm going with business, I think. Maybe marketing. I'm good at getting people to do what I want." Except for Will, maybe.

Will looked up from the business projections and the logo ideas I'd affixed to the outside of the folder. "You've put a lot of time into this."

"Hello, success doesn't just happen, remember?" I folded my arms across my chest, struggling against the urge to pretend I didn't care what he thought.

"So, you want to work together," he said slowly, like I'd suggested we vacation on the dark side of Mars.

I stiffened. "It's not necessary. I can do this on my own." I snatched the folder from him.

"No." He grabbed the folder back. "You're not understanding what I'm—"

"Well, maybe if you'd try to be clearer about it," I said.

He exhaled loudly in frustration, and I braced myself for the next round, already prepping the points I would bring up in response to his arguments. Besides, this *had* to work. What else were we supposed to do? Go around pretending the last three months hadn't happened? That made no sense, and the idea of it made my chest ache. I wasn't who I'd been back then, literally, and I couldn't go back. Nor did I want to.

I was distracted, thinking about all of this, so I didn't notice him leaning over until he took my chin in his hand to turn my face toward him. "It's a good plan," he said, stroking my cheek. "You just have to give me more than ten seconds to think about it. So impatient . . ." Then he kissed me, slow and deep, until I felt like I might float away . . . or melt. *Oh, hello.*

I reached out and wrapped my hands in his T-shirt to anchor myself, but the feel of his warm skin only made things worse . . . and so much better.

"Okay?" he murmured after a long moment.

Yes, yes, definitely okay. I nodded but couldn't stop myself from asking the question that had been nagging at me. "Why not before now?"

He shifted in his seat, pulling back slightly and dropping his gaze.

"I wasn't sure," he said cautiously. "I know you still have to go to school here, and if you want to fit in . . ."

I leaned over and pushed him back in his seat, enjoying the surprise on his face and the heat in his gaze. "Forget them," I whispered, before pressing my mouth against his and doing my very best to make him feel as dizzy and out of control as he'd made me feel.

After a second, he reached out to clutch at my waist, and one of us—no, both of us were trembling. It was, quite simply, one of the best moments of my life—before or after.

"Making out in burner row. I'm a bad influence on you," he said breathlessly when I let him up for air.

"Terrible," I agreed with a smile. And I wouldn't have had it any other way.

DON'T MISS BOOK ONE IN
STACEY KADE'S

PROJECT PAPER DOLL

THE RULES

Ariane Tucker
||||██ || | | ||██| |█|| |█|█

ESTABLISHING A ROUTINE IS ESSENTIAL FOR HIDING IN plain sight. Full-blooded humans are very habitual, as it turns out. They eat the same thing for breakfast for weeks on end, park in the same spaces, and buy the same brand of toothpaste. The best way to blend in was to follow suit. To create my own patterns and follow them without exception. Of course, in my case it was an artificial construction, not the result of naturally occurring preferences or, let's face it, a severe lack of imagination.

But *they* didn't know that.

So, Tuesday morning, first day of my junior year: Tuesday equals cornflakes. Morning, particularly on the first day of school, equals conversation with my father.

In the beginning, these father/pseudo-daughter talks were in preparation for my life outside; to discuss the challenges I would face throughout the day, the exercises I needed to practice, and the plans my father had made to further my assimilation. He worked nights, so morning was the only time available and, conveniently, the only part of the day where I hadn't screwed up yet.

These days, though, our morning conversations were more often just catch-up, with a little, "Hey, remember you're not like everybody else." Like I needed *that* reminder.

But today was different, and it shouldn't have been. It didn't start out that way.

The kitchen TV, positioned on the counter by the sink for optimal viewing, was tuned in to Fox News. The shrill voices of the morning-show hosts debating the latest conspiracy polluted the air with noise, fear, and chaos. As usual.

"Really?" I asked my father, who was already sitting at the table with his bowl of cornflakes.

He grunted noncommittally, his gaze glued to the crawl on the bottom of the screen. He'd been obsessed with the news lately, particularly anything to do with a Senate hearing committee investigating the misappropriation of funds within the Department of Defense. Once a military man, always a military man, I guess.

I took my seat next to him with a sigh. It wasn't that the TV people—who must have received vocal training to hit that perfect blend of righteous outrage and near panic— were wrong, exactly. Their government *was* keeping secrets. I was living proof of that. They were just worried about all the wrong things. All the time. It was frustrating to watch, honestly.

"You know," I said, "studies have shown that watching this stuff makes you ten percent more paranoid and seventy-eight percent more likely to buy an old missile silo and convert it into a personal bunker for post-apocalyptic living."

That caught my father's attention. He gave me a sour look, telling me exactly what he thought of my made-up statistics. "It wouldn't kill you to be more politically aware," he said, pointing his spoon at me.

I reached for the cornflakes. "A lot of things won't kill me," I said. In fact, that list was much longer for me than for a full-blooded human. "But that's not much of a recommendation, is it?" I poured cereal into my bowl and held up one of the flakes. "'Taste this. You'll survive it!' Coming soon to cereal boxes and commercials everywhere."

He rolled his eyes. "Funny."

I grinned. "I can be. Occasionally."

"Less often than you think, kiddo." But he was smiling with a fondness that still occasionally took me by surprise. "So," he said, hitting the mute button on the remote, "first day of school again. Do you have everything you need to—"

His cell phone trilled, a soft but intrusive sound that startled both of us. He didn't often get work calls at home.

He plucked the phone off his belt and squinted at the screen, holding it out at arm's length so he could read it. He'd forgotten his reading glasses again.

I kept eating, waiting for him to declare it a wrong number or to roll his eyes and mutter something about Kagan being an idiot. I had no idea who Kagan was, but apparently, according to my father, he achieved Olympic standards of idiocy on a regular basis.

Instead I watched as the color drained from my father's face.

Fear turned my mouth to sand, the bits of cornflake now unswallowable little rocks. "What's wrong?"

My father shoved back from the table, the phone in his hand. "Stay here," he ordered, and headed toward his den. A moment later I heard the door snap shut.

I put down my spoon with a shaky hand. Other children had nightmares about clowns, monsters, and—in my friend Jenna's case—the Hamburger Helper hand from the commercials. I often dreamed about big black vans pulling soundlessly into our driveway and faceless men snatching me from my bed before I could scream.

I got up and spat my cereal into the sink and rinsed my mouth out with water. My head was spinning with horrible scenarios, each worse than the last, a veritable catalog of everything that could be wrong.

I could have tried to listen in on the conversation—not my father's words, but his thoughts. But that ability—like much of me—didn't function nearly as efficiently as intended. And on top of that, my father was not easy to read. I could get virtually nothing from him unless he wanted me to, thanks to the intensive mental training he'd undergone during his years of service.

Still, there was one thing I knew for sure: if they were coming, it was already too late for me. I'd have time only to hide, not escape, and that would do no good.

In theory, I should have had nothing to fear. A dozen soldiers or "retrieval specialists" were supposed to be a minor obstacle for someone like me. But I wasn't quite up to spec in that regard. At least not anymore.

My heart fluttered unevenly in my chest, reminding me

that, no matter how much I sometimes hated it, I was part human. Weak.

I picked up my spoon and examined my upside-down reflection in the bowl of it. Had someone recognized me?

I look human enough to "pass," of course. All part of the design. Don't want people freaking out about an alien spy/assassin; that might lower the odds of my being able to walk up to someone and pick their brain for information, or, you know, kill them.

But passing wasn't quite the same as blending in. That, I had to work at.

I reviewed the alterations to my appearance in the distorted view, reassuring myself that my camouflage was still intact.

Lowlights in my too-light hair brought it closer to the human range of color. But the texture was off—heavy and soft, but it caught on fingertips like the raw silk shirt Jenna had appropriated from her mom's closet last year—and it grew out with strange bends and kinks in it, which I hated. So I kept it pulled up in a ponytail or in a messy knot that hopefully looked deliberately, artistically disarrayed instead of barely controlled.

Colored lenses made my eyes a murky but human blue, disguising the unnatural darkness of my irises—they were virtually indistinguishable from my pupils.

My skin was slightly too pale, verging on a silvery-gray in some lights, but there was nothing I could do about that. It wasn't enough to be noticeable, really, unless I stood next to someone who'd fake-baked to a Cheeto orange . . . or if you knew what you were looking for.

And there were people who did. Far too many of them.

Was that what the phone call was about? I swallowed, my throat suddenly painfully dry.

My only saving grace so far was that their attention had been focused on locations far from their own backyard. I lived less than ten miles from GenTex Labs, home to Project Paper Doll and site of my very own personal hell.

My father returned to the kitchen, catching me by surprise. I slapped my spoon in place, producing a louder than expected crack, and we both flinched.

"Is everything okay?" I asked.

He nodded wearily, but I could tell he was distracted. He didn't sit down, just leaned forward with his hands braced on the table as if he needed the support.

A pulse of fear sent me to my feet, and my chair tipped over backward. "Do you need your pills? I have them right here on the windowsill." My father was not young. He was still in good shape—thanks, he said, to the regimented training he'd picked up from being Special Forces in his twenties—but he would be fifty-six this year. He'd gone completely gray in the years I'd known him, and while his gaze was as sharp as ever, lately he'd taken to moving as if he carried a heavy weight on his shoulders. Last year, I'd ignored every lesson he'd ever taught me and called 911 when I found him collapsed on the floor in the hall, gasping for air. It turned out to be a panic attack, brought on by stress. He also had spectacularly high blood pressure, another sign that his body was not handling the demands of his life very well. Wonder why.

I started toward him, but he waved me off. "I'm fine. I

already took my meds this morning. Go on to school. You don't want to be late."

No, because that would be a violation of Rule #4: *Keep your head down.* When my father had first given me that rule I'd taken it literally, which hadn't helped matters. A second grader walking around with her head ducked down below her shoulders wasn't exactly normal looking. Hey, you try living in a secret underground lab for the first six years of your life and see if your understanding of the metaphorical isn't a little shaky.

The point is, people notice you when you are late. But they also notice when you are early.

I felt a fresh rush of frustration at walking this so-fine-as-to-be-almost-invisible line. GTX didn't own me, not anymore. But they still controlled my life, down to the smallest details. And sometimes that was the worst part.

I could never have anyone at the house or go over to anyone else's. I had to keep to myself, but not so much that they would worry about my being socially dysfunctional and force me into counseling. I lived with the constant fear of standing out in some way, even if it was for something good. I would be a B student forever even though I'd surpassed the high-school-level curriculum years ago. B's were the perfect nondescript grade, not low enough to attract teacher intervention, and not high enough to rate nomination for the honor society.

I hadn't even been able to go with my father when the ambulance took him to the hospital last year. GTX often lends out their specialists, and one of the doctors might have recognized me.

That was my life. And it would be for the next two interminable years, until I could escape under the cover of all the other graduating seniors.

Once I was gone from Wingate I'd be free. Well, freer, I suppose. I'd never be able to relax completely, never be able to just exist without thinking hard about who or what I was supposed to be. But living farther away from GTX—and the omnipresent sense of danger—would help, at least a little.

I pushed my chair into place, but I didn't leave right away. I had to know. "Are they on to us?" I asked, forcing the words past a sudden lump in my throat. My father still worked for GTX—he had to. Quitting after their prized possession up and disappeared would have looked suspicious. As far as anyone there knew, I was the daughter he'd gained full custody of after the death of his ex-wife in Ohio. And his staying at GTX did provide at least one major advantage: he had sources throughout the company who were usually able to tell him what was in the offing well in advance.

He looked up, startled. "No, Ariane. No. It's nothing like that. Just something I need to handle."

I nodded stiffly. I would die before I'd let GTX take me, or punish my father for helping me.

"You don't have to worry." He reached out and touched my shoulder carefully, gingerly.

I forced myself not to flinch. Sometimes I wasn't so good with being touched. It was yet another way in which I could be caught. Most people didn't avoid a casual touch as if it might cause them to burst into flame. Then again, most people hadn't spent years being poked, prodded, and broken (deliberately) for the sake of scientific advancement.

"Okay." I tried to smile, wishing my father looked more certain or less gray—that was my territory—and pulled away as soon as I could, my heart thundering on the slow-to-fade rush of adrenaline.

Sometimes I could almost forget. Those days in the lab seemed so far away, a nightmare with a little too much detail. Other times . . . well, let's just say today was going to be one of *those* days.